RHODESIA

ZIMBABWE I

RHODESIAN DAWN
ZIMBABWE DARKNESS

Tony Morkel

First published 2004 by Interface ISBN 0-9548194-0-3

Second Edition Published by:

Sable Publishing House
PO Box 52, Ilminster, Somerset TA19 9XY, United Kingdom
Email: SablePublications@yahoo.co.uk

ISBN 0-9549488-0-7

About the Author

Tony Morkel is a third generation Rhodesian, proud of his heritage and family contribution to developing the colony. He received a privileged education at St Andrews Preparatory School and St Andrews College in the Cape Province, and Prince Edward in Salisbury. He is a keen sportsman, angler, photographer, hunter, farmer, and businessman. He reflects on his military experiences during the Rhodesian Terrorist war with honour and with pride.

The family has been dispossessed of all material possessions as a result of government policies and thuggery now rampant in Zimbabwe. Bruised and battle-scarred, but with health and a positive outlook they have begun carving careers in pursuit of new horizons in a foreign land.

Tony's writing reflects historical fact and personal experience, spiced with liberal doses of artistic license, in a setting where place names, times and characters are used with intentional deception so as to shield innocent players in greed inspired brutal conflict of power.

His next novel, the sequel to "Rhodesian Dawn, Zimbabwe Darkness" is a gripping inside tale of events and experiences in the corridors of political power, greed and privilege, and reveals elements of Mugabe's influence, as well as the instruments and psychological manipulation that have inverted a wonderful nation.

Dedication

To Rhodesians and Zimbabweans past and present, who, with honour and integrity created, loved and lost a paradise.

This era presents new friends, new employers, new geography, new culture and a new dawn for every Rhodesian. We will face the sunrise with a fortitude ingrained by our forefathers, and dedicate their example to the eternal goodwill of mankind.

To the dispossessed, suppressed and starving millions that remain prisoners in their homeland, we hope and pray that this cloud of darkness will soon take wing on changing winds.

My trusted friends John and Rosemarie whose literary enthusiasm kick-started my pen into action and corrected my tribal bias to English.

PREFACE

This novel subjectively unwraps human values shown when confronted with varying circumstances. Every character evaluated in these events is described realistically, within the author's understanding of our intrinsic values.

Every event is true in concept with a generous license flavouring details. Every hunt and political decision has been experienced by the author. All characters are real. For reasons of individual respect names and many places have been altered to protect identities.

This narrative unravels a myriad of intentions, misconceptions, and political machinations. It explores financial, matrimonial, physical and mental power, strength and limitations. Fundamental core values reverberate through the people and become seeded in national objectives.

Events are evaluated not in scientific calculation of physical prowess, but emotional, psychological understanding; our comprehension of events and circumstances.

We encounter love, revenge, adversity and challenge during life's journey and every circumstance results in individual reaction. Some unearth scabs of ones self, some reveal unsprung talent and some will nourish evil, eroding the foundations of honour.

Primarily relating to the values and spirit at the core of Rhodesia, this novel traverses hearts and minds, determination and desire. It travels over grasslands and floodplains, through highlands and lowveld, amidst privileged, resilient people, on a journey through challenging circumstances. Fires are fought, hunger is overcome and ravages of drought and flood storms are challenged. Battles are debated, fought, lost and won, revealing strength and burying weakness.

Friendships and loyalties, skills and visions are forged through generations of trials and rewards, tears and laughter, eventually all shattered by the oratorical eloquence of a desperate demagogue.

Political expansion during the reign of Queen Victoria had magnanimous merit and demerit. Her Majesty's island, overloaded with determined people, strategically implanted esteemed individuals, such as Captain Cornwallis Harris, Dr David Livingstone, Florence Nightingale, and Cecil John Rhodes, in foreign lands.

The concept of 'Empire' was the diamond amongst supreme jewels. The muscle and sweat of brave, tenuous men and women became discarded clinker at the ironmonger's forge. The majestic pride of Zulu lieutenants became lumps of dead meat on black powder gunshot. The tough, determined and legendary heroes of Britannia were awarded posthumous recognition with the Victoria Cross.

The savage and untamed traditions, policed from thrones of dead wood polished with cattle dung, is brightly contrasted with the regal thrones elaborately crafted in marble and gold of a *civilized* world. Both realms have emotion, dignity, aggression, tenderness and instinct. Both close their eyes to the smoke of the campfire; both skip light to a laughing infant. One has a reverence for grandeur, the other reveres his descendents and their survival.

Colonial Embryos: Departure Europe, Arrival The Cape

By gracious good fortune we generally have two grandfathers. This genetically enhances particular traits and gives elasticity to others. In the grand design of life, this should improve our make-up by eradicating certain characteristics and heighten those aspects that are socially good.

In my case, one was a spirited Christian preacher of Irish descent; the other was born in the Cape of Good Hope, of a combined German, French, Dutch and Russian ancestry. Pioneering attributes and an impulsive determined spirit of unplanned adventure were deeply implanted into future generations.

Unlike the era when life began at birth, it was rooted deep in us that my life began during the formative years of Grandfather's childhood. Physically a determined man with mental resolve and unilateral purpose, Grandfather set about life at an early age. Through circumstance he became the family defender, provider, planner and decision maker before his twelfth birthday. That circumstance concerned my great-grandfather; was eventful, lustful, shameful and best relegated to a non-recyclable trash sewer. Grandfather's beginnings can be likened to the temperature of Hell being used in the smelt, to separate, purify and refine pure gold. Ore discarded, this process left a man near to social purity and a master craftsman's example of human perfection.

It has to have been a tempered plan in Creation that introduced this element of heritage combining paltry priesthood and powerful pioneer. My priestly maternal Grandparents departed Ireland to spread the Word of God to barbaric tribes of Central East Africa. My paternal Grandfather's European roots departed France through an interesting corridor of fortune, pride and purpose, pasted in power, privilege and pain.

In 1832, two tall, muscular brothers ventured casually to the dock in Calais on a sightseeing excursion. They were exploring new territory with an adventurous eye. On arriving dockside amongst thick ropes, folded sails, cranes, undulating waves, gulls and the smell of fish, the two brothers sat unfolding starchy bread, adjacent were two huge sailing ships.

A youthful crew on each deck was repairing final twists, riveted life rafts, and cracked wooden buckets for long voyages. Jovial banter between the crews from the two ships inspired each of the brothers to straddle over and join in on what appeared to be a joyous social event. That decision resulted in each brother setting a course for all future generations of the De La Harp family.

The younger brother signed up to join a ship called "The Dutch East". The elder brother signed up to sail aboard the other berthed vessel, "The Dutch West". The Dutch West landed three months later in what is now the Boston area of America. The Dutch East ran aground some five months hence while attempting the much feared waters surrounding the Cape of Storms. The entire crew abandoned ship into overfilled life rafts, well provisioned for the short row ashore the Cape of Good Hope. Thus, landed one part of the future family into America, the other part onto untamed, climatically harsh and disease ridden Africa.

Great-grandfather and his brother never met again. Archive information tells us that both lived full lives in pursuit of adventure and family provision. Both brothers went on to produce huge families. In America, a combination of English,

German, French and Cherokee women were their carriers and incubators. The children granted birthrights to that notorious and energetic family of gamblers, mobsters, sailors, pirates, lawyers, bounty hunters, military defectors, draft dodgers and grantees of master and servant labour and supremacy.

In Africa, the thought of procreating amongst the natives was anathema to my ancestry. The bearded old man began his family late in life, in the shady forests at the foot of Table Mountain. Having all his manly creative weaponry set on automatic, in just eight years he fathered into three wives, seven sons and three daughters, whom survived to adult life.

Great Grandfather had thus started the ball rolling, for one of the greatest rugby legend families of all time. They pioneered an adventurous and energetic era as agricultural developers, traders, transporters, miners, inventors and entrepreneurs. They ventured into the unknown regions of Southern Africa and the land of Monomatapa.

ARTHUR

In 1874 in the district of Graaf Reinet in the Cape of Good Hope young Arthur Rubidge De La Harp was born into a paternally void but maternally compassionate family, whose prime livelihood was ostrich farming. Before Arthur was four years old he had two younger brothers, Reginald and Ernest, and a sister, Coral. His father had virtually abandoned his mother in pursuit of urban wealth, easy women and impractical visions.

Arthur journeyed most of his life with little academic prompt nor formal education. His academic inspiration was generated through an inquisitive fascination of everything that crossed his path in life. As a result of instinctive survival and determination of interest, he was almost self reliant. His mother was his mentor and devoted tutor, providing encouragement and assistance. He confidently approached every challenge with an attitude of "learn or teach", "gain or give", "love, be loved", "grant and receive", "in every event, do something, in no event, do nothing".

From a young age Arthur, was dedicated through necessity to work a fifteen hour daily routine. It was soon after the arrival of Arthur's youngest sister that real demands were placed on this energetic young boy. His early morning would start with his obligations. He had been instructed the previous evening during family ensemble in the kitchen, to set out the fowl snares for guinea fowl; gather ostrich eggs before the hens stretched out their wings; milk old Tokkie, the faithful provider of their daily goats milk and ensure that the cows and both calves were near suitable grazing pasture.

Efficiently, always with zest and enthusiasm, young Arthur would attend his responsibilities. His mother was everything in his world, and to please her and receive her gentle smile was his daily objective. He thrived on attending to his responsibilities; and was elated if there were more eggs than budget; overjoyed if the rusty old jam tin dribbled goat milk from being too full. His smile was wide, and his sparkling milk teeth glistened whenever his "herd" had performed well.

Because of his long day lifestyle lacking time for social events, he seldom used a hair comb until early teens. His mother insisted that cleanliness is next to godliness, but daily practicalities placed a wedge in this realm. He was always well groomed last thing at night, but by day was usually stained in a mud or dust. Silly though it may seem, it even appeared that work enjoyed being performed by him. As the world unfolded before him, he was highly regarded for physical perseverance and articulate mental grasp way beyond his years.

As young Arthur chiselled his determination over the hills and through the valleys of life, so he smoothed the edges of an already near perfect childhood, boyhood, and adolescent adulthood.

In the eyes of the community; from the bearded and often illiterate "Boer" (farmer); the "Tannie" (aunt) of the district, and the young studs, both male and female breeding youth; everyone admired Arthur. He was seldom amongst social gatherings because of an inherent commitment to attend his responsibilities.

It should be surprising then, that the local farmers club had a life size portrait of Arthur majestically suspended over the oak boardroom table. In the elaborate gold gargoyle lined frame was a typical scenario; seven people aged three to ten staring into the elevated eyes of a smiling Arthur, authoritative, sitting side-saddle on "Buck Fast" his farm mule.

The artwork was commissioned in 1880, long after the event, and was produced, based on interviews, discussions and the artist's observations. It was locally treasured as a prized work of art. Arthur was acknowledged and personalized in so many ways, but this artwork was an admirable credit to any accomplished statesman, politician and military general or national leader. As a young man Arthur momentarily became coy and timid whenever he had occasion to glance at or pass the portrait. The thick oil based work on canvass portrayed detail, but more skilfully, something about the eyes, smile, and bone structure imparted authority. Youth was delicately acknowledged in the golden blond curls that naturally graced and elaborately enfolded youthful ears and a well worn leather collar.

Formal education facilities were way beyond both the physical and financial reach of the family. Arthur required elementary arithmetic, basic history and superior command of his mother's language, English. His doting mother selected an initial priority to help him get a grip on commanding speech. He rigorously approached the challenge of learning the alphabet. In unison with his mother as tutor, and Tokkie as his listener, he was able to fluently recite A to Z in sequence within a few hours. Then the gruelling challenge of getting his tongue to manipulate around basic words that were spelt in the sand. His blackboard was smooth sand and his scribe tool was a dry stick or finger.

Arthur was led to an early understanding that perfect English was only to be found in the Bible. He studied a single book, the King James Version. He never intentionally marked the pages of this beloved book; this was considered a blasphemous abomination. However, as most of his learning was undertaken during farm chores, his Bible was dog eared, with soiled pages and the pungent aroma of goat.

During the next few years Arthur achieved a deep and compassionate knowledge of the scribes, players and heroes of biblical times. His admiration was deep for commitment as evidenced in characters of Moses, Job, Abraham, Solomon, Jonah, Joseph and all the cast of Old Testament players. The details of the story became a fascination and were alive in his daily conduct; apparent as the compass that would direct his course as a community leader, entrepreneur, farmer and miner. Arthur's roots and spirit had well and truly departed Europe. This magnanimous example of mankind had arrived, to be solidly seeded in dark Africa, initially based in the Cape of Good Hope.

His time of studious devotion and the strong influence of his dutiful mother were to be greatly instrumental in national formation and colonization. It was from this foundation that the First Constitution of the government of Rhodesia was drafted, crafted, penned and presented to Cecil John Rhodes, when Arthur was a mere 23 years old.

Necessity demanded daily food for his beloved mother, brothers and sister. Arthur's formative years instilled finely honed skills of survival. His experiences and grasp were invaluable to his siblings. From an early age he shared his knowledge and taught newfound skills to neighbouring children. This set him in situations of authority; fine tuning his oratory skills, gaining practical experience in addressing others. It also established in him a generous compassion at a very early age. His physical fortitude and dogmatic determination were practiced and perfected through his life.

As a young man Arthur committed very long hours to the needs and goodwill of his mother and family, but also to an expanding community. His world rapidly became smaller and siblings became contributors in domestic supplies. He shared his experiences of administering the medication to calves; identifying ostriches; castrating unsuitable breeding stock and hand milking the cows. His pasture improvement techniques were novel in concept, practical in reality and formation. His time and labour saving livestock feeding practices were intricately explained and demonstrated to anyone signifying an interest. It was not long before his practices were willingly performed by his energetic brothers and sister. Time was rapidly closing in on life with his mother. His book, King James, had taught him that it was expedient that a man should leave his parents and become one with his wife.

One step at a time, please! Leave first! Become one with his wife? Later, much later, when such gracious marvel as could distantly shadow his mother had been created, he may consider this aspect of divine obedience! He was, however, seven months into being a teenager now, leaving it to probability that he could locate such perfection in personage within a few years. For now, at any rate, it was nearing that hour of family farewells and future foundations of manly independence.

Meanwhile, gossip within the farming district was that the prime thrust of local government was to venture into the great interior of Africa, and expand Her Majesty's Colonies.

Already, the Prime Minister of the Cape had dispatched scouts to the north, to evaluate the situation in Monomatapa. Her Majesty, Queen Victoria, had expressed an interest in establishing a rail connection that should link Cape Town to Cairo. Initial probability was that such an undertaking could not realistically be achieved. When Cecil Rhodes was tasked with this challenge, he grasped it with an enthusiasm and a ruthless determination. Amongst the applications requesting employment within his pioneering scouts was a well written letter signed, Arthur De La Harp, aged 14 years. Because of his juvenile status this request for the challenge was declined, in a typewritten document signed by the Treasurer to Parliament, Constantia House, Cape of Good Hope. Naturally, this was sufficient challenge for Arthur who immediately set into plan his big trek to Johannesburg. This comparatively placid stroll was to serve as an apprenticeship for great events and extensive travels. Arthur was now 15, tall and strong. His wide shoulders and muscular torso supported by agile, narrow hips. The golden curls of his youth had turned to sandy blond. His facial features were hard, but this was always made right by his broad and easy smile. His jaw was set solid and square and his wide-apart eyes were alert and full of sparkle.

During the coming months Arthur became pedantic in descriptive details of handing over his duties to his brothers and sister. He continued to depend on that daily acknowledgement, which occurred in the gentle smile from his mother. Her assuring grace never faulted in this new and traumatic development; this preparatory event of her precious and most treasured son "flying" the nest. She continued to provide maternal support that this young warrior had come to depend upon. Her grace, elegance and composure remained affectionately and single mindedly focused on family aspirations. Always with absolute commitment, she demonstrated love and affection from an aura of silent strength and wisdom. Although slight in physique, she was magnanimous in stature and solid in principal foundation. This woman held tightly to her biblical convictions, intolerant of even slight deviance from the teaching of God. She staunchly advocated Christ-like practice to her children and the community. She did not preach but simply conducted her life in a Christ like manner, and lived according to her interpretation of the Will of God. This example of daily conduct imparted a spiritual balm into all who knew her.

This rock of strength, this mountain of spiritual guidance and gracious courage had steered her family through challenging times, as well as fun-filled sport and game days; on horseback; in clean waters and on steep slopes. Her children revered her. Over the coming weeks she was about to falter as young Arthur gathered his span of oxen, and began assembling provisions and a team of wagon drivers. She shed a tear as she observed his powerful hands embrace his rifle, spreading protective lubricant on the inner workings, firing mechanism, magazine and ammunition box. This piece of steel and wood was about to replace her as his companion and support in the impending months.

The planning of his intent was thorough. He discussed with his mother the concept of venturing into the core of Africa. As a family they deliberated long into the night, contemplating the details of provisions, wagons, cattle, guns and men, survival and disease. It was his Mother's idea for Arthur to approach a financial provider to start a transport and small goods delivery service, in support of the ideals of the Prime Minister of the Cape, The Right Honourable Cecil John Rhodes. The two of them discussed this prospect with an established and wealthy trader, Mr. Theophalus Zeederberg. This astute business entrepreneur immediately offered Arthur a job, but he declined in the knowledge that it would be a short-lived opportunity at attainment and commercial success. As an operator in ownership he could achieve well, or fail, but as an employee he would do neither. He would only enrich his master. This could even be at the expense of his own life. His respect for Meneer Zeederberg strengthened with time, but they never did business together. Instead, Arthur was given a letter of introduction, by Mr. Zeederberg, to a man of good honour and worldly wisdom, who traded in Johannesburg. His name was Hubert Davies.

The targets that the family had debated and set for Arthur were demanding; arrived at by stretching ability, tolerance and stamina. Arthur would set off for Johannesburg with a view to raising sufficient investment there to establish a business that would penetrate into Monomatapa, potentially supporting the scouts dispatched by Rhodes. Alternative opportunities were discussed; the developing ivory trade, diamonds and gold. Arthur immediately refused the high rewards offered for dealing in ivory; his sights set to establish the business of wagon transport and subsequent entrepreneurial diversification.

Arthur's plan was to travel to Johannesburg with specially selected drovers, the strongest of trained oxen and sufficient provision for the journey. If he should succeed with an investor in Johannesburg he would proceed, otherwise he would assess alternatives.

As it happened he established a lifelong friendship and business association with the most Honourable of gentlemen, Mr. Hubert Davies. Resultant travels took Arthur to cross the Limpopo River; to hunt in unspoiled terrain; to trade; to own a transport business and to establish a farming and mining business in the prime farmland of the Mazoe river valley.

Arthur deliberated anxiously in the dusk of each departing day. It was a day closer to leaving his herd, his pastures and his family. He was overjoyed at the prospect of an adventure into the dark interior. He gazed long and hard into the eyes of Tokkie and seemed to instil an agreement of absence. Tokkie had accepted being milked by others, especially Coral, who was attentive and maternally delicate in her milking approach. Reg and Ernie specialised with the ostriches and pastures. Cattle management became a joint operation between the three youngest children. Arthur was pleased with the dedication with which everyone attended their responsibilities and slowly withdrew himself from day to day operations. He was now ready to concentrate time and effort on his impending expedition.

The big day dawned, first light seeing Arthur amongst his herd, bidding final farewell to each beak, brow and beard. He was inwardly emotional, but outwardly confident and calm. His mother was weakened, reduced to tears. Members of the local community arrived to witness the departure and volunteer support and encouragement. Eleven boys, varying in age from seven to twenty two, a mother and two teenage girls stood on the veranda of home. Every person waving farewell to the fifteen year old adventurer was moved in either emotional displeasure or profound admiration at his departure. Coral and Reg deemed it necessary not to be present at the farewell gathering. Both were purportedly attending the stock. This was an era when men don't cry, and ladies glow only distant dewdrops.

Arthur's lengthy stride quickened as he approached the drivers to check and tighten down saddle straps; the wagon cover and a few cooking utensils precariously perched on the wagon running board. With a respectful acknowledgement of superior age he asserted authority by a whistle cracking stock whip instruction to the lead driver to "Handei, madoda. Ti-en

– ku Monomatapa." At this command sixteen well trained oxen stepped the first of paces that would become a journey into the unknown; a journey that would cost three of the drovers their lives; and would almost cost Arthur his young life, too.

Arthur had selected his cattle well. The strongest and biggest framed, "Madonsa", with a glistening ivory and silver coloured mantel of horn, could well have achieved several trips to Johannesburg and back. He was youthful and muscular enough to challenge most situations. All of the animals were well-muscled, well-trained at the yoke; rugged, hardy and accustomed to constant handling.

Arthur had his .318 rifle slung high on his shoulder, whilst his senior gun bearer and head driver, Buru, had the .303 below his waist; the glistening .22 rifle stored at the front of the wagon, readily available in event of necessity. The "trek" set out from the yard with Arthur, his two bull terrier bitches at heel, and "Eat'em", the Ridgeback dog leading in front. The team of drovers comprised eight lean, muscular Zulu boys in their teens and early twenties and three elder Zulu men in their thirties. The inventory that now rolled over the grassland to distant horizons was comprehensive but compact. Every man carried his own self made leather stock whip, axe and spear. A single wagon pulled by the oxen carried bags of maize, bags of Nyimo beans, boxes filled with coarse salt, cooking utensils, knives, ammunition and drums, each containing 44 gallons of clean drinking water. On top of the equipment in the first class compartment sat live chickens.

Arthur's desire to turn and wave farewell to his family was suppressed until well out of "reading" distance, so as to retain secrecy of his inner emotions. He carried a heavy heart with concern for his mother, but jubilation overcame quickly as the first rolling hill separated them from the tin roofed house behind. The wagon rode smooth as the soft vlei soil passed rapidly under wheels, gathering swiftly behind.

On the seventh day, when shadows became short, with the sun overhead, Arthur decided to hunt and called a halt. Excitement in everybody was evident. Although it was midday, it was time to set up camp for the night and pursue food for the men. En route to Johannesburg, Arthur needed to travel a minimum of twenty miles on this day. His daily average had been a mere eleven miles and this would mean introducing food rationing if the journey would be completed within the limitations of what was carried aboard. He had set a target of covering a minimum of seventeen miles per day on average. This meant significant increase in momentum. The most appreciated way to achieve this would be another good meat meal. The oxen were out spanned and camp set up. Arthur signalled Buru to prepare a short hunt. Buru's face exploded with delight. His gleaming smile revealed a brilliant brace of shining white ivory, as he tossed his coffee dregs over his shoulder, announcing "Handei, baas, better tina hamba manji", "let's go, boss, better we go now." Time was of the essence, the day shut down with the setting sun. No sunlight meant a time to sleep, not to be attending food preparation or domestic chores. Obedient again to the superior age and experience of Buru, Arthur too discarded his too hot to drink coffee and pulled himself up, smiling, grabbing Buru on the arm. The clenched biceps of this mahogany man in peak fitness lifted Arthur vertical in an instant. Smile acknowledged, the two set course directly into a westerly wind. The idea was to hunt quickly, returning successfully to feed before dark. As Buru led the search, Arthur commanded from the rear, issuing instructions that only a smaller animal would be killed today, as it was too hot to preserve the meat. Excess meat would mean a delay. The ideal size would be an impala, springbok or similar goat size animal. Failure would mean that two of the roosters would become tonight's dinner. As they walked they saw footprints and droppings indicating presence of much of the wild; of Kudu, Eland and Zebra, but nothing of lesser size. They had been gone from camp for about an hour when Buru suddenly stopped, crouched and covered his wide open mouth with both hands. Immediately in front of him, not ten paces, lay three slender, agile looking lion cubs. They had not detected his presence and appeared relaxed. One was inverted, paws folded, limply hung, well overtaken in deep sleep. The others both had crossed paws, staring blankly out to nowhere. In this circumstance Buru cocked his forehead, seeking guidance from his master. Arthur froze momentarily as he took in the gravity of the situation. Immediately to his right, not ten paces away was a huge male lion, with both eyes closed. Then it happened, like greased lightning on a split trip to hell. The dry undergrowth erupted in confusion. Two big lionesses barely fifteen paces to the left, sprang alert into solid defence. Buru swung around, while Arthur instantly unlatched the safety catch on the .318 calibre Mauser. He glanced right, to see the male still at rest, but with alert eyes on search. Then the cause of hysteria, a juvenile hare in full flight with its oversized ears flattened onto fillet, had disrupted the tranquillity and startled the pride into instant alarm. The male didn't move, except to open then close one eye alternately, then the other. The two lionesses stood and stretched, arched their backs; took a wide open yawn and then the bigger cat proceeded to lick the other to restful sleep. The three cubs had hurriedly dispatched themselves, crackling dry leaves and sticks, fortunately, directly into the gentle breeze, away from the hunters. Buru and Arthur lay motionless, central in the boiling pot; the domain of survival of the fittest, amidst the kings and rulers of the continent. Akin to being at court in the

Palace of Herod, having startled centurions to grapple their spears!

Every day the rifles were refreshingly cleaned and the thin film of protective lubricant applied. Each weapon had place of preference in the trek and each was jealously and protectively guarded and cared for by a delegated gun bearer. The scent of gun oil was relaxing to the hunter; it was an assurance that his protector was within reach. Arthur inhaled this sense of security, and then slowly slithered rearward, adopting suitable stance and attitude, so as to diligently depart this arena of the King's court. Buru held a tight eye to the brow of both lionesses, making a regular neck turn, so to laser the thoughts of the sleeping King. As they strategically withdrew, both Buru and Arthur were pleased in the assurance that tranquillity in the pride had completely returned. Gently, but with increasing determination, they simultaneously stood erect, gave a rearward glance and set hurried footprints into the sand. They did not run. Both men knew that this pride of lions had recently eaten; now lethargic to any killing instinct. When they were separated from the drowsy male, by seventy paces, Buru released his barrel of chest filled breath for the first time. Both hunters had feared arousing attention to the sounds of their breathing. This was small quantification of their degree of physical fitness, that they were able to hold breathing and backtrack seventy paces in a vacuum like silence. As they hurried, relieved, from the situation, the second indicator that the lions had eaten, rapidly and mysteriously appeared. A silver backed jackal, with an oversized femur firmly placed between her teeth, sped across their intended path. In hot flight pursuit was a majestic Bataleur Eagle, with outstretched talons and well combed crest. The bird swerved in the air, as a butter paddle might splash through thick cream, to redirect his flight path upon detecting the presence of this human intrusion on his territory.

Africa's equivalent of the sly English Red Fox, the slender jackal, is a reliable solution to after kill contamination in the bush. With carnivorous killing in the African food cycle, there is always a need for the tail end scavenger. After the lion has dispensed with his hunger pangs, the dining facility is clinically corrected in ecological balance. With professional precision the hyena, Bataleur Eagle, vultures and jackal consume their needs. A sampling will be carried to a nest or a lair in consideration of their offspring.

This youthful member of the dog family had intended to return to her lair with bounty. The Bataleur assured otherwise. His needle sharp talons sliced deep into the neck muscle. Her mouth opened wide, screaming, as the femur bone left her tooth grip then skidded to a standstill, pegging into sand. The Eagle landed his razor sharp talons, penetrating deep into muscle, surrounding the neck bone and clamping securely. The agonised jackal tried lamely to bring both rear legs up past her belly, to claw some defence, but barely managed to arch her own back. The fly past was completed by a steep climbing upturn, as the Bataleur glanced down to the shining metal barrel on Arthur's shoulder. The jackal surrendered her life as she hung limp from the talons, and then dropped from the sky. Her broken flesh landed hard and the crackle of breaking bone and splattering belly, blood and brain, all told that this little mother would never voluntarily move again. She didn't, but it was not long before a pair of jet black crows landed softly atop her soft, warm, blood splattered, colourful fur coat, and began dismembering their share of the harvest.

The Bataleur majestically settled on nearby deadwood, in a position of geographical supremacy. She surveyed the situation calmly and then, as smoothly as warmed honey flowing over roasting ribs, she lifted her wings to the breeze and glided gently down to claim her prize from the black raven like scavengers.

Buru and Arthur had experienced an aviation spectacular that is seldom witnessed. They had also glimpsed the end cycle of the clean up process. Virtually every scavenger will enjoy meat from any bird or animal. One exception is that no bird or mammal will eat the flesh of a crow. When a crow dies it is consumed by ants, flies and worms.

Arthur looked up at the sun and decided to return on a circular route to the distant, thin smoke stack which climbed tall to the clouds. This was an indication of virtually no wind and aided the defences of nature, with no breeze to detour the hunters scent or deflect the sounds of crushing leaves and breaking twigs. Thirst was cracking their dried lips and dust was harshly caked on sweat. Arthur decided to return to camp, accepting light hearted ridicule in the failure of the hunt. Buru was more determined.

A rich odour of disembowelled buffalo belly hung in the air. Buru smiled and respectfully suggested a detour round the sleeping pride and the decaying carcass. He skirted a parabolic curve assuring an increased area to seek out a camp meal, pleased with himself for achieving the extra mile of search area, whilst seemingly in consensus with Arthur. In reality, Buru had his own way.

Arthur liked and admired this initiative too. It demonstrated a hungry man's determination, blended with concern for others. In the moment that Buru rescheduled his return route there was mutual understanding and eternal kinship; absolute agreement; unnerving trust and a bonding respect maturing between two people of two continents; two cultures with totally opposing spiritual foundation. The binding force of mutual disappointment and a shared anxiety were all contributors to this master and servant relationship. It forged a bond between diverse personalities; Arthur, a revered master;

Buru, profoundly loyal and uncomplicated in decisive sincerity.

These manly giants were bonded through the grit and determination in attending to wagons and rifles, hunger and thirst; together they had looked death in the eye.

Arthur and Buru returned to camp to radiant smiles in acknowledgement of their effort. Buru had found five porcupine quills pierced into the dried skull and skin remains of a Serval cat. He skilfully twisted the quills between thumb and forefinger as he settled aside the smoking log fire, ready to share moments from his afternoon experiences. His masterful recall of events that had not quite occurred added unnecessary colour to the picture he was painting. Smoke hung low around the camp fire. The evening had no sign of air movement. Tadarera sauntered off to the chicken coop, laughing. His eleven inch knife shone silver bright, as he honed it on coarse sand in an effort to achieve new sharpness. He proudly claimed honour in being the only capable meal provider of the day. Buru quickly claimed status as the only eyeball communicator with the King of the jungle. Arthur mused as Buru recounted the event "surrounded by lions, too big and too many to mention". The fact that three kittens fled from the hare was conveniently, amusingly misrepresented. Three lions looked him straight in the eye and vanished like expended lightning, desperate in fear of the strength of Buru. All drovers listened intently hanging on to every word, frown and facial muscle twitch of this majestic looking Zulu. He unfolded his version of the Bataleur aviation excellence and of a dangling

Jackal, performing freefall moves on his plummet to bone crushed retrieval.

Buru's deep and descriptive baritone was interrupted by a squawking rooster having his neck wrung. The second rooster was not so talkative. His neck was instantly severed with the vice like grasp of Tadarera, gripping the bird between forefinger and thumb. Both roosters were gutted, stripped of their feathers, head and spurs, and placed into boiling water in a three legged cast iron pot on the fire. Like traditional "stone soup" they nourished and flavoured the water to edible accompaniment for the time honoured staple food of Africa, sadza. A hard porridge, prepared from coarse ground meal of maize or sorghum. It was not long before the camp fell into exhausted silence. Arthur and his two terrier bitches shared a blanket. "Eat'em", the Ridgeback preferred to sit on the camp periphery, back leg down, on tall standing front legs. He was shivering as if cold, staring intently into the night. Occasionally he realigned his stance and periodically curled down to sleep, but seldom for long. He neither barked nor growled, but something in that black void kept his attention through the night.

The shrill of crickets and the owl's hoot, the nightjar's whistle and the jackal cry melodiously symphonised into the night, harmonizing with the varied breathing tones of the drovers, the dogs, the oxen and batwing flaps. Lion and hyena made their presence known, although their sounds were wailed from distance. The cattle were constantly alert to all predators' aggression but on this night they had no fear as the kill in the vicinity had tempered the night sounds, permeating an atmosphere of jungle tranquillity. So much for the planned 17 miles per day. The hunt would have to continue the following morning. It did - and everyone shared an abundance of char grilled impala steak, sadza and thick gravy.

The remaining trip to Johannesburg was completed with single minded determination. Daily distances increased as the terrain levelled and operational routines developed into second nature. On occasions, Arthur would select a drover, varying according to degree of meat needed and walk ahead of the wagons in search of a suitable animal for the pot. These ventures provided opportunity for Arthur to develop intrinsic understanding of individual drovers. He listened intently as they revealed matters of their own inner commitment and belief. He developed intense interest in the subject matter these men would select and he learned to understand each individual from a different perspective. Together and in isolation, the team gained respectful knowledge of each other, developing strengths and desires; together overcoming fears, inabilities, offering support and providing encouragement. Arthur was regularly advising and guiding, solving the issues that were foremost inhibitors to some of their plans. His counsel was sought in matters of hunting and family, courting and breeding, seasons and storms and war and peace and fire and fortune. He gained insight and wisdom from their ancestral experiences and systems of cultural governance and communal contribution. Their practices of satellite decisions, communal consensus and unselfish energetic exertions distinguished their objectives distinctly apart from the greed and aggression of the boardroom selfishness of western civilization. Their world was simple in a fashion of honour and respect. They placed an esteemed value on being physically strong, fit and humble. Their ambitions had narrow horizons in a commercial environment, but full oceans of desire at the roots of their village.

Their travels continued with occasional disruption. A wheel on the wagon inadvertently rolled over an angled granite slab and the immense weight of tare pushed hard at an angle, forcing the wheel to slide, angle, buckle and break. Two spokes were shattered and needed repair and a bush lathe was assembled. Making replacement spokes took time and the chore was keenly attended at the edge of the campfire. Every drover contributed and was deservedly pleased with the team work. It was Tadarera whose craftsmanship proved superior. His wheel maker skills were well honed. Whilst the wagon was empty it was carried by the drovers to level ground, Tadarera changed all the hub stubs of the axles and tightly secured the outer steel rim to the wooden wheel. This involved a precision craftsman who could achieve specific measure to the circumference of the wheel. With an unusual skill, the steel rim had to be heated so as to expand sufficiently to fit the wheel. The steel contracted squeezing tightly to the wood rim of the wheel. When all was complete it was wood pegged into place and the wagon reloaded for an early departure.

This proved sufficient repairs and maintenance for the remainder of the trip to Johannesburg. The wagon with new wheel hubs travelled lighter, with less strain on the oxen but had added two days to the journey. Revitalized the oxen and drovers were glad of the break and stepped off on the third day with renewed vigour and strength. Crossing a series of small rivers and bigger waterways was a time deflecting hurdle, but the travel was smooth and without much ado.

The walk into Johannesburg was eerie for these bush men. Tall buildings, narrow streets and high mine dumps with strong smelling cyanide extraction plants were all foreign to this group of wiry bush travellers. They were surrounded by children, barking dogs and an abundance of people. This was all out of place to their rural environs. Wagon travel here required regulated direction and control on the oxen that were unaccustomed to urban hustle and bustle. The routes were all dust, devoid of vegetation. People peered from buildings, through windows and doors. There were Greek owned grocery stores and Indian haberdashery; a Devonian bakery, adjacent to the Dutch tobacconist and the wagon repair business where the owners spoke Italian. This busy repair centre normally had five wagons each week, pulling in for repair. The road was well signposted, with colourful signage inviting shoe repairs, whiskey, softened steaks and tough steaks at half price. The hotel boasted two saloons and a bathroom away from the dust. The main street was straight and long, providing an urban gauntlet for these bush hardened men.

Locating the trading facility of Hubert Davies was quick. It was a huge imposing three storey building at the far end of the main street. There was an elaborate sign, painted in gold on a green background. HUBERT DAVIES, MINE SUPPLIES & MACHINERY.

The front oxen followed Arthur in a curve to the entrance, and then Buru took charge of the column. There was a sign over a concrete trough advising "Livestock water point. Welcome, Welkom". The oxen needed no encouragement to move to the trough. Buru restrained them and quickly unyoked the front four animals. Arthur observed, then approved and moved off to the wide doors of the building. He kicked the dust off his boots and beat his trouser legs as clean as he could. He entered into the foyer to be met by a suited elderly gentleman with a monocle. Arthur walked tall and brisk paced with his right arm extended in friendship. "May I help?" questioned the man with the monocle. Had to be of direct English descent thought Arthur, and yes, he was right. This sales manager was correct personified, sharp tongued, knowing just what to say before deciding to offer tea or showing you the door. He was disturbed by an inferior emotion as Arthur requested to see Mr. Hubert Davies.

"Aah, yes, I mean, sorry, No because he is not here. He is expected back within a week or two. He has travelled far to the trading port in Lorenzo Marques. He's been gone five weeks." Arthur had not anticipated this delay, but could occupy a little waiting time well. He left a message that he would return in a week, giving a time and date. He passed on a kind greeting from Theophalus Zeederberg and walked out. He talked fast to his men and they all moved off at speed. The unyoked oxen were left to be driven separately and their yoke was bundled into the wagon. They needed to move fast to be sufficiently distant from this rat race. Arthur moved in a north westerly direction, in the hope of crossing the Kyalami River. He pushed the men and the oxen hard for the remainder of the day. In the late afternoon they were surrounded by low rock outcrops and short flat topped thorn trees intermittently growing in grassland vlei and swamp area. There were many pools of water in the black clay soil and the cattle could be well satisfied. They set up a quick camp, merely to spend the night.

When they awoke in the morning they had been joined by a horse, fully saddled with a tight girth strap, saddle bags and a short rein dangling loose to her knees. Arthur approached with the skill of a whisperer and she merely adjusted her weight off her right leg, transferring it onto her left. He talked "horse" with his tongue and his actions. This was a well ridden animal that had been well cared for. It had obviously lost its owner and was seeking civil company. Arthur loosened the girth strap and removed the saddle. It was extraordinarily heavy. He placed it over the trunk of a fallen tree. He called for a handful of maize meal and held this under her chin. She sniffed and lipped her way through this small handful of pleasure, wasting most of it onto the floor. They tied her rein onto a tree and settled into the task of breaking the camp. Buru tried lifting the saddle onto the wagon, amazed at the weight.

He opened the saddle bags to see what could be so heavy. Each bag contained a lump of silver grey metal the size of a junior rugby ball and almost the same shape. Arthur realized the severity of his situation and his plan for the day now changed. He had no mining experience, but he knew that this was an exceptional metal that was developing the towns and the dumps and the head gears, generating employment for hundreds of workers. It was as near to purified gold as a layman could get without high tech smelting and furnaces.

He removed the metal from the bags and placed it into the larder box in the wagon, buried deep in the meal, amongst the KWV, the chicken eggs and the boxes of ammunition.

Arthur saddled up the horse. He sliced and plaited temporary repairs to the reins. Sitting near the fire in the early dawn he poured a mug of coffee and contemplated his day. Then he set out on horseback to back track the route into the main street of Johannesburg. His horse was strong and well trained, obedient to his every command. When he arrived at the offices of Hubert Davies, the sun was just a quarter high in the sky. He pulled up and the horse seemed to know where to go. It stood adjacent to the frame where the rein could secure to the halt hooks. Arthur dismounted and secured the reins to the beam. He walked quickly into the front doors of the building. The suited man approached him in an identical manner and in the same sequence as the previous day, spluttering identical words. When he recognized Arthur he delighted in telling him that Mr. Davies' had returned from his travels. He would be in the building in a very short while and would Arthur like to wait or return later. Arthur explained his urgency and that he would wait, or preferably, would go direct to where he may locate Mr. Davies. The monocled man hesitated and then explained the directions to locate Mr. Davies home. Arthur thanked him, expedited out and onto the horse; leaving a cloud of dust and galloped away as if on the final stretch of a race track. He stopped abruptly outside the gates of an imposing Dutch gabled home, set amongst shaded lawns and well kept gardens. A black horse drawn carriage was parked near the front door and the horses stood relaxed, altering their weight from one leg to the other. Arthur jogged up to the front door, greeting the horse hand as he passed. He knocked on the front door only an instant before Mr. Davies opened it. Arthur introduced himself and explained the urgency; the gold amalgam in the horse saddle; the reason for being in Johannesburg and a brief reason for his call on Mr. Davies. He then handed over the sealed letter from Mr. Zeederberg and stepped back a pace. The letter was opened and read with intense concentration. Mr. Davies' face broadened as he read and enjoying the content of the letter. He extended his hand in the friendliest of gestures; sealing the beginnings of a lifelong camaraderie, business partnership and mutually agreeable friendship. He reversed into the hallway of his home and invited Arthur to sit in a teak riempie stool in the foyer. They sat in chairs close to each other and spoke in low voices.

The gold amalgam would almost certainly belong to someone known to Mr. Davies and the rightful owner would receive his goods as soon as he could be located. Maybe the horse would be recognized by someone who would identify the owner. The matter would not be advertised, but the metal would be stored in the vault at the office of Mr. Davies.

Banter effervesced as if they had known each other a lifetime. They spoke quickly on matters of ostriches, the Cape trading facilities, mining and transport. The day unfolded quickly, with a series of changed plans. Together, Arthur and Uncle Hubert rode fresh horses out to the campsite, instructing the drovers to pack up camp and return to town in the morning. They collected the amalgam and returned to the offices of Hubert Davies and Co. Arthur became a guest in the home of the Davies, with Mrs. Davies looking into his eyes; his soul; with a passion and kindness known only to a mother. She attached an emotion and friendship that was shared with her husband and Arthur became as a son to the family.

The gold amalgam had quantified the honesty entrenched in the marrow of Arthur, expected of everyone, but seldom revealed in this manner. This was instrumental in bonding an eternal friendship based on a handshake.

Arthur remained at the stately home of Hubert and May Davies whilst finalizing preparations for the big trek into the interior. May had taken him to the local tailor and haberdashery section of several outfitters. He became well presented at formal functions hosted by the Davies household and was always seated in the place of preference when hosting influential members of the Transvaal administration or business community.

Together with May and Hubert they planned and acquired all necessary provisions, everything being financed and recorded through the accounts section of the Hubert Davies administration department. As a parting gift to the drovers May had presented each of them with two sets of shorts and two khaki shirts each. Without success she tried to persuade them to take footwear.

Like a boy attending boarding school for the first time, Arthur was well presented in his new clothing from the Indian Market. He had established several important contacts that would contribute to his future planning and entrepreneurial intentions. Everything was ready for the big trek. He cabled his mother with the time and date of departure. He gave good account of the exceptional hospitality afforded him by May and Hubert and was able to confirm details of his financial plan and return schedule.

The horse that intruded Arthur's camp was now tethered at the water point and word had been disseminated throughout the community of the reason for the horse being in the custody of Mr. Hubert Davies. Ten days had elapsed and no owner had come forward to claim the horse.

In addition to the full provisions and draught power that he had started with at Graaf Reinet, Arthur now had additional oxen, saddlery, two horses and four wagons. Each new wagon carried 100 bags of maize and was yoked to 16 well selected, fresh oxen.

The atmosphere was jovial, with a pioneering spirit emanating from the wagons and the men. Local neighbours and more distant community members turned up to see, encourage and bid fond farewell, with messages of fortune to the adventurous travellers. The day had just begun to glow a faint light on the horizon and it was cold.

With an ear piercing whistle and crack of the whip, the men stepped forward in unison with the oxen. Arthur strolled out from under the ornate gabled entrance of the house and closed the door behind him. He waved at the crowd lining the driveway as he walked through them and heard many messages of goodwill.

With pride in his pace, he strode briskly up to the tail wagon running board and climbed aboard. He turned from this elevated position and faced the crowd. He had a panoramic view of the mine headgears reaching tall on the Johannesburg horizons. The wheels at the top were turning and little wagons moved both up and down the dump slopes. The dumps of discard soil from the mining operations were small hills now, significantly changing the skyline of the city. A trail of spectators folded into the road behind them as the trek of 72 oxen, two horses and five wagons rolled down the main street, heading in a northerly direction.

Control of the trek was now firmly established with Buru leading. He walked with the authority of chieftainship, in undeniable control of his responsibilities. The final outward bound segment of the big trek had commenced.

The sun was radiating a bright orange, as it hurried to bed below the baobab on the western horizon. It rapidly turned to a rose red, and reflected a myriad of colours on low transparent clouds. Vegetation brightened from an array of amber, reflecting the dry season, the ochre and the crackle brown bake in the soil. It was that seasonal expectation that livened the country, revived harshness to kindness, and gave energy to lethargy. The animals became jittery in anticipation of the end of those long dry, harsh months. Butterflies pranced from leaf to bark gum; from stone to mirage, and elegantly fluttered by, passing on to other elusions. It was that time of year when butterflies are the most nourishing of food available to birds, reptiles and rodents. It was the dry season, sometime experienced as an open hot hole facing direct into hell. This is Africa. Vegetation is brittle; wildlife seems tired; heat haze projects mirages and cool shade breeze is seldom. The heat shimmer is persuasive that your mouth should be dry and your body needs rest. An unlikely attribute during this season is that most animals in this particular part of the country seem to achieve exceptional physical condition. Their skin seems drum tight and muscle protrudes as if in youthful athletic prime. October in the lowveld is hot and nature is designed to cope. Arthur was camped in the low lying areas overlooking a sand pool on a tributary of the Limpopo River.

Tadarera and Buru had both strapped fly beads around their forehead. An ingenious idea, a strap is secured to the head tightly, above the brow. From each half inch of this strap dangles several two inch long strips that have weights attached. A slight neck jerk or constant headshake disrupts any landing insects. This provides an effective repellent to the many insects seeking moisture from human lip, eye and nostril. The Mopani fly is best known of these, and they become very persistent when needing intake of that moisture! The discomfort experienced when these little creatures seek eye-lid moisture is an annoyance that can have far-reaching impact. Animals can run, and be stampeded to exhaustion; people to claustrophobia and birds to swift flight, if this tiny winged nuisance be too prevalent. It is this little terror that gave need for animals to have a tail; for some to have very extended mane, or face hair. This discomfort is a camp-fire topic on every possible occasion, with a new concept, new experiences and repellent design plan being spat forth at every opportunity. These little nuisance insects have generated exhaustive camp-fire entertainment and brain-stretchers. Most travellers to these areas quickly determine efficient insect repelling techniques – and in a hurry, too.

Three vultures circled high above the camp. Observing the effortless aviation skills of these far flying birds can be inspiration and therapeutic tonic. Arthur shielded his eyes from the rose red sun as he arched his neck to look skyward. His mind was alert and becoming wizened: being sharpened, but was this in matters of flying..... Or matters of survival? This young man had the adventurous and engineering competence to evaluate aviation techniques, but now was not the time. These scavenging giant birds spoke volumes in their daily routine. To the ripened old men of tropical survival their presence told of wind and of weather; food, feast and famine; of success and of failure and all that physical living is about. The vulture has been scorned and ridiculed as scavenger, beggar and ugly parasite. Arthur saw none of this. Rather, he saw an incredible flying mobility, tenacious agility, compassionate parenting, and a clinical vacuum cleaning machine, all designed into a single species of God's aviation genius. But he was observing something that was to have long reaching impact on his life. He was being directed to the rescue of another adventuring traveller!

As the sun continued towards its destination, Arthur detected the vultures were planning to land. He whistled for Eat-em, Gyps and Star. They hurriedly joined him; Star from under the wagon; a guilty looking Gyps from the back of a wagon, and Eat-em who had been asleep, with his nose wrapped amidst wing feathers of the old rooster that had become dinner the previous afternoon. His wishful thinking had merely become dreams, as he fell into midday sleep, bathed in wagon shade and fowl feathers. Like bearers at the ready, Arthur set off, rifle on shoulder, with three dogs at heel, a laughing Buru and excited Tadarera joining the walk. They left camp in a hurry, in a flurry of light hearted humour. Everyone knew why. Tadarera had a handful of coal grilled, unshelled peanuts which he was throwing like a masterful juggler, into his mouth as he ran to catch up. Arthur headed straight towards the vultures' landing ground. It was a short fast walk with an abrupt stop! Treetops overloaded, branches bent like well sprung gymnastic leguanas under starter's orders. The vultures were everywhere; in the trees, on the ground, in the air landing and taking off and immediately overhead. This human stripe of sudden intrusion into their silent and waiting world had caused panic and frantic fright into flight.

Young warriors were always ready to act quickly, but none of these did. They were calm in the knowledge of no immediate danger. Even Eat-em and Gyps were not too alarmed in the flurry. Star, on the other hand, misread the situation. Her stump tail at once tried to hide under her belly; her back arched as every high speed instinct was put into gear. Star accelerated instantly to full gallop. She had no idea as to what, why, who or how things had happened. She only knew that she had to be far away this instant. She achieved maximum thrust as she sped off, out of sight, amidst feathers, dust and confusion. Suddenly, just five paces away, Arthur realised that they had stumbled into an alarming situation. A crudely parked ox wagon was standing askew, with one wheel lying on the ground. Vultures had been startled from their perch on the wagon edge. An old, silver bearded man was soundly sleeping, propped up against a nearby Mopani tree. He had been oblivious to the hustle and bustle in his immediate vicinity. The vultures had sensed imminent death, gathering, to await his final heartbeat. The startled panic of birds, Buru and the dogs, the guns and dust all contributed. The old man slowly sat up-right and stroked his hands through his beard, to his eyes. He looked too fragile for this environment. His glare momentarily fixed on Arthur's chest, then slid aground, as he crawled over to a more comforting sand patch. His wrinkled old skin showed signs of a lifetime beneath Africa's sun. His arm flapped as if to tell Arthur "get out'a my planet, go away".

Arthur gave orders and Tadarera keenly responded with a leap towards a nearby forked stick. His strength was evident as his knife sliced the purple black heart of one of the worlds' hardest trees, the Mopani. In a few quick minutes Buru and Tadarera had crafted and plaited a stretcher. A piece of hessian sackcloth from near the extinguished campfire was used as the mattress hang strap. Arthur stooped enquiringly over the old man. The old eyes lacked life but his body temperature said otherwise. His frail appearance was deceptive. Stooping over each end of his body length, Buru locked onto the shrivelled skin around his ankles, while Arthur and Tadarera formed a chair-like backrest with interlocked arms, and positioned themselves to receive his weight. Like an alert angry adder, the old silver beard came alive with resistance as the old man spat out dry words of hatred, in Afrikaans. His body language instructed that he be left alone. The full strength of three athletic adult men was required to overpower this frail old man, and hold him to the "stretcher." His strength faded quickly, but it had been quite a lesson to these three hardcore men of the bush. It was late. The sun had slid below the horizon. The return to camp would be in moonlit darkness.

Surrounding the old man's silver eyebrows the outer eye muscles were swollen hugely out of proportion. His forehead was painfully swollen. The rest of his face was drawn and sullen. His lips were cracked to bleeding and his teeth were newly broken.

The man was seriously consumed by one of Africa's many ailments. He probably had malaria, but his swollen eyes were not helping in diagnosis. When the stretcher bearers got back to camp the old man was shivering with cold yet dripping perspiration from his chest and facial extremities. He needed to sit close to the camp fire. This confirmed the diagnosis. Arthur grappled darkness to find the quinine medication. It was in powder form and had to be carefully measured in a sewing thimble. The dosage was one quarter thimble of powder per estimated portion of bodyweight that equalled an unopened bag of salt. Arthur measured out one and a half thimbles of powder, and mixed this with water into a paste. The old mans determination at resistance had to be physically restrained by an additional three men to hold him, whilst the centre finger knuckle bone of both Buru and Tadarera had to form a clamp on the upper jaw; mid way between lower jawbone and outer eye slit. The old man mumbled complaint, but had no options against this manly mechanics of jungle body repairs. The quinine paste was plastered against the deepest part of his throat and his mouth filled with water. His lips had to be held closed with the clasp of two hands, while Arthur skilfully monitored breath intake, then sealed both nostrils tightly. It was a case of swallow ... or swallow. With well informed commanders, there was no alternative and zero tolerance, the general rule that successfully colonized the world and won two World Wars. The old man could die, but if his physical resistance was the yardstick, then long life would be his benchmark. He now owed his life to the non negotiable decisions of Arthur and the physical strength of those surrounding him.

In the morning the old man stared deliriously into the flames and smoking embers. He was warmed at his feet by the two terriers and his back, by Eat'um. Mphofu, a youthful drover, had risen early and stoked the coals, adding coffee granules and water to the three legged cast iron coffee pot. He poured a sickly sweet cup of strong brew for the old man, handing it over with his left hand clasped to his right wrist, in a demonstration of respect. Mphofu was shamed and frightened by the arrogant refusal from the contemptuous old man.

Mphofu set the metal mug a safe distance from the fire to ensure it stayed warm, but not too hot. Arthur had witnessed this event and was surprised. He moved closer into the firelight, sitting nearer than normal to Mphofu. He thought quickly and made a decision. The old man was not being rude, but simply expressing anger. Arthur understood. He walked back to his wagon, untied the thong closure and manoeuvred his hand, sifting through a steel trunk filled with maize meal. Buried deep inside the trunk, protected in the maize meal, was a bottle with the inscription:-

KWV – Smaaklike Brandewyn KWV – Refined Brandy Spirit Kaap van Goie Hoop. Cape of Good Hope

Arthur approached the camp fire again, but this time with researched confidence. He sat close to the silver hair and long silver beard. He secured the brandy bottle between his own rib cage and biceps. He held the warm coffee cup in the full clasp of both hands. Then, he poured out half the coffee, and stared deep into the eyes of this unwell and elderly man. He smiled. The old man returned a hard, solemn glare. Arthur discarded the top from the bottle and filled the metal cup. The aroma was vile to him, but a distinct tonic to this old man, who grabbed the cup in both hands and consumed the entire contents in three swift overfilled mouthfuls. He looked at Arthur from behind an angry, wrinkled mask and coughed up large, deep seated dark brown sputum. He expelled this with a marksman's precision, at the fireside edge of the foot of Mphofu. This was a statement clearly understood. It needed no explanation to anyone raised abreast racial hatred and encouragement. The old man had still not uttered a discernible word, but indicated need for another drink. Mphofu again filled the cup with tar like coffee, while Arthur put out his hand to collect the bottle. The old man moved as a viper to prey. In an instant the coffee splashed into the flame; the cup lay inverted in sand and the bottle was tightly sucking its way through a silver moustache, deep into his mouth. Today's first sign of thirsty Mopani flies was seen alighting a coffee drenched log. As Arthur looked on in amazement, the old man drained the bottle of its last drop of liquid, tucking the dry bottle into his belt. This degree of alcohol intake would kill any unseasoned novice, but it was a tonic to this sun hardy, leathery cadaver that now sat staring at nothing. His eyes suddenly became filled with life, and he rolled over in protest at the presence of his onlookers. Within minutes he was in deep sleep on cold ashes and sand. As the sun rose in the sky the drovers had all worked together to make shade so that old Silver Beard would not become burned in the heat. They had planted two fork sticks two paces apart, and placed a beam pole from one to the other. Arthur sensed that the fever had harmed this old man in the brain, and he chose to stay close for the day. When the old man awoke to a sitting position soon after midday Arthur called his team to perform another administration of quinine. The energised old man was still unable to fight off six strong men, but not before putting up formidable effort. Then Arthur deemed it expedient to award him with another short shot of brandy. This time he brought out a hip flask size bottle indicating that they could share it. No such luck. When seen and in reach, the lightning speed of these muscles was no match for the unsuspecting Arthur. As the speed of a cracking whip, so it was that yet again, the bottle seemed determined to swallow itself into his gullet. Arthur carried brandy only as a form of bush anaesthetic, so was quite happy to not partake. The quarter bottle was quickly devoured, and again, within minutes the man was sleeping motionless, this time snoring loudly. He was oblivious to the Mopani flies, and needed no warming. He did not wake that afternoon and so it was that the camp settled into another night in the heat of Baobab country, somewhere between the Limpopo and the Zambezi Rivers.

Before dawn the next morning one of the younger drovers knelt beside Arthur, and spoke with urgency in his trembling speech. The old man had vanished, could not be found anywhere. The camp all gathered around the fire. Everyone was nervous. Buru laughed in amazement. It was as if someone had risen from the dead. The respect for this achievement was piled high on "doctor" Arthur. The old man was gone and so had the empty bottles. His spirit seemed to remain by virtue of an unexplained aura penetrating the camp mood. Everyone was silent until the first sign of daylight nudged itself into the stars. With a clear dawn and full warmth from too much coffee, everyone went in search of the silver bearded man, of respectable strength. Buru and Tadarera went straight to where his oxcart had been parked. It had moved. Fresh cattle footprints, droppings and a discarded label of KWV indicated that the old man was back in control. The wheel to his wagon had been restored. There was no evidence of anything else nearby. They returned to report their findings to Arthur, who laughed jovially acknowledging a divine intervention in the repair of broken human bodies. The boys all wanted to follow the cattle tracks and rescue the man who had become known simply as "Mdala", "Old Man." Arthur forbade this as a transgression into the private world of an aged traveller. He had left the group in admiration for his resilience and human strength in extreme adversity and he had left a KWV label.

The journey continued. Several weeks passed. As the column of oxen, the wagons and the drovers snaked through the harsh mountainous terrain, past huge granite boulders, hills, valleys, rivers, forests and geographical obstacles, dry riverbed after dry riverbed, so camp fire unity became deeply entrenched amongst everyone. Even the dogs seemed as equally attached to each other as they were to Arthur and the drovers, the cattle and the chickens. Thirst had played a role in all lives, and it was here that the chickens clucked, and suffered most. The column had had to split and a wagon made light to return south for three full days, and then back again with full water drums. This was part of the professional pioneer learning curve that was experienced by many. The temptation to travel light, without water was seldom wise. The remainder of this, Arthur's first trip to Fort Salisbury was uneventful. When he arrived to tumultuous greeting from the elderly chief of Monomatapa, Chief Mbare, he was elated, and gratified to conclude his first major financial transaction. This was the sale of all 450 bags of maize that he had bought at the Hubert Davies mill in Johannesburg. He had not yet paid for it, but by virtue of his agreement he was about to own his first ever £2,000. He had purchased the maize at 12/6^{d} per bag and had sold the entire consignment to S. Sloman and Co. Millers, for a gratifying £5 per bag. The actual cash transaction would be direct between Sloman and Davies; Arthur would feel his dues directly from Hubert Davies.

Time was needed for repairs to wheels and to rebuild the ox muscle draught power. Now, business completed, replenishment energy restored in a matter of five days, the trek south to Johannesburg began. The actual departure from the kopje (hill) area of Chief Mbare was a joyous occasion. The chief had greeted Arthur with elaborate kindness, and had invited him to return "checha, sterek" or with "much haste" but for a longer time. The power of the chief rested in his tribal support and livestock wealth. His living arrangements were quantifiable evaluation of his grandeur; his assets and attire demonstrated the feelings of his people towards him as their leader. This day he was regal in stature, grand in eloquence, shiny in sweat and elaborate in humour. A tall agile leader was dressed for the farewell occasion in the belief that he would soon be hosting his new found friends from the south. He wore a shoulder cover of pale grey leopard skin and had a 'Sam Brown' of charcoal coloured sable skin. His skirt cover was tailored from the close-stripe sections of young Zebra. His breast plate and head gear were not symmetrical but certainly crafted by a devoted crown and garment specialist. It was predominantly the chest skin of a young lioness, with inclusions of segments of the skin of red impala; pure white from sable belly and a shining blue/black from the back skin of a young wildebeest. This garment was constructed to portray excitement, joy and joviality. The mood was created to set the tone for a joyful return of his visitors. Yes, the chief was resplendent in appearance and composed in stature. His gestures showed warmth and appreciation toward his visitors. He indicated a genuine eagerness for Arthur's return and it was entrenched that their friendship had cemented deep into all warriors.

Farewells behind them, all minds were clearly set on the 600 mile journey back. The oxen had made the journey and individual characteristics and competencies were now evident to the drovers. The return was light travel and should not take more than six weeks. The heavy loaded wagons had tired the north bound oxen. The 13 week northbound trip could be much reduced on the empty southbound return.

For ten quick days the time passed without event. On the morning of the eleventh day as camp was being assembled, one of the younger drovers, Patulani, walked 200 paces from camp. This was the general routine in fulfilment of daily ablution tasks. He returned hurriedly; his face drained, from the natural purple ebony to a reddish brown. He had stumbled across an ox wagon, four sleek looking oxen still tethered in pairs to their yoke and a sleeping, silver bearded old man. Patulani could not contain his youthful enthusiasm. "Baas, baas buya checha, lo Mdala ena pendukili", "Sir, sir, come quick, the old man has returned." Arthur jumped and ran to Patulani. "Show me, let's go". Camp scurry included the three dogs. Arthur approached respectfully. Mdala was hunched low, breaking twigs and blowing on a newly lit fire. He seemed angry but looked incredibly well, except for one eye. This was swollen and painful. Arthur kindly extended a friendly handshake which was ignored, as Mdala turned to billow the flames. Arthur signalled the boys to return to camp and two of the dogs joined them. Arthur rolled a nearby dry stump closer to Mdala, and sat. He looked at Mdala and smiled. The disinterest was waning, and Mdala looked in anticipation of KWV. Arthur offered coffee and food. Surprisingly, Mdala stood erect over the small flame and proceeded to urinate, killing the flame. He then kicked sand to cover all smoking embers and turned to face where Arthur had come from. He led the way. Arthur followed. The walk was brisk, but Mdala had a slight favouring of one leg over the other. Neither spoke, but the fact that Mdala was agile and youthful beneath those wrinkles spoke volumes. Mdala had just arrived in the area, having journeyed through a bright moonlight night. He was setting up to rest through the day. Arthur had disturbed his plan, but Mdala was pleased, as this meant less food preparation and more KWV.

Mdala seemed to know exactly where to go and what to do. He led to the fire and glared at Buru, who immediately stood, respectfully. The stare and solid sternness said it all. Those gathered at the fireside immediately left. Mdala sat in Arthur's leather strip seat. Arthur chose an inverted wooden box. Tadarera returned, and poured a thick, black brew into two metal containers and added sugar. By swirling the cup in a circular motion the sugar partly dissolved. Mdala swallowed the piping hot brew, and then proceeded to fill his pipe with tobacco while remaining silent. Young Arthur spoke with respect to this wise old traveller, and not a word was returned, until the third draw on the cracked, home made pipe. Then Arthur realised the man was of German origin, but with South Africa well ingrained. His stories developed slowly, but with unexpected wisdom, supported by a lifetime of experiences. His latest had occurred, and continued as an ongoing saga. The depth of spiritual connotations was alarming. He had experienced three separate incidents spread over some 900 miles, involving the very bowels and aura of Satan himself.

Mdala had set up camp some three months prior, on the north bank of the Limpopo River. (The significance of this camping spot being a foreign land was to impact Arthur much later.) In clearing a campsite, Mdala had been moving logs, rocks, stumps and soil and filling holes and depressions. During this exercise, his native gun-bearer "Peleele" had disturbed a nesting place of the much feared African Black Cobra. This snake is known in Afrikaans as "Rinkaals." This snake is highly regarded by African tradition as physical, living representation of Satan himself. It is feared not only for spiritual reasons, but also for its lightning speed; accuracy and violent aggression; skilfully penetrating thin bone where necessary to disarm, destroy and annihilate any intrusion on its territory.

The snake erected itself to equal height, looking Peleele straight in the eye. Experience was quick to react. Peleele shielded his direct line of sight from the Cobra. In an instant the venom dripped off his arm in a spoonful quantity. Mdala turned, to look directly at the hooded head from the back. Devils are said to have eyes in their back and this seemed so. Mdala grabbed his stock whip, attempting a speed of sound contact with the snake's neck. Rinkaals' was too quick, slithering into dry grass, her head carried high through the initial disappearing surge. Her departing eye contact with Mdala conveyed a clear message, "I'll get you." But for now she was gone. Camp construction continued and the fire was lit.

Peleele laughed as he trembled and finger-flicked the liquid from his forearm. "Ai, baas, nyamusha ena doozi." – "Hey, Boss, today that was close." Mdala and Peleele continued camp action, cooking, preparing and planning. Mdala laughed at and ridiculed Peleele for being in the line of fire. It humoured them both, and shamed old Peleele. He was embarrassed enough, but Mdala enjoyed making him squirm. When all was calm and the two men relaxed around the flames appreciating the campsite Mdala noticed a shine slither back from the grass. She was back and the two men froze, momentarily motionless. Mdala slowly reached for his stock-whip. Too quick. She vanished as quick and as quiet as she had arrived – into a nearby stump. Mdala grappled a burning truncheon sized dry log, and rammed its glowing flame and embers into the hole where Rinkaals had disappeared. Obsessed with her destruction they both gathered dry grass and set alight the remaining stump. All brightly aglow, they were now certain she could not escape. It was a stump partly obscure, partly buried, partly alive with rooted shoots, and partly dead. The route taken by Rinkaals delved into deep earthly bowels, and she accessed an unseen corridor and alighted the far end. She had left behind a nest of 14 two inch long cobra babies. When Mdala saw her come out, his anger rose, he was determined to destroy the complete stump. They dug together, and uncovered the full and very active nest of 14 writhing, wriggling worm-like mini-vampires. Mdala excitedly thrust another burning log containing glowing coals atop this nest of vipers. As he looked up he saw a tall standing black shine vanish again into tinder dry undergrowth. The two men set the area to flame. As they settled back fire-side, Peleele knowledgeably revealed that Satan is most comforted amongst glowing embers. He was afraid that destroying her young was a mistake. Mdala believed the problem was over. Peleele believed it had just begun.

Ten days passed, and Mdala and Peleele had travelled well and comparatively uneventfully, making about 22 miles per day. The undulating open grassland of the midland area was under the chieftainship of an elderly wrinkled old man, known as Sekuru Somabula. Sekuru means "Elder". "Somabula" means "Same level". This was a geographical name given to the sub-chief who ruled over flat plains and flat topped trees.

Mdala selected a crop topped acacia tree under which to camp, and Peleele was pleased with the campsite. It was only 70 paces to a small trickle of clean water. His secret hope was that they would base up for a few days, or even weeks. They flattened the surrounding grass, and formed it into a carpet. Peleele cleared a patch, and lit a fire using dry bark from the lone acacia tree, and broke off a long dead, very dry branch and placed it central amongst the flame. The bark had been lit under a big section of dead Acacia tree. It would burn for at least three days. He was pleased with the temperate climate, open spaces, herds of kudu, sable, wildebeest, of reedbuck families, impala, warthog and guinea fowl, and proximity to water. And some of those virginal looking mothers breasting snotty nostrils in the kraal of Chief Somabula also had place in his thoughts. Yes, they could be very comfortable here for several weeks.

The oxen were out-spanned. The oxcart had few contents, and was light to manoeuvre. Mdala was smoking his favourite "Voortrekker" pipe blend and attending to a deep cut on the back of his hand – that meat between thumb and forefinger, had been deep cut that week when the disselboom of the wagon lodged between two rocks while crossing a stream. Mdala had attempted to lift at the moment the oxen stepped forward. This squashed his hand between rock and rim wheel steel. The steel remained shining, and the rock became bloodstained. He was now drying out the wound by inserting coarse salt deep into flesh; rubbing, massaging – and gritting his teeth. His hardwood pipe barely survived the grip from his lips and the clench of teeth. He was staring over the grassy plains. He stood to stretch his vision over several horizons, and realised he was looking at just another horizon. The sting in his hand was subsiding. He turned back and knelt near the fire to shake the coals alive. He picked up the burning log that was an overhang straddling the flames. The main trunk was now burned through, and was hollow. Mdala and Peleele together lifted the heavy trunk, and eased it closer to the fire. This opened the log to being tunnel-like for a good length. Deep inside, amidst smoke and heat – and shielded by flickering flame Peleele heard a noise that made his watch-spring type hair curls to stand out straight. His exclamation prompted Mdala's inquisitive assessment. Together they rolled the trunk to reveal the source of noise. Four eyes looked with one keenness. Their heads and arms were touching; sweat creaming itself from one to the other. The log-sound could have been boiling sap, or gum from the tree. It was a sabre type rattle, which neither hissed nor growled, but was somewhere in that void. At the instant of log pivotal rollover, Mdala learned a lesson. The venom splashed directly central on the bridge of his nose. Both eyes filled equally with this killer substance, as Mdala writhed in agony trying to remove whatever was flowing into, and trickling out of his agonised vision. It was a thin liquid substance, thinner than Spirit, but sticky. He screamed in agony as the liquid penetrated the gash in his hand, and his arm became uncontrollably erect; his jaw bone clenched acknowledging agony and his eyes seemed to be housing coals on fire.

Peleele was distraught. It was always him that this white man doctored. Now the role was reversed. Peleele knew what had to be done, but a meagre black servant had no right to do it. He had to urinate into dry bark of the offending tree, and pour this into his master's eyes. Persuasion in Africa is harsh and final. The weak have to subside and surrender to the strong. In the moment of agony Mdala had no strength nor virility, nor statement or argument. He limply surrendered a shivering lump of human flesh to Peleele, now the butcher! Peleele was desperate for his master, as he too had experienced this psychological agony. He had never had venom in his eye, but he had been laughed at and ridiculed for being cobra spit hit on the arm. That pain was enough!

Peleele bathed his warm urine into, over, under and behind the eyes that seemed to be on fire. Looking into these now bloodshot spheres of his master was painful. Looking out of these eyes was even more so. Mdala was trembling in agony, but was otherwise totally obedient and passively subservient to every instruction from Peleele. Peleele nervously accepted command of the situation, and performed medical miracles. His knowledge and experience had been gleaned from a lifetime of campfire stories. This is what saved the eyes of his master.

Peleele tried his hand with the .303 calibre rifle, but could never resolve even how to load it. Mdala tried giving instructions from his blinded position, but the project was a hopeless non-starter. They were destined to have no fresh meat for the duration of Mdala being sore-eye. This was harsh reality to them both! Peleele tried his fishing skills in the trickle puddle that skirted the camp. He made fine fish-hooks from acacia thorn, and plaited fine nets from the inner skin of tree bark. He excelled in elation when his hook ensnared an adult frog, and he was infuriated when chief Somabula told him that the river contained no fish as it dried up every year, for eight months.

After three weeks of total darkness, and excruciating eye-pain Mdala sensed some relief with gentle pastel light seeming to appear. The regular wash in urine had significantly eased the pain, and Mdala waited keenly for this five time a day ritual. Each bathing seemed to relieve pain and provide slight experience of light. Peleele had also advised the people in the village of Chief Somabula of the agony of his master, and the response had been overwhelming. The elder women in the village had prescribed bathing with warm goat milk and rapid cure would be obtained if some of the young mothers would provide direct injections of breast-milk without it being containerized. This was regularly done, at least three times each week, directly dripped into wide open eyes, by several young mothers. The relief was gratifying. Milk was precious and the giving of it was at the expense of child health, but it was necessary to help this old man. The village had truly given from deep in the heart; given of their inner warmth and demonstrated deep human compassion.

Then, one morning Mdala awoke and had vision. He could see more than light. He could detect movement and this provided an invigorating reason to bathe his eyes more often. So much so that the two men were having difficulty between them in producing enough urine. Mdala would joke with Peleele that he was not much of a urinator. Peleele would determine to prove his master wrong, and dribble into a container barely enough to perform the bath. Then he would challenge his master to do better, and he seldom could. It was light hearted, jovial banter.

Eventually Mdala had vision that could distinguish people from animals, pots from rocks and bullets from sticks. They decided to move forward. Peleele needed one last visit to the kraal of Chief Somabula. He told Mdala it was simply to bid his farewell! He set off early, and usually returned within two hours. Peleele had been gone more than twenty four hours. Mdala fumbled around the camp and prepared himself a strong brew of hot black drink. He was anxious. Peleele had been away too long. There were few hazards in this part. The lion population was small and there was ample game-meat to feed them. Cheetah was in abundance; could reliably be seen two or three times every day, but never had these animals ever shown sign of aggression to people in the district of Chief Somabula. Mdala was lost in this thought when he heard high pitch giggles from a short distance. Then he was amazed to see Peleele holding one of the little teenage girls possessively. He told the others they could go, and they did. He then gingerly approached his master with a fully prepared statement. He needed someone to help him. The work of Doctor, Cook, washer, drover and head-urinator were too much. He had therefore recruited Shupiwe to accompany them as cook and pot washer. Mdala was incensed and expressed his contempt. Peleele pleaded and said he would release her in just one month, to make her own way back to her ancestral village. Mdala had no options. The camp and trek continued, with Shupiwe behaving as a daughter to Mdala. She was very afraid to be alone at night, and so the gallant Peleele condescended to have her share his bedding.

They stayed on at this camp for five weeks in all, whilst recuperating the vicious Cobra attack. Then they moved on.

The first night in new camp was comforting and very pleasant as they had travelled only eleven miles, and found a huge pool on a somewhat bigger river. Peleele wanted to base up here for a while. It seemed an excellent place for honeymoon purposes, and he was sure there were fish in the pool. They had not been successful in hunting since Rinkaals visit, and they desperately needed protein. Mdala agreed that they would remain here for three days, if fishing was successful. His eyes were still not capable of hunting success, and his forehead was painfully swollen. Camp was set up on the bank immediately overlooking the pool, in the shade of five well-canopied Mfuti trees. Peleele was in his element, and hooked his first success within three hours of arriving at camp. It was a slippery, slimy, long whiskered Catfish. He was so excited and screamed with joy when finally, landing had occurred. Shupiwe and Mdala were summoned to enjoy the event. As they walked closer for the poor vision of Mdala, they witnessed an excitement generally reserved for five year olds. Peleele grabbed his fish in both hands and jubilantly lifted it over his head. It gave a curt wriggle and slithered from his hand, to the floor – and one wriggle later, it splashed and vanished into deep water, leaving a short farewell swirl on the water surface, and puppy like drooped ear disappointment all over Peleele. His arms swung wildly as he expelled every type of traditional expletive. No one felt sorrier for poor old Peleele than Peleele. To the rest of the world this was either funny or indifferent.

The following morning Mdala decided it was time to leave. Peleele was devastated; physically too complex in his bond with Shupiwe, he could not leave her. He could not argue with his master and felt he could not abandon him either. These decisions were now far too complex. Peleele decided on the only practical option. That evening, when all oxen were in-spanned, and the trek was moving, he would quietly take his bride into the dark, and allow his master to travel on. His plan was actioned when the moon had fully developed in the early evening, and the oxen continued in the same direction, and without leadership. Mdala lay in the wagon as the oxen trundled through the night. Mdala was mystified when he realized that Peleele was no longer part of his team. He realized too, how Peleele had been persuaded. What she had to offer was more powerful than what Mdala paid. He understood. It was now weeks later, and he had set up camp in the shade of a huge Baobab tree. It was here that Patulani had discovered him whilst attending to morning ablutions.

Mdala never spoke of his family or history, except in regard to his experience with Rinkaals and Peleele. He had genuine deep seated fear of Rinkaals, and gut feeling intuition that Rinkaals had descended into this world to disturb and distress his travels and his companionship with Peleele. Arthur adopted a sympathetic attitude to this man of otherwise good experience and practical wisdom. But he could have no impact on his pitiful fear of this eternally determined satanic predator that haunted old Mdala. These two pioneering spirited giants of an unfolding Africa parted company in mutual admiration and a genuine respect for each other.

It was to be 40 months before Arthur would finally grasp understanding of this old man, and his spiritual fears.

Arthur had established his home and several business interests in this land now called Rhodesia. He had contracted to supply hardwood timber to several mining companies. The biggest was known as The Globe Gold Company. The other was The Phoenix Mining Corporation. Arthur had recruited forty men from amongst several villages in the district of Chief Gweru and Chief Somabula. He had in-spanned thirty two oxen to five wagons and travelled deep to the west, down the Zambezi Escarpment, into vast forest areas of Teak and Ebony and Mahogany and the high gloss craftsman's pride, the brown and white steel hard Mukwa tree.

With weary drovers and hungry hewers Arthur had to hunt for tonight's pot. He summoned Tadarera to accompany him, and left Buru in charge of setting up camp. With dogs at the heel they set a demanding stride. Within seven hundred paces of camp Tadarera stooped low on his haunch, and indicated into a nearby thicket. Arthur had a very keen eye in this terrain but today he was beaten. Tadarera had seen what Arthur could not – until the twitch of an ear alerted him. They were idle and distinctly not alert. This was the result of the midday heat. The old bull stood tall as if cast in bronze. His pair of three curve horns was a proud possession, statuesquely on display. His ladies were elegantly scattered, seemingly surrounding him. A few young bulls with barely a curve in the horn were on the periphery. Arthur selected a bull from the herd, took aim from a dead-rest "V" in a convenient green-stick, and slowly squeezed death into the barrel of his .318 calibre rifle. Neither an eye nor an ear had detected these two stealth warriors in action. The hunt was over, and the camp was in meat. The shot-sound had been heard from the camp, and the certain impact thud had told the men that they would have meat tonight. Eleven younger athletes sprinted out of camp, hurriedly to offer their services in retrieving the meat. Arthur and Tadarera were pleased to receive help, and walked slowly back to base. Vultures were again in evidence circling casually, at quite a distance. Arthur cocked brow to observe. Together they stopped. This grand flock of beauty in ugliness was busy. They returned to camp at a brisk walk where Tadarera quickly summoned several young men. He showed them the landing vultures and instructed they should hasten to see what had attracted these birds. As athletes in prime, these young Matabele men set course and into action at canter. It was not long before two returned. One was hysterical; the other just flapped his abundant lips in disbelief. They had left three men at the site. Arthur received a quick brief, jumped for his rifle and ran. What these men had seen was alarming, at least! Arthur arrived to a scene of despair. The men that had remained were afraid. They had been chasing the vultures away from two ox carcasses. The oxen had been dead for several hours, both still secured in their in-span yoke. The vultures had started devouring the carcasses. A pair of Bataleur eagles was grounded some thirty paces from the oxcart. The trees were filled to bending the branches; large bellied partly bald vultures and a lone Marabou stork. The ox wagon beam was pointing high to the heavens, and in sitting position just eleven paces away, sat a silver haired man with his hand positioned firm into his long silver beard. Arthur rushed to his side. The man had no life in his eyes but his body had warmth. There was no pulse, and a frown was deep seated. Two severe lacerations had sliced deep into his jugular, and a thin clear liquid trickled and mingled in blood-furrows down into his bent elbow. The prospect of surviving a cobra bite to the neck was zero. Arthur stood to take in the reality. His eyes panned into and over the wagon. There were a few meagre possessions; an axe; a pot; an empty salt sack and a dried out skin from a huge golden leopard. Protectively standing, proud and erect in the far corner of the wagon stood an eighteen inch section of shining black cobra, with her hood flared out wide as a plate; her fork tongue smoothly agile, alert and active; her two inch diameter muscle of girth had been severely scarred by fire; her slender muscles and remaining six foot of body length coiled protectively around seventeen little vipers. She held Arthur's eye contact – seeming to smile – and planted a clear bush message. "You stand on *my* land, not yours" – "Touch my babies – you will surely die." – "Hurt us – and I'll see you in Hell."

VENISON, VERMIN, VENOM AND VULTURES

Arthur was deeply committed in his quest for excellence; his vision of involvement, an inner determination and desire to be remembered for positive contribution and regional significance. He set personal goals with tough objectives and worked steadfastly to surpass his own very demanding schedule. His business acumen cemented a life long friendship with his most generous sponsor, Hubert Davies, in Johannesburg. The first of Arthur's trips to Fort Salisbury was wholly financed by H Davies and Co. partly through a gift of five wagons, as well as twenty eight oxen, and sufficient cash to pay monthly wages to the drovers. It was Mr. Davies who arranged the agreement whereby Arthur would transport maize to Fort Salisbury and sell it to S Sloman and Co. who had set up a trading post on the southern bank of the Mukuvisi River. The business agreement was neither documented nor legalized. This huge investment transaction was put in place between two men that had never met each other, by a third person – Hubert Davies – who spoke only high regard and grand honour of both Arthur and Solly Sloman. The eventual result was mutual appreciation of each other with both Arthur and Solly being very lucratively rewarded.

Arthur had returned three times, and decided when he left the Kraal of Chief Mbare on this occasion that he would return all the way to his home; to his Tokkie and to his family. He had a yearning to be amongst the hills of his youth. His determination to confirm his manly competence as a pioneering adventurer had been fulfilled; his bank balance was far greater than he had anticipated and all of his remaining travel team were ready to return. They had been away from home for 20 months, and their routine needed a little home-grown female inclusion. Gyp had twice miscarried; Star showed no inclination towards breeding and Eat-em seemed content to protect the camp. All three dogs were exceptional trackers, and all had many memories of the hunt; the win and some thorny rewards. The hunt had left certain physical scars on all of them, and success had left a spirited determination and eagerness. These were three exceptional dogs that were much enjoyed by everyone on trek and certainly each dog had been contributor on many an occasion, when the hunting party had accepted failure, the dogs would seek out and find.

All but one of the wagons would remain in the Johannesburg milling yard at S Sloman and Co. when the group returned to the Cape. Arthur also made the decision to return old Madonsa back to pastures from whence he had come. He had shown no sign of fatigue on the entire travels, but a decision was made to rest him for the immediate future.

They set off all in-spanned for this third return to Johannesburg, feeling overconfident; becoming deep slotted in routine and repetitive in action. In reality they were starting on the most eventful of journeys; Buru and Tadarera both coming close to death, and Arthur deciding for the first time in his young life that maybe death be a better option than the Fever. As they travelled the midland plains of Rhodesia they all experienced a tranquillity; an inner assurance of traversing this continent with ease. The flat topped thorn trees and vast open grasslands interspersed with regular sightings of zebra, wildebeest, impala, kudu and reedbuck were all contributions in the mental diaries of each. The trials, however, of traversing Africa were about to unfold.

It started that afternoon. Tadarera securing a tourniquet tightly around his head just above the eye brow was the first indicator. This was a known relief of head-ache, and seldom failed. The severity of head pain was measured or indicated in the tightness, and Tadarera was putting extra pressure into his knot. Buru seldom showed the emotion that his eye propelled across the campfire this day. He knew what Tadarera would be experiencing, and his sympathy cells became energised. Tadarera had beads of perspiration straddling his upper lip, and a very wet forehead. Arthur was not at the camp fire, but his rifle was. This separation had never occurred before. Star, Gyp and Eat-em were also gone. Patulani became anxious and strode with determined gait and hard-heavy stride from the fire. He walked to the fire of the drovers and noticed several with the same beads of perspiration that were on Tadarera. All were sitting on a long dry stump, and three had secured bandoleers to their heads. The headache fever had hit, but such sudden effect to so many was unusual. Patulani tried comforting the drovers. They were not moved and indicated as such. Talk was shallow and sombre; laughter non-existent; abnormal disinterest in food. Why? Malaria could not affect so many so quickly – so simultaneously. But all symptoms indicated malaria. Then Patulani detected it. An engorged, very bloated shiny blue tick amongst a cluster of Bontleg striped thin flat ticks deeply embedded behind the ear of one of the drovers. He reached for his knife secured against his rump, and began the process of "shaving" the ticks from the flesh of his companion. The head of each tick is buried deeply subcutaneous, whilst the blood suction action externally bloats the tick's abdomen. To pull the tick away results in severing the embedded head from the body. The head remaining in the human body results in nasty septic eruption. The least harmful way to remove a tick is to prize the head from its internal lodging. This is best achieved by hooking a knife blade into the tick as close to the head as possible. An extracting motion sucks the tick head out, and by gently "shaving," each tick is totally removed. Unfortunately for man, no amount of human skill or science can remove the fluid deposit in the tick quest for survival. This venom is toxic, causing an extreme fever. Virtually the entire camp had succumbed in some degree to this potential killer.

Buru appeared unaffected, as did four drovers. Arthur was not in camp and this was a matter of dire concern. He would routinely not be separated from his rifle, so why now?

Arthur maintained deep concern for the anxieties and emotions that others spoke about and endured. When he detected his own body give way to the venom of mosquito or tick or cobra, he decided to leave the camp so as not to intrude the recuperation time of his men. Domestic matters of cooking fires, coffee and meals could be ably prepared by Buru or any of the drovers that had not been affected by the wretched venomous toxins from whatever source. Arthur drunkenly staggered, walked, staggered, fell and regained himself – for ten minutes. He was in a distant world of extreme head-pain blending with muscle fatigue and a high body temperature. He needed warmth – blankets, hides or whatever would provide that warmth, his temperature was now way over 104°F but his body shivered violently with the sensation of being cold. The body fluids oozing from his perspiring forehead, dripping from his upper face and forming rivulets down his unshaven bone structure had tasted like recycled, over-boiled, regurgitated raw dried out, slimy nasal excrement. He had taken in the full dosage of quinine, and had quenched and relieved that vile taste by gulping down quarter of a mug of KWV Brandy. Direct sun rays were his present provider of warmth and he made his way down a steep embankment, into the dry river bed. He buried the full length of his body into the baking dry river sand and delighted in the warmth that filled his soul. He relished the moment of warmth, and momentarily he was relieved of that excruciating head-pain and exhausted muscle surrender that encased his mind and his bones. For a few short moments he relaxed and calmed, then surrendered into unconsciousness. When he awoke later that afternoon he felt energized and refreshed and sat upright and alert. He was not in the river-bed, but in the shade atop the banks of the river. His reprieve from delirium was short, and he again felt the curse of the cold overcoming his sweat wet body. He had no energy to return to anywhere and lay outstretched in the sun to regain that feeling of warmth. Again, he passed into a world of darkness, hoping that he would never awaken to such a nightmare from hell. Showing no sign of consciousness or life for many hours he lost that part of his life. Never would he recall events of the following two days. When he finally gained semi coherent thought he opened his eyes to the most horrific smells, his focus landing amidst vultures defecating, squawking, dancing and clutching around him. He lay motionless, experiencing visions of being in a waiting room to the furnaces of eternal hell. He closed his eyes and the birds squabble, gurgle and screech became louder demonstrating frenzied excitement. He panicked but did not have the mental alertness or physical strength to move. He felt the feather flapping disturbances and opened his eyes. He thought he caught a glimpse of Buru, but this faded as he lost consciousness.

Many hours later Arthur awoke to a ghostly silence of normality. The sun had been replaced by a full moon, and Buru spoke quietly in his deep Zulu baritone. He laughed gently as he explained to young Kapipi that the fever had departed and Arthur would soon mend. Having no recollection as to how he had moved from his warmth in the sand he gathered his bearings and returned to the wagons for another dose of the vile but life-saving quinine. His return was memorable in that he looked into the eyes of anxiety, the disappointed vultures, as he passed flocks perching treetops along his path. The birds were silent, twisting their necks to get a better view of their disappearing "meal." Arthur imagined himself being carried away bellied in vulture, ending up splattered on cliff faces throughout the land! He was grateful to be walking. Buru and Kapipi slowly followed behind at a respectful distance, for after all, Arthur had virtually been raised from the dead. The pair of them had maintained purposeful guard over his painful body and protected him from the hungry birds. Hyena and jackal had also attempted a taste of morsel of Arthur during his weakest moments. All vultures and vermin had to contend with the spear, axe, kiri and possessiveness of Buru and the drovers. The devoted Buru divided his time between feeding the unwell men at camp, and supervising the guards protecting the body of Arthur. Without this protection Arthur would have been broken to morsels by the power-vice jaws of the hyena, jackal and vultures. As it happened not one of them touched him.

In the master plan of recycling and cleaning the African continent, there is a well defined "pecking order" that is seldom transgressed. When a body is definitely void of life it is usually well surrounded by the cleaners and scavengers of the wild. No vulture will partake of any part of a carcass until the king of the air, the Bataleur Eagle has consumed his choice selection. It is usually the eyes that appeal first, but he then approaches the soft under skin near the tail of wild animals. Arthur was thinking this through on his return to the wagons and his belly revolted, his sphincter muscle, reacted and he vomited a yellow vile smelling liquid of putrefaction onto his path. He hadn't walked 15 paces when a slender young jackal slinked in from nowhere and lapped up this litre of stench and gravel. Buru and Kapipi had observed this from a distance and both spat in expression of disgust. They were revolted by this event, but both knew not to interfere with the recycling events of the bush. Just as the vultures had not eaten the dying man because the Bataleur had not agreed nor consumed his rightful 'first fruits', so it was that these wild warriors had respected the wild laws. They did not disturb the jackal at his hors d'oeuvre.

Arthur was mending, but the affected drovers were all terribly unwell; some of them appearing close to death. They had been treated with quinine, but this was not working. Temperatures were too high, and head pain was excruciating. They had all soiled themselves; their clothing drenched in their own urine. The dogs were lying in the shade and the oxen were disinterested in drink or feed. The surviving chickens were all together, scuffing the soil as if looking for lost gems. All animals were in shade, some regurgitating cud and re-chewing, others with closed eyes or just calm and relaxed. Arthur was exhausted, weak and suffering. He tried to re-energize his strength by pouring a mug of thick, black bittersweet coffee but he couldn't drink it. He offered it to Mongwe, the youngest in the group. He was grateful and sipped it slowly, having poured it into his own tin mug. The sugar seemed to immediately invigorate him, and he found energy to walk far enough to urinate outside the designated area. He had wet himself and was inwardly shamed. As he leaned against a tree appreciating the wet earth in front of him, the coffee overpowered him, and shot out as a liquid projectile from the base of his belly. It was one distinct movement from start to stop. He wiped his mouth, but it was dry and he felt a little better. He now had energy to sleep!!

Arthur decided that all the sick needed prevention from dehydration. He mixed strong solutions of salt water. This he insisted they all swallowed, but some could not be woken from delirium. It was a task that he left for Buru and Kapipi to administer. Arthur unrolled his bedding and spread it under one of the wagons. Gyp and Star beat him to it but he shared the space and instantly passed into peaceful tranquillity and deep sleep. He did not move for twenty hours, and during that time both Buru and Kapipi shared watch over all the sick and the dying, ensuring safety and comfort as best they could.

Arthur was mending rapidly, with regular intake of quinine. He was forcing quinine down all the unwell men, but it seemed to have no effect. The drovers had tick fever which was debilitating. Two died within days of each other and were buried in very deep graves on the upper banks of the river. Arthur bade them farewell with a reading from his book of Psalms, acknowledging that "He makes us lie down in green pastures and He leads us beside quiet waters, where He restores our Soul". The other Drovers commiserated by scattering ashes thrown in the wind and chanting traditional gurgle to departed forefathers.

All other Drovers and Arthur recovered to full health, but regaining the necessary energy and physical motivation was a long and tedious process.

Athletics practice on the farm. The Author aged 13. The cleared height 12’8”
The National record at that time 12’6”

On “Twin Rivers” walking with wildlife – an enjoyable aspect of 1960’s life in Rhodesia

Alouette helicopters were an essential and incredibly resilient part of the Bush War

Young Lieutenant with Trooper Ozzie le Bronne – Operation Hurricane

SOUTHEY

Southey had enjoyed ten years of private school, excelling in all aspects. He had travelled from Shamva in the Northern Province in Rhodesia on a three day train journey to and from school for ten years, three trips per year. School was St Andrews College in Grahamstown, in the Cape Province of South Africa. It was 2000 miles from home. He had been awarded colours for cricket and athletics, as well as achieving the all round "proficiency tie." He had just written his matriculation exams, and was not enjoying the prevailing "farewell" atmosphere. Boarding school excitement was at the normal end-of-year peak. All exams had been completed, and the dormitory was in packing disorder. Tin trunks were scattered in non conforming disunity, and all beds were spread with clean pressed laundry neatly folded, ready to pack. The hostel air permeated end of term moth balls and echoed empty cupboards, and news print discard.

The jovial atmosphere was interrupted by the entrance of the head of hostel, and roll-call. Afterwards he called out the mail, amongst which was a telegram for Southey De La Harp. Telegrams were not common. The Morse-code system of telegraphic transfer was expensive and used only as a last resort in emergency. Southey was eager. He sliced open the telegram seal, thinking there must be a serious problem at home. The worst went through his mind. But then it was soon to be his birthday, so maybe this was some special surprise. He was relieved but numbed at the content as he read.....

Son

Train ticket not available for return. Have contacted Stirk & Son. Two push bikes set aside for immediate collection. Suggest you arrange a friend to accompany you. Your house-master will advise you the detail. Anticipating your arrival in Shamva 30 days from term end. Good luck. Happy birthday. Love Dad.

There was nothing to negotiate, no alternative, so planning began. Southey had a mathematical mind and quickly saw a cycle of 70 miles every day for thirty days. This was quite some challenge that involved climbing from sea level to an altitude of nearly 5000 ft.

Who, at such short notice, could accompany him? His peers were all committed in work or social obligations. It would require a quick thinking adventurous personality to be persuaded for this challenge. He approached his very good friend, Des Burke to join him. Without hesitation Des agreed and action commenced.

Des Burke had been a year ahead of Southey at school. He played an excellent game of rugby and cricket, and they often played fives or tennis against each other. This final year Des wrote his post- matriculation examination so as to improve his past results. His interest in school sport had also persuaded him to stay on an extra year at school.

His natural leadership had been well developed. He had political aspirations, but his prime interest was to serve his country in the legal profession. Southey had similar intentions.

Daily average distance covered was 164 miles. In view of the harsh terrain, excessive heat and torrential thunderstorms this was considered an exceptional achievement.

The cycling journey to Shamva in Rhodesia was an experience they both enjoyed. His physical exertions had been demanding in an enjoyable way. They camped and cooked together, planning the daily challenges, allowing time for adventurous lateral hikes, mountain climbing and riverine walks.

BRETT

Southey matured into a life of physical and mental endurance, action, determination and fulfilment. Youthful physical projects should expose an adventurous determination and unfold a life of lawful excitement and achievement. He had cycled from Grahamstown to Shamva, some 2000 miles as an 18 year old. He needed his son to do something that would illustrate, quantify and substantiate his own self determination, fortitude and the grit of life. Little Brett had lead a tough but privileged life as his father's constant companion.

Shortly before Brett's birth there was evidence of irreconcilable difference between Southey and his wife. They had been married just ten years, and were about to have their third child. Southey had just acquired 30,000 acres of ranch land in the midlands of the country, and the land was raw, untamed, no roads, buildings, purified water or greengrocer. No bridges, telephone, dams, cream cakes or fashion parades. Daily routines were demanding, hours of mental and physical gristle. The rural lifestyle of the ranch suited Southey but his bride, friend and soul-mate could not be persuaded that dust, isolation, and wood-smoke would be a grand prospect. This saddened Southey desperately. As a realist, though, he approached this situation from a pragmatic perspective.

He doted on his wife, and assured her every need was actioned so as to ease her stay in the maternity hospital. That era was social pioneering and emotional bonding because of mutual isolation and a community in development. Southey's family had cultivated close friendship with the family doctor, his wife and their children. Their relationship included regular sessions with a bottle of whiskey, or lunchtime gin and tonic. So it was when Sybil went to hospital that Southey stayed the first night in town at the home of his friend, the family doctor, John Adlington. Events moved fast. Brett was born with John Adlington at the bedside. Sybil had planned in silence. She had reserved her flight aboard Central African Airways to return to her mother in Nairobi. She stayed in maternity care for five days, which was a very short time in that era of developing colonial Africa. Without a word to Southey, John Adlington or any nursing staff, Sybil packed her belongings and caught a taxi to the railway station. Here she boarded a train with a pre-paid ticket, bound for the capital city, Salisbury. Her luggage and her baby were carried on board with ease, as she had left all her maternity discards at the hospital. Her baby was in the pram, which also contained all of her selected worldly possessions. She was travelling light, and running fast. Early the following morning she arrived at Salisbury rail station. She took a taxi to Belvedere Airport, where she boarded a timely flight to Nairobi, having to wait just two hours for departure. She was met at the Nairobi airport by her broad and beefy mother, Toby. So it was that she had journeyed over several countries, covering several thousand miles, when Southey arrived at the hospital to see her and his baby, Brett.

The medical staff were amazed at his ignorance that his wife and baby had left the hospital the previous morning. Events were numerous and emotions were monotonous, beginning the new life of Southey De La Harp as a single parent, devoted to provision of an optimum life for his special little daughter and his two boys. The legal formalities of the divorce and child custody were attended with efficiency and aptitude that only a very determined and skilful person could accomplish. Southey had been a legal practitioner and was a most determined parent and provider. He was no match for any adversary in matters that so closely touched his marrow as security of his children. Returning his son from the dusty suburbs of Nairobi to that rightful place in life, the vast grasslands and woodlands of the African bush, required just six weeks. Southey went to the Belvedere airport, where a tearful air hostess handed this six week old bundle of life to a youthful and very anxious, now delighted Southey. This remarkably beautiful hostess could well replace the black, male maid Southey had engaged to look after his son. But then again, no person in this world could ever replace the woman he had selected to be the mother of his children, and no-one ever would.

Brett arrived to homely warmth, compassion and an abundance of love. This love was not only from within the colonial advantaged people in the surrounding community within many miles of home, but from the ranch hands, foreman, stockmen, maids, gardeners and the domestic servants. Extravaganza was routine from his earliest memories, and included such social events as Trooping of the Colour, Presidential Inauguration in the VIP section of seating, and many social events that occurred on stately lawns and well shaded gardens trodden by presidents, queens, kings and state rulers from around the world. He was witness to board meetings from a very young age, and was seldom excluded from adult conversation.

He was trained and finely honed, skilled in the challenges of the hunter, the art of the horseman, the love of nature and the freeness, freshness and vibrancy of rural life in developing Africa. He was nurtured and cared for by warrior-type men of the Ndebele tribe. He learned leather craft and bush-craft, survival and the inner tribal social systems as known through the generations of this hunting tribe that descends from Zulu origins. Brett was never far from his father's attention, but was in the constant care of several Ndebele carers whilst Southey attended the daily rigours of ranch development. Brett literally grew up in the saddle of the horse; experienced the embracing arms and the goodwill heart of the Matabele and the Zulu people; walked with them the grasslands, the hills and the valleys of the savannah, the sandveld and the lowveld, encountering diverse and challenging circumstances as daily events. He learned the mood of nature, with sometimes a slow breeze indicating severe storms, and sometimes a beautiful coloured sky may alert him to a migrant departure or arrival, or to thirst or change in the forecast. He learned bodily nourishment at the same time as keeping his own physique at optimum fitness. Everything was learned as a result of practical daily activities amongst the finest human examples of African determination and survival. He learned evasive techniques and the aggressive, the productive and the destructive. He learned self sufficiency and he learned the values of dependence and independence. He learned the value of giving and the benefits of discussion. He learned to kill and to heal; to attack and retreat; to hunt and to hide; to give and to help; to run and to crawl; to sing and to cry, but above all the survival essentials he learned to love….to give and to receive. He learned that to like is a privilege and to hate is a curse, and he learned that throughout his life he would never be more than a mere custodian of anything. That everything belongs to future generations. He learned that he could create, achieve and succeed, or he could destroy, hurt and fail. His words could breathe joy, happiness and laughter or deprivation and tears; his actions could generate life or accelerate death. Brett was observant of these tribal beliefs and lived amongst the African people in total acceptance of their simple guidelines. His senses were always alert to explore, expand, develop, create and to contribute. His life had realistically not involved ladies, women, girls, a mother or sister for any ongoing time. He had lived with his father and brother, and established friendship and play with children of the ranch. Through circumstance of being an heir to the ranch, Brett had admiration and a revered respect from all ranch employees. He was at ease giving instructions to his seniors as well as his peers. His authority had never been disputed nor challenged, his decisions were unquestioned.

Southey had three children. The eldest was his only daughter and he relished every opportunity to demonstrate gentlemanly kindness to her every need and wish. She was kind and thoughtful, exceptionally intellectual; very alert and intelligent, with acid and venom readily available in her magazine of verbal and emotional ammunition. She was articulate in usage; her aggression and determination made her a fearful opponent or valuable ally. Southey's legal mind had mastered the skills of argument at the highest level of legal debate, but his little girl never lost either debate, argument, dispute, or respect. She won everything ever discussed, because, if not, then Vesuvius' volcanic eruptions were preferable to the vermin sounding, venomous viper vernacular that replaced the angelic pristine little treasure of his heart. His love and care for her was paramount. She was amongst three males, with no feminine backstop, and Southey could never permit her suppression. She lived most of her school life with her mother but visited her two brothers and her father on the ranch every Christmas holiday. Her visit was always relished, keenly anticipated. From a young age she imparted determination. When Brett heard the nursery rhyme about sugar and spice he differed. His sister was formed and crafted in chilli pips and scorpions secretions; she was dynamite; pent up energy and brilliance all parcelled in butterflies' wings and pastel pinks. She was the type who would peak betting odds favourably to lose her virginity before 13, break ten hearts by

16, do cigarettes and athletics for her country, refuse a university scholarship; travel the desert in an ambulance; hike in polar weather and probably even climb Mt Kilamanjaro. She could certainly sail through medical school; win every beauty competition; and probably end in "happy ever after" marriage, with five impossible children, and a string of happy and adulterous memories. She was energy, alert, fun and a fountain of vibrant effervescence. She knew how to be happy, make happy and feign sad. She was the mistress inventor of manipulating people, and seldom failed any endeavour.

The next of Southey's children was Norman, an academic and artistic hero to his family and peers. He would not fail any of life's pursuits. From a very young age Norman was content with his own company so long as he had paint or pencil to express his colourful imagination and love of nature. He was attentive, kind, and generous and spent unending energy helping and guiding his little brother. Both boys were convincing marksmen; successful hunters; devoted and loyal in every circumstance. They were likeable, athletic, energetic, artistic and kind. Brett was smaller than his age group, but agile and swift. Norman was asthmatic and academic, but went on to smash school athletic records, long distance and cross country, representing his school in the competitive South African inter provincial Triangular athletics. Norman was also the school chess champion and played third team rugby. Brett was number two to his elder brother in the chess team; represented his school, club and country in athletics field events; tennis, squash and long distance. Both boys were above average in most subjects in school and both captained some or other sporting discipline. Norman had climbed the Hogsback mountain peak during the Cape Province snow storm in 1964, and had walked the end of year 110 mile school expedition through the forests, hills and riverine of the Tsitsikama forest. The boys were well prepared for the adventures of life. Brett's preparation was strongly moulded in the Ndebele tribal ways. Norman was cast in the artistic modern skills of the 20th century. Both being well rounded, physically capable, psychologically balanced, leadership material. Southey had set determined objectives for his life and had achieved most of these targets. He was deeply satisfied, proud and encouraged by his children.

Africa is a harsh continent that can be paradise or purgatory; pride or prejudice; success or destruction; affluence or deprivation; killer or killed, always to be respected for the principal value of zero tolerance. Beautiful, wild, torrential, fast flowing, venomous, deadly protective yet arranged amongst the most tranquil pink sunsets, calm waters, green pastures, shaded cool breeze, gentle giant elephant, serene giraffe, all friendly, uncompromising, protective and unforgiving. The weak will be consumed by the strong. That is the bush law of Africa. Time now, for Brett to fly the nest and substantiate his efficiency; to experience the values of independence, determination, strength and resilience.

It was midnight when Brett woke to the sound of clinking tea cups and a low baritone voice calling from the passage. "Baas Brett, vuka, wena hamba manji," – "Boss, Brett, wake up, you are going now."

In break-neck speed he was out of bed and fully dressed in shorts and khaki shirt, no socks; boots slung over his shoulder, suspended by long laces, all within 20 seconds. He slumped back on the bed and accepted the coffee from Jemus, the long serving head chef. Passing fingers through his hair, he thanked Jemus, "tatenda Jemus" and excitedly called out of his bedroom window to Hennery. “Mangwanani madoda” – “morning guys.”

The response was jovial and assuring – everybody except Brett and the big boss, Southey, were ready to leave. They were all warming around a small fire, turning and toasting some dried out flattened sadza – a thick meal porridge that forms the staple food of the Shona people. They were coal grilling it to toast – (known as m’Potogai) for later consumption.

Brett slowly sipped his coffee, draining the last quarter and filled another mug. He absorbed the night sounds; the cricket, the night-jar, the gecko and the occasional desperate shrill of something – becoming a meal to an owl or a cat. The smell of m’Potogai and the quiet, deep base voices around the fire mesmerized Brett into spellbound emotional fascination. The men around the fire were utterly reliable, dedicated and a most loyal people. They could be relied upon in circumstances of death, to volunteer their own soul for a cause they admired. All four men at the fire were Brett’s age or a little older. All were employed on the ranch, and all were absolutely trustworthy unto death. Brett was their master and they were his friends, allies and hunting companions.

He gathered his rolled-up kaross (a blanket of patchwork back-skins of a multitude of small animals – rock rabbits, hares, squirrels, steenbok, duiker, serval cats, otter; and from the unborn foetus of a Zebra whose mother had been trapped in a snare, and put out of her misery by Brett with a single shot with the .22 rifle held between her tear filled blinking eyes, against her head). With his kaross strap and boots slung over his shoulder he joined the “makomana” – the young men at the fire.

He perched himself on his own heels, absorbing the warmth in his body and the smoke in his eyes. "Ja, Baas, lo Satan ena boneele wean nyamusha" – "Yes, Boss, Satan has seen you today." The Ndebele people have deep suspicion. Fire smoke is theoretically targeted towards that person that the devil himself is looking at, at that moment. "Better pasop" retorted Brett as he closed his eyes to the smoke, and gritted his teeth. The flowing gentle wafting carried puffs of thin veiled smoke equally to everyone as it escaped the circle of men, and climbed and floated away in the early morning breeze. Brett grabbed a piece of m'Potogai from the coals, blew on it and eased it into his mouth. He winced at the bitterness, but enjoyed it and washed it down finishing his mug of coffee. He barked instructions for everyone to get in the vehicle and threw his bootlaces and kaross string to Gauto.

Hennery cocked his head taunting Brett. "Eene 'ndaba, mfan?" – "What's the matter little boy?" Brett intoned. "Are we going in jungle and you so stupid you going to remember to forget your gun, sir?"

Brett was always ready for Hennery, because they knew each others every thought, idea, pain, passion, strength and weakness. "m'Boriako, wena!" and Hennery spat on the ground, and burst out laughing. Brett slapped him on each shoulder and ran off to the gun cabinet to collect the rifles.

They were gone! Southey was waiting near the Fargo truck, talking to Jemus, and something was said that filled Jemus with a roar of laughter. Southey smiled, and the little fox terrier, Blackie, jumped onto the back of the truck. Gypsy, the bitch of many breeds with a stumpy tail stood close to Jemus, and then she too jumped onto the back running board.

Debate was now serious as to what the dogs should do. They did not know in to what terrain they were headed, and in the event of difficulties they would not find the way home. Brett arrived in the darkness and announced that Gypsy had to stay because she was too heavily pregnant; Blackie could come. Debate, Decide, Do! It was done. Everybody on the truck?

Jemus laughed as he inserted the crank handle into the front bumper slot and awaited instructions to crank. "Gaia!" instructed Southey and the old man lifted his bent body to a full stretch, pumping the handle up to speed. The engine fired and Southey revved up slowly. Jemus threatened to keep the crank handle, wished them well and waved as the vehicle drove out of the yard. Gypsy trotted off to sulk behind the house, while Jemus cleared up the coffee tray and made up Brett's bed.

As he left the house to return to his quarters he heard the Grandfather clock chime out the sounds of Big Ben. It was 12:30am and the sky was radiant and light with sparkle and twinkle of every colour.

Blackie was leaning over the right back truck edge, with closed mouth and slit eyes, immediately behind Southey's arm, hanging out of the driver's window. Southey had selected a part of the country that he considered to be the harshest available from the aspect of untamed geographical terrain. It was that area of Rhodesia that had an abundance of game with tributaries of reliable river bed from where water could be located. The area was known in 1890 as "Hills of the Elephant" – "Gomo ye Nzo" – but changing cultures, cosmopolitan developments, migratory settlers from Portuguese East Africa, Nyasaland, South Africa as well as Italian, German, Jew and Indian mining and trading tentacles spreading into the heart of Africa like well fertilized roots of a wart, or the searching nerve ends of fast growing cancer, the name slowly changed – now known as "Gona-re-zhow" which translates in the Portuguese dialect to "Sleeping Boat."

This 20th century *Big Trek* had begun. Southey's boy was about to prove himself a man – or succumb to the ravages and savages of the wildest, untamed terrain anywhere in the 1960's world. The world of the Beatles, JF Kennedy, Space dreams and Sputnik forgotten in that place on earth where lions feed, buffalo roam in herds of hundreds; crocodiles bask their 18 foot bodies on hot, dry riverbeds, awaiting thirst to porter their meals to the very tip of their tongue; Roan and shiny black Sable protect their snow-white belly-skin from the claws of the leopard; rhino have no fear of sex mad money changers and traders, and elephant reign supreme. This was land that mining prospectors had abandoned, farmers had dusted their feet on the granite boulders, sneered at the lack of good soil, and moved to greener pasture. Traders by-passed as quickly as possible. The entire area of several thousand square miles was virtually uninhabited, with the exception of isolated nomadic hunters who had built seasonal villages for occasional excursions from the low-lying flood plains in coastal areas north of Lorenco Marques, and other areas. Brett had no idea what challenge lay before him, but he did know that he was ready to take on whatever may develop.

In prime physical fitness, with his bush eyes focused and shiny, fine tuned; nose and ear senses alert to every detail, Brett sat in the passenger seat of the Fargo truck beside his father. His nine inch sheath knife straddled his thigh, and he removed it to again test the slice of his arm-hair, confirming it to be as sharp as or sharper than anything ever machined by Gillette. The vehicle load was light, with four very excited ebony coloured men, several rolls of blankets and a few pots. He had a tin of 12ozs of yellow quinine powder and a red unopened tin marked "Fitzsimmons snake bite kit." They had 40lbs of maize meal, packs of coarse salt, his kaross, water bottles, two rifles and two card-boxes of ammunition. Things were strewn anywhere, being sat upon or slept on, or used as pillows. Beside him Brett had the .318 rifle that Grandfather Arthur had used on his trek expeditions from the Cape, which now belonged to Southey. The .22 rifle was behind the vehicle seat, wrapped in a blanket. "Gee, Dad, ten days walk with only ten rounds of .318 ammo, are you serious? What about rifle zeroing? What if I miss just a couple of times? What do we eat? I think you should give me at least 40 rounds for the .318 and 50 for the .22 – please Dad. There will be four mouths to feed." Southey enjoyed the spirit of enthusiasm and the plan, but the purpose of this exercise was to ensure Brett could overcome difficult odds, face the challenge, assess and overcome every hurdle. "Actually, son, I want you to carry five rounds of .318 and ten for the .22. Any more than that will make this just a stroll in the valley." Brett believed the tease and decided to accept gratefully what he was given. After all, the four of them could live very comfortably for ten days on the meat from just a single animal.

Southey travelled the long, uneven dust road south from the Ranch, through Umvuma, joining the strip tar road to Fort Victoria; down past Ngundu halt and onto the Lundi River about mid distance between Fort Victoria and Beit Bridge. The eastern horizon was beginning the glow of dawn. Arrival at the low level bridge meant big things to everyone, but to Brett this was *the* moment of life. This was the setting cement of trust; acknowledgement of parental recognition; the precipice of adventure, that eagle moment of jumping the rock to discover that "yes", you can fly or "no", you can't. If you can't, the fall to the valley will be tumbling, bumbling, bashing painful and crushing. If you can, the impending soar to the heavens, through the clouds, high, observing the world from outstretched wings, where floating to anything and anywhere is a mere wing-flap away. His feathers were ruffled, if not a little messy, but he would soon be amongst giants in the quest to see the world from above; to command from high stature; to determine and decide from that elevation of overall view. He lifted his foot to the truck running board, thrust it into his boot and inwardly grinned at the prospects of forthcoming days. His belly muscle looked and worked like mating cobra in a bank bag; his biceps balled up like a cricket ball as he lifted and slung his kit into place. Southey was standing with his foot on the back bumper, bidding affectionate farewell to Blackie. He would miss his little friend, his constant ranch companion at heel. "No, damn-it" he decided, his companion would not be sent to the lions den. He would return home with Blackie, and reluctantly Brett agreed. Farewells seemed to linger as Brett was anxious to move. Southey repeated some words of good fortune, wished everyone well and climbed into the Fargo, suddenly noticing that all four men had surrounded Brett. "Oh no, Nyamata wena kwela, my boy" "Oh no son, you climb on, my boy" directed at Gauto, who had hoped to join the *real men.* He had not come prepared for travel of any duration, but just a blanket and sling-shot was all he wanted. He glanced at Brett like a scolded puppy might search for protection, and Brett turned to his father. "Hey, Dad, you scared to go back to the ranch alone? You need Gauto that bad? You must be getting a bit long in the tooth, or old in the bones. Show me if you can make it alone, or if only we young bulls can mount? Leave Gauto, Dad, you'll be OK. Swap you Blackie for Gauto? Hey, Gauto, crank up the old man, let him return in peace." With that he threw the crank-handle to the front and laughed as Gauto's grip tightened and he begun to crank the Fargo back into life. That deep regal 'purrrrr' of the eight cylinder engine was a tonic to hear, and it was much anticipated when the journey ended in Villa Salazar in about ten days. Southey smiled as he turned the Fargo to face north.

"Phone me as soon as you get to the customs post. I'll collect you the following day". As he accelerated away he handed a sealed shoe box out of the window, into the waiting hands of Hennery. Written on the outside was an instruction, "Open only if in need." Dust from the accelerating truck surrounded the boys, causing laughter and relief. They were now dependent on the rifles, their skills and the winds of fortune for the immediate future. Brett lifted his .318 rifle onto his shoulder, and Hennery held the .22 wood-stock in his left hand, central, at hip height. All these young warriors had often walked the grasslands, valleys and hills together, as friends, hunters, master and servants. They all knew each virtually from birth, and they had individual identity. Loyalty was a very bonding attribute demonstrated by all. Braziwa took the lead, demonstrating his lowveld knowledge; you don't move in the midday heat. Daily travels should be more than half way when the sun is quarter high in the sky. From that hour to well after midday the heat decides whether to push forward or rest up.

The journey was planned to follow the Lundi River for most of the way, but Southey knew the impracticalities of continually walking through the cliffs and valleys and dense intertwined river undergrowth or the steep, near vertical terrain. Time was not a factor; a week either side of the plan made no difference and Southey had set a hard task for the trip to be completed in ten days. It was 110 mapped miles but that did not account for the difficult terrain, climbing, pulling on vines, sliding back down well worn game trails on gravel, and the regular back-track return when confronted with unexpected cliff faces or impenetrable vegetation. The hike was not possible in a direct, "ruler on a map" route and needed to be better planned. Southey was aware that he had metaphorically thrown his son into the crocodile's jaws by plotting the route so directly, but he needed his son to evaluate everything as events unfolded, and take appropriate corrective measures. It was easy plotting a pencil line by hand following the river, but reality on the ground was a little different. He knew his son was responsible for the safety and welfare of his bearers, and that he had every skill and physical attribute to accomplish what he had set out to do.

After a quick brewed coffee break Brett determined a rifle target at the downstream side of this dry river-bed. It was brilliant white bird-splash on the fore side of a charcoal section of hardwood, just five feet above ground. The backdrop was an embankment in the river-bend. No chance of a stray bullet going wrong here. He measured out 100 paces of dry sand and moved sideways into a shallow depression. Hennery handed him a short fork stick as thick as his wrist which he plunged into the sand. He spread-eagled himself in ideal leopard crawl position in front of the fork and gently rested his rifle woodstock into the 'V' top of the forked stick and slowly took aim at the selected white spot. There was already slight indication of heat haze shimmering off the warm sand bank, and Brett knew to compensate for the rising air current. He aimed direct at the centre point of the white spot and slowly exhaled his full chest of breath. With a surgeon's precision he squeezed the trigger, and with a golfer's commitment, he held his position until well after the bullet had struck. He was pleased with the shot and confident of his accuracy. Hennery ran forward to the spot and placed his index fingernail on the point of impact…..central in the splash-mark. There had been no allowance for either distance or wind as there was no need, distance being compensated by the slight rising heat. Hennery returned with a pride and respectful exclamation in acknowledgement of the master marksman skills. "Aaah, Baas, budi wena kwanisa, shuwa" "Aaaah, boss, but you are able, surely." His admiration was always hugely magnified because he had never been able to duplicate this sort of accuracy. Hennery could not close one eye and had to aim with confused interrupted focus. He was occasionally able to hit an outstretched, full-open grain bag at 100 paces, but with a grouping of never better than three out of five shots hitting the target. Brett passed the .22 rifle to Gauto, and took the .318 down to the aim. Placing this into the 'V' he repeated the zeroing action of this heavy powered rifle with equal tenacity, aplomb and accuracy. Gauto ran forward quickly but was ankle-tapped into a mouthful sand-sprawling submission, as

Hennery overtook and laughed, as he observed over-shoulder that little half brother surrendered the race, and arose slowly to spit sand, and dust out his eyes, in brotherly humiliation. "Pastardi, Wena, m'Boriako." With laughing mouth he trotted up to the target. Hennery was already returning, laughing and taunting, and proffered a punch on the chest as Gauto baulked past. They were not only blood brothers but exceptional friends. Their love was equally shared between all five men together this day. With confidence that both rifles were true to the squeeze of the master, Brett ordered Braziwa to lead downstream to an area well mapped with wide pools. From these they would cook sadza, recharge water bottles and rest through the midday heat. Unfortunately that place so brilliantly river blue on the map transpired in reality to being wide river black-mud, contaminated in buffalo manure and a urea pungency. No hope of consuming water here, and Brett became anxious. His decision to proceed quickly was inspiration to his bearers but alarming to him. He still had full bottles of water but if this was how the river was in "blue" parts, how was it further down? Walk fast but conserve water. As they proceeded and the sun rose higher and the heat haze shimmered and the bird sounds echoed distant there developed a silence between these men. They now had a single purpose – locate water. Their mouths were dry and the Mopani flies became irksome in the mouth outer edges and moist outer eye zone. This indicated that water was far. Braziwa was not worried and assured everyone that all was OK. The entire walk had been amongst rock cliffs and troops of baboons and trees alive with vervet monkeys. Hennery provokingly suggested that the brain of the monkey must be better than that of Peleele-Pasi as they knew exactly where to find water! "Aaah, nyarara, wena, broer ka lo bloe mchendi" – "Aaah, shut up you, brother of Blue Balls." This was in reference to the brightly coloured genitals of the human-like features of monkeys. "Monkey, maybe my brother, but then you must be the brother of Donkey" retorted Hennery. "Ja, true" said Peleele proudly, and the sun climbed hotter and hotter into a bright blue, cloudless sky.

The heat became excessive, sapping their energy and Brett decided to rest up in the shade of a riverbank fig tree. The roots had been partly exposed by flood erosion and the tree appeared wizened and aged. Braziwa explained this tree as a "she" because the fruit was sweet, the aroma relaxing, and her shade gave comfort to everyone. The upper branches were humming with energetic tones of worker bees and green pigeons warily observing the intruders. Brett stretched out his full length on the cool of a flat granite boulder. Hennery and Gauto leaned back on the tree trunk. Braziwa and Peleele-Pasi climbed down the steep embankment some thirty feet below, to a bed of golden river sand. They sat on a well rooted section of driftwood as hard as the granite above. They were debating the prospect of water. Braziwa opened his bottle and consumed the last of his liquid, and assured Peleele-Pasi that they would find liquid nourishment before nightfall. There was too much life on cliff faces and trees despite that the pools were all dry. There was no stress amongst the birds or the baboons and the animals were plentiful and in very good condition, too.

The midday sun passed slowly, giving rest to the weary bodies of Brett, Hennery and Gauto who all went into deep sleep for twenty or thirty minutes. They were woken by the flurry and wing-sound of the rapidly departing squadron of green pigeons. Their departure had been occasioned by the arrival of a Bataleur eagle alighting the enormous upper branches of the fig tree. The proud eagle perched as if in command of his squadron, seeking salutations first over his left shoulder, and then from his right. And then, like royalty needing privacy, he unceremoniously plied his majestic crown down into the foliage below his feet. As an artist atop the trapeze wire, he seemed to fall, float and sail to a lower branch, canopied over in cool shade. There was a majestic aura to this king of the African air, beaming a message of confidence. He was clutching a loose, fur wrapped chunk of blood-dripping fresh meat in one claw. Brett lifted himself onto his elbow, looking over to Hennery and Gauto, all trying to waken. "Where are Braziwa and Peleele-Pasi?" Silence. Brett called in the mid-day heat and his call rang out loud through the high cliffs and crevices, bouncing as a yodel through forest and granite and tree-tops and dead-wood, echoing back through the canyons a deep megaphone base. The Bataleur turned his head on one side, observing down to three vertical bodies, blinked one eye, then proceeded to tear mouthfuls out of the flesh in his grip. Hennery lay on his back observing this action and noted a freshness in the thin-blooded meat. "That animal has just died, within minutes" noted Hennery, and Gauto agreed. At that moment, from across the river their eyes were attracted to Braziwa and Peleele-Pasi, who had witnessed the Bataleur rise from the carcass. It was a young Klipspringer, that most agile of timid antelope, that had fallen probably 80 feet from an upper rock ledge, and had landed heavily on a ledge, crushing his skull, and breaking his back. The two men arrived at this warm broken body within seconds of his death – detected by flowing blood and body heat – but had been beaten to the carcass by the eagle eye of the Bataleur, who ripped off a broken section of back leg before a fly had arrived. They decided that the carcass would be suitable dinner for everybody. It was immediately gutted in the river-bed, cut up, salted and char-grilled in the shade of the fig tree. Everyone ate burnt offerings, raw on the inner flesh, salted, hot and tasting good. Brett thought to himself that today he had dined in the very presence of the king of the air, amidst the finest princes and warriors, partaking of the freshest provisions available anywhere. He lay back and enjoyed the light hearted banter of satisfied men that were boys in prime youth at the peak of life's journey. He was satisfied that everyone had eaten; had enough ready meal for the morrow, and he had only used two bullets out of sixty. Water became a priority, but all except Braziwa had ample for the remainder of the day. As soon as digestion had occurred the walk would continue. Five men stared silently into the dying embers as the shadows started to lengthen; the sun turning down on its journey to set.

Gently, but eagerly the valley awakened. The Bataleur above arose to the treetop, ejected himself with fifteen fast wing-flaps of his six foot wingspan, diving steep in the valley, gathering air-speed then lifting to glide, sailing effortlessly, high to the heavens. His under-wing silver shone out to the world showing his kingdom his armour at ready. His occasional head-turn bid farewell to his guests as he continued to survey his valley.

The men all stood up as one body, and extended themselves in a cat-stretching action that loosened tight muscles. The back-arching, wide open arm-stretch performed by Brett revealed a well fit and very comfortable body, ready for action. Hennery tightened his muscles and re-flexed his every tendon, and now he too was ready to kill. Each slung his responsibility over his shoulder or hip-belt and fell in line behind Braziwa who was well nourished and raring to go.

Brett was pleased with progress and allowed his poetic mind to absorb the red rock cliff edges; wild, almost prehistoric vegetation that clung in the crevices; wide open blue sky and chattering monkey at play. He noticed the occasional vulture in circling flight and the bee-eaters darting from dry mud-bank to tree twig; and swallows in seemingly urgent flight. The distant call of the ring-neck dove as he told the world of peace and love; and the elegant overhanging brachystigia branches that shed pods to feed troops of monkeys or baboons with eager mouths below inquisitive eyes watching active hands splitting pods, invariably dropping the fruits to the forest floor. No worries! The men continued at pace, selecting hard ground in the river bed as their path. The determined pace was being set so as to get to water as soon as possible, and select a suitable camp site that would afford protection from the elements and the ever searching predators so numerous in this terrain. They walked hard and fast for three full hours without stopping. They had today covered a distance of about 18 miles since the farewells with Southey. They were pleased with progress and ready to set camp for the night, but they needed water.

Brett was amazed by the length of buffalo grass as tall as the shoulder of a stallion giraffe, and he pined for the artistic skills of big brother, Norman. As the sun lay longer shadows in their path, the cooling afternoon became more active, and the walk-pace increased. They were walking in the river bed, direct to a rock cliff-face that indicated a sharp turn in the river. Braziwa turned a corner of narrow river bed, and dropped to the sand in disbelief. He lifted his palm to stop more intrusion, and they all stared in disbelief at the sight. The sheer cliff-rock overhang on both banks of the Lundi River unfolded into a wide flat plain of unexpected grassland and river-pan.

Below them was a low overhanging river-rock jutting out over a deep and well shaded pool of crystal clear water, some 25 feet below. The pool floor was as clear as a filtered swimming pool about the length of a polo field, widening onto granite walls that climbed a bank to exposed roots of the hardwood river verges. The shaded pool was as picturesque as any sight ever seen by Brett or Hennery or Gauto or Peleele or Braziwa. The sight of water was exhilarating, but the crystal clear water framed in this scenic, panoramic vision was breathtaking. The roots of a waterberry tree were entwined around the rock, supporting the mammoth growth of this giant evergreen tree. On a vertical branch as thick as the chest of a horse, at a lower level than these intruders, relaxing in parental moments of bliss, lounged the gold and black spotted body of a mother leopard and her two playful kittens. Over the pool about a mile distant was the unbelievable sight of a herd of 1000 buffalo moving in a slow motion solidarity toward the huge expanse of brown water pan. Behind them, forming the horizon rose a sheer red cliff face, finishing the frame to poetic perfection. This sight was too awesome for comment or movement. The leopard no more than ten paces away, playfully good-natured, calm, composed and content; her

kittens jumping; landing inverted on top of her; playful and carefree; silent but fun-filled. The backdrop of buffalo; the evergreen foliage of entwined water-berry trees; ancient rooted rocks and the clear pool waters was all too much to absorb. These five men of the wild had surely experienced insight through a window of Heaven. This panorama was in the heart of uninhabited, hitherto unwanted land in the south east corner of Rhodesia.

The eastern horizon glowed faint indication of first light. Brett and Braziwa were fluffing the coals and cracking brittle-twig onto the fire. The Lundi river valley was a vast open grassland below them, and the aroma of dawn floated through buffalo dust and dawn-smoke of hardwoods. The intense morning star shone brightly and a few wispy clouds idled overhead. Brett blew gently onto his tin mug, inhaling the refreshing blends of this sub-tropical sunrise. Apart from the low breathing sounds of Hennery and Gauto, and occasional sharp shrill of the nightjar the morning was silent. Peleele-Pasi was blanketed over his head, but his bare feet, belly and buttocks were open. It had been a warm night at the highest pinnacle of cliff face overlooking the vast plains in the Lundi river valley. Brett selected this sleep-place because he did not want the leopard to be able to approach them from above. Elevation always makes the higher one seem strong! The steep climb to the top had taken two hours of rock-climbing team work to elevate them onto this platform view of the world. Deadwood lay scattered around and a fire was quickly in place. Remains of the klipspringer was boiled and a pot full of sadza prepared. Coffee, campfire, clear skies and bright stars relaxed them into the first night. Brett passed into sleep with his hand on the stock of the .318, which was leaning in a green-fork next to his sand pillow. They were all exhausted; slept well.

The last of the boiled coffee was tipped onto the glowing coals, and in the group tradition Braziwa and Gauto both urinated to kill the fire. It is believed that unless you are bladder sufficient to kill the fire you do not deserve to leave camp, but to remain, clean, cook and be slept with. This age-group of men had sincere commitment to this supposition and it was taken seriously always. And, present company considered, there was no way any of these men was going to be slept with! All water bottles were emptied into the steam-smoke, onto the coals, and the descent of the cliff slope began.

Descent was demanding to the upper body muscles as it was optimized by vine-grip and swing-down, by wrist clenching team work, by standing on shoulders, and body-rope linking to lower each other. But it was quick. They were now arm-locked on each other while Brett linked his right arm through a lower branch of a tree and linked his left arm through that of Hennery, who was foot-locked onto a small section of vertical rock, with Gauto below him and Braziwa below that. At the bottom of the chain was Peleele-Pasi who could barely reach water to fill the bottles. The fill and hand-back process for two gallons of water took no less than 40 minutes before they were all assembled atop the smooth rock wall lining the pool.

As they sat debating the plan of the day, and absorbing this most pristine of sites, a troop of monkeys were chattering and swinging on the opposite bank tree-tops. With commando type uniformity and precision they quickly decided to go to the waters edge for the morning drink. They traversed the edge to a place of vine type undergrowth where they proceeded to a lower ledge, from where they could barely lap water. One lost his grip on the crack in the rock-face; plummeted head first into the pool. His swim skills were tested to the limit, as every attempt to climb up the smooth rock resulted in slippery descent and a ducking. The agonized men looked on silently, hoping for respite in the trials. Realizing the futile situation, Brett grabbed some deadwood and swung it with both arms, spinning as an Olympian may do with the discus. The log landed near to the exhausted little monkey, and he tried to escape from the fright. He turned to the log and clamped both forearms around a narrow section, pulling his back leg up and onto the log. He was drenched, shivering, exhausted but safe. He looked across the pool as if to say "thank you" and then up to the tree he had come from. There was no sign of any of his troop. They had scattered on seeing his problem, disappearing into the trees. He was alone, now, shivering, trembling and petrified; on his own little raft, in the heart of his homeland, a heavenly dream place of men. Probably from embarrassment more than preen value, he started to lick himself dry. This episode had delayed the departure of Brett and his men by nearly two hours. It now looked as if the monkey was dry and would soon jump to safety. The men stood up to leave, and monkey took a flying jump against the rock face and slid straight back into the pool. He climbed back onto his raft with difficulty; the log seeming more unstable to his grip kept rolling over. Then his care seemed to drift as he lifted his rump over his head, and upended the log with himself full under the water. Brett stood and left hurriedly, so as to not disturb additional attempts at self rescue. They climbed, weaved, and strode through the dense vegetation eventually reaching the far end of the pool. To everyone's delight monkey was on top of his life-raft, privately preening himself, and enjoying the sun.

Brett took the lead with much increased pace, walking directly to the cliff face on the eastern horizon. They walked through an extended area of ankle high grass, crossing the path of yesterday's buffalo trek. Soft dung pads were liberally splattered. The area was buzzing with flies; every soft-pad being home to hundreds. It is a fascination of the wild that whenever walking amongst a trail of nature, the thousands upon thousands of flies are of virtually no consequence. They prefer the provisions of nature to making demands on the faces, eyes and body excretions of man.

They crossed the vast open grassland where small herds of Zebra had passed, now resting in shaded tranquillity. After walking for several hours Brett seemed no closer to the cliff face than when they departed the pool. A tree-line had appeared between them and the horizon. This was in a gentle slope valley that had literally been overlooked. Brett established his bearings as the trees came closer, and was pleased at the prospect of shade. The heat was now intense, with the sun blazing directly into their faces. The men moved in silence with expressionless faces and eagerly looked to the shade. The Lundi River was now many miles to their left, mid way to the northern horizon. They had water but needed to rest up in shade. A final hard thrust was necessary as Brett accelerated the pace. Shadows became directly underfoot, and the tree line was a few miles away. The red cliff faces had disappeared behind the tree line but they needed to reach them by late afternoon. An unexpected valley, a tributary of the big river appeared, and necessitated revision of plan. This walk would be hard. The gentle downhill slope aided the speed. Brett looked back over his shoulder to observe the path of the day. Expecting to see the high cliffs of their sleep place as a faint dot on the western horizon, it instead appeared as if he could stretch out an arm and touch them. He felt betrayed by his expended energy; disappointed that his body had not carried him further; concern at his travel target not being achieved. But with an enthusiasm and a jovial smile he suggested to Hennery that they return to the cliffs, swim out with monkey, relax and revive like the leopard soaking the shade and the cool-breeze. Hennery snatched the opportunity to taunt Brett. "Aaaaii, but you white men! You have nose like a shrew, you look backwards to apes! You cry on the comforts and you fear at the future. The nose of a shrew only leads to a hole, sir, and straight hair indicates a life in the cold." Brett absorbed these quick words of banter in fun, but realized that this unschooled bush man had so concisely penetrated some deep truths. He concentrated without comment and Hennery pulled up beside him. They walked fast and Hennery offered to shoulder some of the weight from Brett. He took hold of the .318 rifle which freed Brett to swing in his walk. This would get a few extra miles behind them. They walked side by side, joking and enjoying, reminiscing and laughing out loud. Braziwa and Gauto joined them, while Peleele-Pasi strolled up the rear in a world of his own. The countryside rambled and rolled, but with well cropped grass cover, having been home to huge numbers of animals. Evidence of these was in every clump of grass, rock or bush, with footpaths meandering. The skies were blue, occupied by an isolated Bataleur, a Wharlbergs eagle, or a Peregrine falcon, all regularly sharing airspace with singular vultures, or spiralling flocks searching for food. A lone tree stood out in front and was distinctly misplaced. It was a date-palm and could be seen for miles …. From every horizon. It was strategically placed on the verge of a descent into the valley. It grew profusely; evergreen and was reliably watered from the entrapments of an adjacent depression in the black clay soil. This geographical and vegetationally misplaced lonely old tree magnetized these men of the bush. Without verbal mention they redirected towards this imposing, eye-catching tree of phenomenal botanical and geographical interest.

In the midday shade of this well matured tree Brett suddenly remembered a vision, a camp fire gem of fact. Excitedly, he stood from his sprawled out position and scanned the horizon. The heat haze was at worst in this midday lowveld. The shimmering illusion of water horizons intruded his vision. He would have to wait for the mirage to subside and he decided that they would camp right here for the night. He instructed his men accordingly, and then insignificantly planned a short afternoon excursion in search of a small roast for the pot. He left the .318 leaning against the date-palm and instructed Hennery to gather wood for the night fire and clear all the droppings from under the tree; a space for the camp. Brett, Braziwa and Gauto left. Hennery and Peleele-Pasi remained. As they departed Hennery had to distance himself from the campsite, for a necessary daily routine. He moved off some 200 yards and squatted, deliberating the plan of the morrow. The insistent chirp-sing of a honey-guide attracted his gaze and attention. He returned an acknowledging whistle which silenced the bird for an instant. His mission ablutions completed, he stood and approached the honey-guide. She was prancing and jumping, chirping, screeching, active in non-stop agility, excitement and quick movement. As he approached her and whistled she dropped low in the air, swiftly gliding with an occasional flap then glide, and landed atop a tall tree two hundred yards away, almost returning to campsite. She again commenced her fairy type war dance and silenced to the whistle of Hennery. He approached and changed his shriek-whistle tone to one of continuous, low-whistle and the melodious sound of a gentle breeze wafting rocky crevices. Then his eyes detected the quarry; a swarm of very active bees, angry and anxious to buzz. They were hovering, surveying, over a flat rock that was held upright and horizontal by a tree root. He observed with experience. Something had disturbed this swarm to anger. He approached and took closer inspection, rebuffing the occasional sting. He called back to camp for some matches, which were quickly brought by Peleele-Pasi, who raked up some dry grass and tinder. Together they sat close to the swarming mass of agitated bees and placed green leaf onto the flames. This provided billows of smoke-screen which they carried to the heart of the swarm. Peleele was pained by the stings but Hennery seemed not to notice. Together they lifted the flat-rock, and the swarm came alive with a fire-sounding "whoosh", like an enraged hippopotamus venting anger, charging enraged through the reeds. The stings overpowered Peleele-Pasi, who ran from the scene, flapping arms and hands around his head, and torso. He ran to the original fire, grabbing branches, thrashing the air with the leaves. The fire was big and smoke was billowing upward. He stood directly over the flame, feeding his inside thigh-skin directly onto the flame, jumping and thrashing and running, but staying and jumping, now screaming. From deep in the catchment of blue smoke he felt relief and abatement of the swarm. He shielded his body in the smoke, selecting to burn rather than be stung. The flames came close but he knew what to do with that, and smoke was necessary to keep the stingers away. He called out at the top of his voice, as if to be covering distance. Hennery replied from no more than five paces, with a grunt and deep throated rumble. He was OK, disappointed at the volume of honey. "How are you, my friend?" "Aaah, cheesa, cheesa, cheeesa" – "Aaaah, hot, hot, burning" replied Peleele, but he laughed and assured Hennery that all would be OK by the morrow.

Peleele-Pasi had absorbed the venom of no less than 200 bees in his head. His eyes and lips and cheeks and hands were swollen. He was sore but amazed at the toughness of Hennery.

Hennery moved some eighty paces and lit another fire piled high with green leaves. They sat either side of the now well caught fire that was turning the green leaves to smoke. Apart from the occasional sting, events had calmed and a mound of honey-comb lay dripping and broken and crawling, with bees honey-drowned and wing-stuck, walking heavy honey-footed to nowhere. They searched quickly for the dried outer bark of softwood, and located it upright, holding to rock. Hennery pried it away and lay it flat near the comb on the rock. He cleaned and filled it with dripping comb until it could hold no more and he placed everything remaining at the foot of the tree from where the honey-guide performed her trance and sang out her scream. This is the bush-code agreement. It was, after all, her just fare share of the bounty. Peleele observed from within the billowing smoke and immorally thought to take on his cat-sling and shoot the bird dead in her trance. He knew never to fall prey to this temptation. The mistrust would never be forgotten and could result in the honey-guide taking an unsuspecting searcher of honey straight into the nest of a cobra, python or wounded leopard.

Brett, Gauto and Braziwa were gone just two hours, returning with a Guinea fowl, alive and alert, clutched tightly by Gauto. They had had unbelievable fortune to surprise a small flock of parenting hens that were wing-spread and sprawling and dust-bathing, fluffing the sand. Brett knelt on one knee, lifting his .22 rifle to aim. The birds were not three paces from them oblivious to their presence. Brett noticed that one of the hens was bleeding from its eye and in obvious pain. It lay to one side looking socially rejected. Slowly, without breath-sound or movement he lowered his rifle as Gauto secured a marble size stone in his slingshot. Brett smiled, and let Gauto take sight on this bird. He pulled back the red inner tubing to the full extent of his arm-stretch, and then loosed his hold on the leather patch holding the stone. The guinea fowl flock took instant departure, running, weaving and neck bending through the undergrowth, and disappeared into scrub. Masterful precision and ongoing practice had assured pinpoint accuracy. The stone struck hard on the crown of the bird and Gauto leapt at the sight. The bird flapped hopelessly, with legs cutting air as if sprinting at hurried full pace. It was side flapping, gasping then instantly silent, but quivering. Gauto landed both hands firm into feathers and knotted the feet in his fingers. It had been stunned, momentarily unconscious by the blow, sufficient for arrest by the hunter. Gauto was so pleased, proudly clasping the big hen under his arm. Braziwa secured the bird by the neck and blew warm-breath into the eye wound, revealing a thorn protruding from deep at the base of the eye. It needed his tooth-grip to remove the thorn, and hopefully provide small measure of relief. He pulled down a branch of a young msasa tree, peeling off the hard outer bark. The tender young inner bark was moist and cold, and he rolled it on the palms of his hands, into a thin string of tough rope. He secured the feet of the hen tightly together, and looped the bush-rope through the sling-shot on Gauto's neck with a simple twist-knot.

Their return startled Hennery as he had not heard the sound of the rifle and their hunger meant that they had no right to return. Gauto was wide eyed, open mouthed and full faced as he whistled his version of events, explaining his agility, brilliance, expertise and virility. Yesterday they had eaten fresh meat of dead-buck. His efforts had now brought in really fresh meat, still working a heart-beat.

Gauto held the plump hen in his left arm and clasped his right hand middle and forefinger tight around its neck. The bulbous ends of his finger tips met under the beak-jaw. He released his left arm-grip and brought down his right hand into a slicing action that severed the head from the neck at the join. The flapping carcass was inverted and Peleele-Pasi took charge. He gutted and plucked and salted and potted the bird. It would make an excellent relish; accompaniment for the sadza tonight.

Brett listened intently to the retold versions of events. He witnessed an intensity of pleasure and pride being expressed with agile virility. The bees and the birds of the African people had roosted close to his heart today. The stories were re-told several times with interjections and humorous additions from Braziwa and Hennery. Brett enjoyed being able to relax amongst the unimportance of such light-hearted uneventful events. He rose from the fireside and again scanned the horizon, as he had done at midday. The mirage had gone. His eyes narrowed in concentration as he took in the reality. Yes, it was true! Very excited, he called Hennery and Peleele to see. On the northern horizon as clear as if it were seen through a telescopic eye-piece was the silhouette of the trees, the date-palm, surrounding in particular the tallest of giants of this little known variety of vegetation. He turned through 180° to observe the opposite horizon and true to his expectation there it was again, but this time it was a bigger area appearing as a plantation.

By virtue of his marriage to Shupiwe the daughter of Chief Somabula, Peleele was an Honourable man. His life had accomplished great travels ranging from Johannesburg highveld through to the Zambezi River; to the shores of the east coast of Africa; to the highlands of the Drakensberg; to the deserts of the Namib and the Bechuana salt pans. He was filled with a lifetime of action experiences. His recent years were in the employ of Southey on the Ranch. Many of his illustrious campfire revelations were merely discarded, but his wisdom and penetrating attention to detail was captivated; fascinating. He was fluent in the dialects of the Shona, Kore-kore, n'Debele, Tswana, Tambuka and Chewa people. He had had dialogue with the mysterious two-toed people of the Zambezi valley and he had intimate experiences that transgressed many boundaries. Brett had absorbed much from this wise old man of great experience.

Brett was now chilled in the confirming knowledge that this very place had been walked on and traversed with wagons and adventurers, slaves and their masters many hundreds of years before. With powerful recall; the detail and facial expression on the well wrinkled face of Peleele, (the father of Peleele-Pasi) Brett shared the historical relevance of this centuries old tree. He quietly lived through those ancient times as his mind reflected; bouncing on travel and gold; slaves and power; caravans and camels; wealth and work; leaders and politics; people and passion and the power of women.

History had many untold events. The growth and relevance of this tree was a little known but strategically important advent in developing Africa. Centuries old, this tree had survived harsh extremes of the African lowveld. Events as recalled through camp-fire tales were generally suspect in detail but accepted in principle. *This* detail remained accurate, especially in the knowledge that Peleele had probably never ventured to this south east part of Rhodesia; unlikely to ever have experienced the sight of the tree.

Brett took pleasure in sharing his knowledge. The date palms on the horizon were pointed out and the story explained, giving full credit for this knowledge to Peleele. Probably 2000 years before that there had been great expeditions in search of herbs and spices and valuable treasures. It was believed by the local ancient men of wisdom that during the biggest exploration of all time, ships had sailed from distant places, possibly the east or possibly the north. The origins of these great travellers was not known, but it was known that their leader was a goddess, supreme among humans. Her name was Sheba, and she was queen of all the world. Peleele-Pasi was bewildered; intrigued at the fact that this information had passed on through his own roots!!

The ships carried hundreds of men the majority of whom were shackled slaves, secured in columns together. They landed deep into the floodwaters of the Sabi and Zambezi rivers mouth, where the ships were left, secured to firm ground. As regional flood was so seldom, it could take years before these ships would be restored to sea-worthiness. Like beached whales on dry land these huge carcass like, tall mast caverns became almost reverently known as the "Gona-re-zhow" – "Sleeping Boat". The occupants penetrated deep into the areas of Monomatapa and beyond, inland to the granite verges of open grass plains. On instructions from their Queen these well muscled men were to construct for her pleasure, a retreat in an area of desirable lifestyle, and a fortress to protect her treasures of great value. It was with this in mind that the ancient ruins of Zimbabwe were structured.

Legend has retained little detail of these great explorations. It is told that the ships were stranded upstream in the rivers, sometimes for ten years or more, as they could only return to the sea on floodwaters. In order that following battalions of workers could arrive on the worksite it was necessary to establish permanent markers for the slavers to follow. This is the origin of these date-palm plantations. From two coastal sources, one near the mouth of the Zambezi and the other near the mouth of the Sabi there is planted on each horizon for the duration of distance to the structure of the Zimbabwe ruins, a plantation of date-palm. To this very day, every horizon en route from the river sources to the ruins still has the plantations which can be seen distinctly from the preceding horizon plantation. It is now known that the origin of these plantations is from a variety of very tall date-palm trees native to Egypt.

It is a legendary commonplace that a considerable portion of her vast worldly wealth was stored for posterity amongst the granite and high hills surrounding the ruined structure of Zimbabwe. That palatial encampment; the never completed fortress which was over 100 years in construction now forms the base of the Rhodesian insignia and is a revered place of gathering for ancestral worship.

The planting of appropriate markers to survive through the centuries was an exemplary concept. This feat of engineering is fast forgotten in modern civilizations, to be contemptuously discarded onto a trash-heap of legend of ignorant savages. The Egyptian engineers and doctors, scientists, generals, architects, the lieutenants, the slaves and tellers of fortune have been eternally able to land-journey direct to the ruins. All they had to do was follow the date-palm planted by explorers who rejected this land on behalf of their queen.

The guinea fowl boiled, and boiled and ……. boiled. Gauto and Peleele kept adding water as the steam evaporated from the three legged pot. Hennery and Peleele had laboured long hours to remove every grub, stick and live bee from the honey. They sat distant from the camp sufficient so as not to be attracting the bees. They had cleaned out a fresh strip of green-bark and were selecting prime sections of honeycomb, gently placing these onto the bark. When preparation was over they sat whistling, humming and gorging. Brett was at the fireside, observing the boiling pot, imagining who, what and when must have journeyed this very spot. His mind was deep into yesteryear when the whistling Peleele penetrated at high pitch, bringing him back 2000 years to the present. The four black men were sitting on top of a sloped rock and Brett looked across at the team. Fine men, he thought, as he moved quietly over to join them. They had put the very best sections of pure honeycomb onto a section of clean bark and set it aside for their master. As Brett approached Peleele joyously handed it over. He spat out a full mouth of crushed honeycomb, oblivious to his earlier pain. His face was big, lips even bigger and his nose flattened into his cheeks. The four of them enjoying the cool of the day, squandered well over an hour at this honeycomb end of their rainbow. They laughed, talked, sang, hummed and even danced a tribal "thank you" whilst imitating their honey-guide. Between the four they all overindulged, consuming volumes that are not medically good. Their palate and fun time and sweet golden dripping; the laughs and the songs and the fowl and the slingshot; the monkey, the leopard and clear calm waters; the buffalo dust and his majesty Bataleur had all struck impressions deep rooted today.

Never had Brett known anyone to take in the volumes of honey these men had consumed. By judgment of full buckets he estimated they had devoured at least 2lbs of honey each. This was beyond the ability of anyone he had met before. Juicy syrup was dripping down the rock and off twigs and the bowl of the bark was filled to capacity of crystal clear thick liquid syrup, but they could take no more. Brett told them to join him at the fire to eat. Gauto prepared a generous portion of sadza to eat with the stew. Brett had to dampen the dancing fireside enthusiasm for fear of getting grit on his honey-comb. He had enjoyed a full mouth of the sweetness, but needed the intake of food for the muscles before he could take in this food for the soul.

The full-moon rose over the cliffs that were tomorrow's objective. It shone so bright it was almost like daylight. In the lowveld heat of the early evening with a blanket protecting against mosquitoes and bright light, Brett slept little and lightly; his visions extending the annals of history. His college professors had been civilized gentry, from the upper echelons of society, and they tutored the decision makers of tomorrow – the land barons, politicians, mining magnates and all of that society that could achieve nothing unaided. Brett had learned about a battle of Hastings, 1066, and somewhere, some achievements at a place called Stonehenge. He couldn't recall too much of that lesson, except he failed that section of the test. The wrinkled old brown man sucking his pipe, who Brett knew as "Finish" (interpretation of Peleele) had unwittingly unfolded a deep divide between gentry and savage. Without the slightest debate the old wrinkled savage had been a superior, proud, humble, articulate mentor in every relevance of friendship and survival. Yes, the gentry had contributed to a civil comprehension of developed society: of silk and gold and diamonds and privilege and palaces. Peleele had only explained how to survive lions and flood storms; cold nights and crocodiles; hunger and snake bite; thirst and thistles – a humble example of reverence and service to all of mankind. Peleele would never be awarded tangible recognition of loyal devotion, knowledge and tutoring competence. He would not be remembered on the pages of history, but he would be revered forever in the minds of the ignorant, the peasant, the savage and immediate community. He sought only a life of sharing and fun; survival and good health; of communal contribution, conservation and goodwill for the future. Everything he owned was available to anyone in need, and everything he knew was painstakingly shared.

Brett concluded that there is universal imbalance in wealth and in comforts, and the server is always subservient to the master. There is no barometric measure of inner emotion; no tangible acknowledgement of the back-breaking determination and goodwill of our servers. For on-spreading the words of the battle of Hastings the rewards to professors were huge. For sharing the traditions and ancestral wisdom from a platform of illiterate kindness, the rewards to Peleele are zero.

Brett lay confused, eventually handing over to a light sleep in the cool of the evening stars.

Physically, the buffalo is the toughest, strongest, most resilient, most powerful animal in the African wild. This peace loving beast is gregarious and plentiful throughout the lowlands and grasslands of the African savannah. It has the resources to fend off attack from all African predators, but is still the most hunted and preyed upon animal. The day ahead was sure to take them to buffalo country and Brett felt a keenness of mind.

Brett awoke late in the night. His coffee mug had been filled by Peleele-Pasi, and placed at the butt of the .318 rifle. He lifted himself up on his elbow, surveying the distant horizons. The bright moonlight lit up the horizons, and camp was like day. The tall palm-trees were reviewing the territory from their grandstands of dexterity. Brett felt that emotion that may be experienced by druids on first sight of the towering, balancing structures at Stonehenge. He tilted his head in recognition of the superior man-skills and knowledge that were responsible for these trees; these incredible beacons and this tree immediately above him, and the smaller scrub-type juvenile palms stretching up to their senior. He would treasure these memories; these moments of civilized insignificance – confined to the dustbins of savages!

He swigged at his coffee cup to straw-draw the liquid. Direct sipping would burn. He talked with Peleele in quiet whispers because the crew were asleep. Peleele had recovered from the pain of the bee stings, but severe swelling remained. They talked for an hour reflecting on varied topics, but always returning to the wise, well stored memories of Peleele. When they decided to sleep the moon was quarter high, bright, throwing a silver light from horizon to horizon. It was not yet midnight, but must be pretty close.

The whipper-whirl sounds of the night were relaxing; the world's best medication for the sleepless. As they rolled over to take hold of their sleep there was a thunderous, echoing roar from a lion that seemed no further than the length of a playing field. Brett sat erect. Peleele wrapped tight in his blanket. Hennery awoke together with Braziwa, but both lay motionless, listening. Was it a dream? Silence. Even the roaches and whistlers, the insects and night-sounds were silenced. Hennery rose quietly, and moved close to the fire, breathing with a wide open mouth so to be silent. Everyone was alert, except Gauto who was dreaming of guinea fowl. All others had ears, nose and back hair in action; alert. Silence prevailed prompting Braziwa to close in near his master. Brett was now holding his .318 Mauser across his chest, and eased a round into the chamber. He spat throat phlegm on the back-sight so as to give it shine in the dark. He sliced his thumb-nail through the 'V' groove, checking it to be clear and ready for use. Hennery drew close, holding the .22. Suddenly, like a bolt out of heaven, like thunder and lightning, like a meteor, crashed a rock to the ground, not ten paces away. All eyes were alerted to the movement to one side, and it happened! The roar of the lion was deafening like a thunderous command from on high.

Gauto awoke in a stupor, running amok. He headed straight for the beehive, ten paces as one; back over the rock to the palm tree, and up ten feet in a flash. He climbed as if ape-man had taught him. Then the ground trembled, and a big herd moved to a canter, and suddenly stopped. Another roar from the deep; bellows of chest and the throat of the king vibrated the night to a stop. The moon shone bright, painting splashes of silver across the short cropped grass in the vlei. The herd of buffalo seen the previous afternoon had been to the river and were now returning to graze on the plains. The pride of lion had rested up for the day in the shade of the surrounding trees, in full expectation of surprising the returning herd. The outcrops of rock provided a cooling rest for the pride. The lion had strategically placed themselves; two of the females had elevated positions on the far trees framing the grass. The other five, including the long maned male remained this side of the vlei. All seven slept through the day, well into the early evening. The cat-plan was well established; the ambush strategically designed to allow time to rest and rejuvenate the muscles. The wait had just begun. As the herd slowly grazed its way through the vlei one of the pride occasionally opened an eye or an ear, flopping lazily back to rest. As the sun dipped down over the western horizon the pride started preening themselves in readiness.

Tension was deep – to the marrow of every living creature for miles around. The silence was hair-raising. Brett looked up at Gauto who had an excellent view way down the vlei, sitting gingerly on a flat concave well spiked palm branch, with the bulk of his weight in a notch in the skin of the tree. He was 20 feet up the tree, and comfortable, with his arms hugging tight around the stem. His right hand was tight clasped to his left wrist. He viewed the battle arena as a centurion may view from his gallery. Brett smiled and Gauto invited everyone to join him up the date-palm. He could climb higher making way for others to share this lower branch, although the nature of growth was such that each branch required no more than two people, one up and one down, providing they held tight to the stem.

A deep bellow and roar some distance away indicated the battle plan about to be sprung. The rumble and tremble and dust that ensued was quake strength to the camp. A pot fell from the rock, to the ground, and Braziwa made quick his climb, sharing the branch with Gauto. Brett directed Peleele to follow. He needed leg-up assistance from Hennery, who shouldered the .22 rifle, and the two of them climbed in tandem. Peleele climbed to the most elevated place, skilfully passing Braziwa and Gauto. All four up the tree each directly one above the other, Brett eased back ten paces behind an outcrop of granite boulders. He lay flat as a marksman at range, holding his .318 rifle at ready. He smeared spit and a pure white piece of bird drop onto the front sight of his rifle. This would aid quick night-sighting, bringing the white into position at speed. The rumble and hoof-sound was building; crescendo had to be seconds away. Gauto put his hand over his wide open mouth as if to stifle amazement. The dust rose high in the sky, and then spread like low level nimbus. The front-runners of the herd were in sight now, and it seemed as if the horizon was a giant wave of anger; rumble; rage and thunder all crashing directly toward them. Moonlight washed over the battlefield, giving floodlit view to the spectators – clinging to their grandstand. Hennery called loudly to Brett, demanding his immediate climb up the tree. He shouted that the raging river of buffalo was too vicious a storm to challenge. Brett smiled, sent back a "thumbs up" and called back, shaking his head, but his shouted refusal was drowned out by the herd. He had his .318 rifle at ready; was bull faced and focused as always; ready, whatever may happen.

The front runners of the herd entered the arena of low cropped grass immediately in front of them, and dust filled the air all around. This stampede was invigorating. The herd seemed in jovial canter, cavorting, bucking and kicking as they moved from Brett's right to his left. Brett stood in amazement, overtaken by the physical power, the speed, the action and the slow motion might of events. The herd was now 20 paces away, out in the grass, moving at high pace. Suddenly, unbelievable, drastic and urgent the entire herd halted immediately as if on command from a general. A sleek lioness had run in from the far side, way over to the left, turning at high speed, face on, charging straight into the face of the herd. She made no attempt at concealment; like lightning going into the kill. Behind and on the far side her back-up approached at speed on her left. The battle had truly commenced; the kill about to occur and Brett was just paces away. Both killer predators stopped quick, and flattened themselves on the floor, just paces from the herd.

The herd stopped abruptly and the sound of their panting was loud. The snorting and bull-base throat-rasping sound impacted like thunder. Silence, except for the breathing, then a thunderous roar from the right. The king of this region commanded, but the buffalo stood their ground. They were amazingly positioned in laager, with horns bashing together, and their rumps pointing inward in a series of huge circles, maybe 700 beasts in a laager. The young calves were central, fully protected and surrounded by outward looking elders and the burly beasts faced their predators straight on. This initial front charging lioness was lying low in the grass to the left, crouched flat to the ground holding eye contact with a selected protective mother buffalo, whose udder swung full-milk beneath her. Like lightning moving over the low grass, she sliced into the herd at quite unbelievable speed with power straight into the face of her determined adversary. Flying at the speed of a vampire, her mouth hit the target central, her paws slicing air on either side of the animal's neck; her back legs were curled under and forward in flight; her teeth cutting deep into the black flesh of the buffalo nose. Her front claws turned their target to blood streams; pumping, gushing down the buffalo's neck. Her teeth bedded deep into the fleshy nose muscle. Blood squirted under pressure some eight or ten feet into the air – and around and down to drip off the grass. This mighty beast lunged forward with the lion clinging hard to remain, trying to pull his head down under and between his front legs to get him down. The resolve and strength of the buffalo locked his forelegs straight and wide apart. He was determined to stand. The boss of the buffalo horn brought down a mighty blow, bashing and beating and angry, she smashed the chest of the lioness a hard blow. The immediate action of the big bull beside her showed team work in action. He lowered his head to the ground and lunged forward, flicking his mighty neck, propelling his boss upward spiking the lioness on the tip of his horn, hooking and spooning her, flinging her high into the air. She landed hard, back on all feet but in pain, just in front. The other lioness, her support, came in to her aid, joining the fight. The big bull again used the over-size boss of his horns ramming hard into the chest of the supportive big cat. Both lionesses moved quickly away, and in shame, to tend, momentarily defeated, to their pain. Three buffalo lunged forward to head-butt the lions and both lionesses retreated and lay down in the grass. The herd stormed their direction. The sleek and aggressive big cat stroked a paw across her snout and her eye, and quickly stood proud to receive the buffalo attack face on, but as they approached just a short pace away the proud lionesses accepted defeat and trotted back to the tree line, then turned, facing the herd and lay flat, with their ears flattened against their skulls, and their tails twitching a signal. The herd bellowed and brayed; stood four square solid shaking their necks and snorting and ready for more. The laager of encircled young calves remained tightly secure. The huge male lion, as tall as a buffalo at the withers appeared from inside the near side tree line. His regal command of the battle was reflected in his stride, as he reviewed the defences and power of the buffalo. A huge black bull with a chip off his horn lunged forward towards the lion, and swung his enormously muscular neck, so as to smash the skull of the lion. With every tense muscle alert and in action the lion turned and faced directly at Brett, straight into the on-looking barrel of his rifle. It had not expected to see anything there; surprised; entrapped between the man and the beasts – and took instant and severe retreat back into the trees. It was fast and low slung as it vanished from sight behind a mound of granite where he skidded around and lay flat to observe the scene – for an instant.

There were four other lions on the battlefield on the far side, quite distant from the two lionesses that were observing from the far tree-line. Brett had his rifle trained in the direction of the big male as this animal was in a battlefield state of aggressive alertness, enraged and determined to kill, spontaneously acting on instinct. From the treetop above he heard a bellow from Hennery; the lion had long gone and was now crossing the vlei between two big circular laagers of buffalo. Sudden calm seemed too eerie but Brett felt his senses returning to calm. The dust was hanging still in the air and the buffalo bellowed as they swished their tails and snorted and regrouped and waited. It was exactly as a ranch scene, with the cattle waiting to be herded through the dip-tank. The sounds and the smells were identical. For dust-filled moments.

The silhouette of the men in the tree had a backdrop of bright moon casting silvery floodlight, brightly illuminating the entire arena. The men had all engorged themselves with excesses of honey, and this had now worked its way through. Pure liquid honey, removed from the wax is the most potent of laxatives known. From the most high pitched screams at the top of the tree Brett detected an unexpected urgency; an instruction for all the men to move in a hurry. Peleele was screaming as if an elephant had stood on his toe. Brett held his rifle at ready, but moved seven more paces distant from the tree to observe what had happened to Peleele-Pasi. Desperation was scribbled all over his face, but just an inaudible scream belted down. His anxiety filled face was contorted and he looked close to tears.

Suddenly from well in the trees a lion growled from deep in the back of its throat. It was part of the predators' teamwork to alert the herd into tension. In an instant the bellowing buffalo stopped swishing their tails and the silenced herd was ready. Brett was directly between the lion and the herd. He hurriedly faced the direction of the roar, holding his rifle in place. He moved behind cover of moon-shade and rocks and lay flat, his right shoulder to the vlei full of buffalo. The lioness appeared not five paces in front and to his left. She was young and stood calm, observing her larder. She was twitching her tail, but standing tall and alert. Brett had the rifle trained on her skull at that point of imaginary cross on the line drawn between her left ear and right eye; right ear and left eye. He did not want to kill this feline in prime but his nerves were stretched and the tension was at peak. She had a wide scar on her neck, as wide and as long as an outstretched hand. It was certain to be the horn of a buffalo that had ripped skin and gouged flesh, but let her go free. It was dried out; well repaired but she distinctly had mental recall of the event. She was standing back this time round, leaving such bashing for others. Although Brett was in front of her, she had been observing with a focus and concentration that centred her vision past Brett. She flattened herself on the ground and her ears lay flat. Her tail kept twitching from left to right, and then it happened! Like lightning connected from her nose to the herd she streaked straight to the big bull on guard. Her muscular body shot past the far side of the date-palm, only two paces from the base. The bull came forward to head-butt and she veered off to one side. Before she could settle to regain her composure the lunging charge of two big bulls changed her mind; she hastily retreated to the trees behind Brett, and the bulls reversed back into laager defence.

Peleele-Pasi clung tight to the girth of the date-palm, ensuring not to let go at all. His desperation was extreme as he clenched his teeth in a speechless plea. He had partly removed his short loin cover, giving final notice to the warriors below. They could not move, save to surrender down to the ground and the pride and the herd. They could not believe his actions as the burst of diarrhoea rained down. Peleele's agonized desperation turned to gut busting laughter as the pressure released. The liquid spray fanned out into the airborne dust and descended down in bursts. Braziwa looked up to see what was happening, his face full frontal to the rear end of Peleele-Pasi. The first burst caught him full in the face, dripping like lumps in hot syrup. With rapid fire on constant repeat Peleele abandoned all effort to stop. The relief was too good, let it go … and he did … again and again and again. Sitting above the event did not mean his escape of the drama. Running down his leg, dripping from his ankles to the head of Gauto the trickle persisted. Gauto was mortified as he realized what was happening. His back had been full splashed as a swathe of foam, and it ran and dripped off his buttocks. He too looked up in defence and caught the next burst full in the face. That quickly shut him up and he arched his neck down to look low. More kept dripping on the crown of his head, and Peleele-Pasi could only laugh from his crows nest grandstand.

The smell was acidic of rotting offal of steenbok and guinea fowl; the consistency of gut rotted hot syrup, decomposing. It was a blend of the sour rot of gall and the vomit of cats filled with rats. And it was smeared on the faces of Braziwa and

Gauto, and it was now slipping off the shoulder of Hennery, dripping onto the ground. Brett witnessed it all. He was disgusted, revolted, incensed, shamed, displeased, but very amused, laughing.

His attention remained amongst buffalo, lion and dust but he roared with laughter – together with and almost as loud as a nervous Peleele-Pasi who was oblivious to any swelling of bee-stings or prowling lion or buffalo stampede, or enraged comrades, brothers and friends.

As if signal was called through electric command, the buffalo laagers all came together. The circles blended, as pools of smooth table top water may join to become one. The huge herd of buffalo was now gathered immediately in front of the camp-ash and light smoke, and a misplaced silence returned. Then slowly the buffalo tails began swishing. The herd was alert and ready, regaining an attacking composure. The occasional bull-stamp of front feet crashing hard to the ground seemed to issue a challenge to all on-looking predators.

Then, like a truce had been signed, the buffalo all simultaneously turned to face south, and started at a slow canter, with their huge necks swaying, lifting and dropping, bellowing and occasional double-kicking of back-legs, cavorting and swaying the herd moved away. Then the female lions all joined in the slow canter, surrounding the herd as if leading to slaughter. Brett had had no eye contact with the male for too long. He remained in the moon-shade, but lifted his body to increase his vision span across the vlei, searching for the king in command. Sudden movement to his right diverted his attention from the progress of the cantering herd. The huge male lion was moving in from the open grass, and coming directly, in a straight line towards Brett. But its vision was concentrated over its own right shoulder, rustling the herd into place. It had not seen Brett, but was now getting too close, a mere 30 paces or so. The huge inelegant mane that distinguished his kingly authority was waving in unruly direction. Brett moved his rifle sight so as to strike a flat granite outcrop in front and to the side of the cantering king. He did not want to wound or to kill unless to save a life. He squeezed the trigger of his .318 and an unbelievable explosion erupted into the night. Brett was quick in action, and another round was in the chamber, immediate! The bullet ricocheted off the granite, splashing splinters of granite deep into the foot-pad of the lion. He lunged upward, and out into a virtual back somersault, into the grass of the known, rather than into the trees where things were unknown. His speed was immense, his tail trailing directly behind, covering 100 stretched man paces in just three seconds, as he crossed the vlei and into the far side tree-line. The rifle shot had alarmed everything, and the buffalo immediately engaged a full gallop, their heads single-mindedly lashing forward, tails outstretched, in a hurry, they raced, without reference or thought for each other. The lions had surrounded the herd, trotting like herdsmen. The rifle thunder had belted them a shocking, nerve-racking bewilderment, and they too, abandoned the chase. They all made instant very high speed, low level urgent departure from the vlei and disappeared into the far side tree-line, away from the direction of gun-sound. Brett had dealt Nature an abrupt shock-blow and he was pleased that he had. The rumble of 5,000 buffalo hooves; the roar of the lions and the dust and the high speed action of hunters and hunted, all faded away into a bright moonlit night, towards the south.

The moon moved shadow away from Brett, and he stood and strolled back to the embers. His rifle was slung low, not at ready. He called to his boys to come down from the tree and he moved a big dry log on top of the coals. He knelt to blow the coals into flames then abruptly stopped with the smell now too strong. He barked to the guys to get a grip on themselves and go far off and clean up in a scrubbing sand bath. Like scolded hyena they came down from the tree, slithering down, then away from the fire. They were nervous and stank, and had to go into the night, ashamedly peeling off in opposite directions. Hennery went to his bee-side fire and started it back into flame. He gathered much deadwood and stoked it into being a big, raging camp-fire. The light would repel any predators, while he sat fireside and removed all his clothes. He rubbed his whole being with coarse sand and repeated the action several times. He buried his clothes in the sand and then rolled sand over cloth over sand, occasionally sensing the slimy sour smelling syrup, mixing it in with more sand and more rub. Nothing less than a very long swim in deep running water could help. He felt humbled to the depths of the deepest canyon, but could not remove the stench from his world. He rolled in the sand and smothered sand in his hair, but nothing would remove the horrendous acidic gut-rotting smell from his being.

Brett had established another big fire and moved his kaross some 50 long paces away, and the pot was in place, full of water. He was brewing a well deserved pot of coffee. Then he sauntered over to Braziwa and Peleele-Pasi trying desperate tactics of smearing thick steak-like crushed aloe leaves over each other as desperation of the stench overtook them. The smell had distinctly abated and he moved over to see Hennery. He was a sight and Brett burst out laughing. The fire light was bright, lighting his eyes and highlighting the shine of his teeth. "Aaaah, Baas, lo bleddy sheet ka lo Peleele." The insinuation was that no maiden could ever be pleased at his muscles; this rot was destined to stay on him for ever. Brett assured him that it was almost cleaned up, and Hennery was pleased to be allowed to return to the camp fire, to be slowly joined by the others.

The morning glow on the eastern horizon had started. It was to be a very hot cloudless day. They gathered their thoughts around the campfire in silence. That Brett had remained in the heart of the rage had bewildered the gun bearers. They were amazed at his lack of fear and ongoing courage as events unfolded. When the lion had looked down the barrel of his rifle at the ready, Hennery had been ready to jump down to his rescue, and almost fell from the tree with the crack of the rifle sound. The moon had now set and the night became dark for a short while. As the horizon became brighter in a glow of red radiance, they dissected events of the night. They enjoyed having witnessed the defence mechanisms of the buffalo; the power and determination when confronted with threat; the close up aggression and speed of the predators; the agility of wildlife planning in action, the precision of team work and response to command. They had not anticipated witnessing the surrender of the lions or the violent reaction of the honey so quickly. Braziwa and Gauto were now alerted to the call of nature and both moved off quietly into the night, squeezing tightly their buttocks, and walking gingerly upright with very determined short paces. Gauto managed just 20 short paces but the delay in seating himself properly necessitated another sand bath as the syrup substance trickled all the way from his rounded buttock, down to his calf muscle and dripped onto the ground. The power of the squirt direct from the depth of his bowels was strong. He pushed and enjoyed the relief, and filled one hand with sand from his side. He smeared this into the syrup like liquid clinging onto his skin, and rubbed it onto his flesh. He was enraged at his own lack of control, but the relief was overpowering. He burst into deep laughter as gallons of syrup-type liquid squirted itself out of him onto the ground, and into the sand.

When they returned Brett was pouring himself a last mug of coffee. They would start their walk as soon as everyone was ready. They had not slept, but none showed sign of need. The urgency of getting to pools of water was paramount in their minds.

With blankets rolled and utensils gathered Brett took firm hold of his .318 rifle and Hennery the .22. They moved off in single file, directly into the glow of dawn, with Brett taking the lead. This was easy but fast walking. It remained cool with a gentle breeze into their front, bringing the scent of the wild right into their nostrils. As daylight widened the horizon there was a lot of evidence of duiker, steenbok, reedbuck, and a herd of seven kudu. As the big red cliffs of the river drew closer, Brett swapped rifles with Hennery. He wanted to get something small for the pot, his plan being to clean up and swim, refresh and relax during the heat of the day, and move off refreshed into the early afternoon.

Frustration developed as the river approached. An abundance of animals was to be seen at every turn. Those that were relaxed and at peace were the bigger animals; the kudu herd, a sable bull, several Nyala, and buffalo. All these presented themselves as suitable targets, but the steenbok and duiker seemed knowingly energized and accelerated away into dense riverine undergrowth, or slipped into camouflaged non-existence. The walk pace increased with the nearness of water, and attempts to stalk quietly were abandoned. Walking the river bank was hard. The undergrowth was thick with animal tracks; paths penetrating through, down into the dry riverbed. They could not remain in the riverbed because of excess of rock and reeds and mud that all combined to force them to walk downstream through the undergrowth, making regular observation back to the riverbed. Braziwa moved up to lead and assessed the locality of water. He climbed away from the river and set direction across a huge vlei, towards a series of big rock outcrops. The river turned against the cliff face, leaving dry beds of golden sand, and cavern type erosion deep into the rock. As they climbed the crest of the wide grass area a huge bull elephant stepped out from the trees, showing them his rump, walking diagonally forward partly crossing their intended path. He was about 500 paces away, making towards the same place as Brett. The men grouped together and debated. They did not want to break ground over the expanse of open grass area in confrontational approach to the elephant. They moved back into the tree-line and broke into a slow trot, with rifles and axes and spears swinging below the hips. Their plan was to arrive unseen in front of the elephant, and hurriedly get to the pool. Although the huge bull was walking gently, they could not match his speed, in time to the water.

The pools were several but small. The elephant was near the water's edge, breaking green foliage from a young waterberry bush, so the boys had to skirt around, through dry river bed and down the far bank, down into the water. It was murky, but refreshing as they drank plenty and filled bottles and the three legged pot. When this was over, the four splattered men walked chest deep into the water, splashing and ducking and laughing. Brett sat on the small beach, overlooking the jovial atmosphere. Suddenly he jumped and screamed instruction at the four fun-filled laughing black men, ducking and splashing each other. A crocodile about four feet long had slithered from the sand bank on the far side of the pool, and into the water. Hastily the four retreated, trying to run, splashing, tripping and laughing, determined to get out of the water in a hurry. They were lucky this time. This was a non-event, treated lightly, the same as most of their crocodile situations!

Brett moved up the bank to the shade of an acacia tree and selected an appropriate river-washed root as his seat. The ground in front was a massive, solid flat-rock which became an excellent place to spread out and look at the map. They had only been walking for three days but had covered nearly half of the distance to Villa Salazar. This well shaded place of good water, and tranquillity was surrounded by abundant plains game from which they could select a cuisine as if they were city tourists in hotel residence. The men had not slept the previous night and could use some hours of good sleep. Observing the map, walking his fingers across, he calculated that a few steep areas remained to be crossed, but the back of the distance was broken. They could afford to strike camp and relax, while Brett went in search for the pot. With elephant in the area they would need to locate a flat sleeping area elevated up on a steep slope that would not be an elephant path or foraging ground. The ideal place was found high on the river-bank in the overhang of several Mahogany trees. Surprisingly thick grass was flattened and the camp fire was lit. Brett spread out his kaross indicating his sleep-place of preference. The others moved some ten paces away and spread out their area so as to sleep in a group. Brett stretched out on his bed, with his hands clasping elbow behind his head, as a pillow. He closed his eyes and his mind drifted back to the past. If only that queen had located this place the world may have been different. Smoke wafted over his head, working its way up through the leaves. He would ease gently through the heat of the day just exactly where he was, and would go out in search of filling the pot later. Looking skyward he relaxed into thought of the past; old man Peleele, whip-cracking centurions; ivory traders, mauling lions, beached ships and raging rivers. He felt centre stage in events of yesteryear, playing to a stately audience of Bataleur and circling vultures. The mid day heat massaged his tension, and relaxed him into a short light sleep.

Brett woke suddenly, jumped upright, and looked across at the other four men. They were staring at him, and all had smiles of anticipation, hoping it would be he that was summoned to go on the hunt. Brett studied each face in turn then relegated Hennery to housemaid and cleaner, Peleele-Pasi to the rank of chief of ablutions, and Gauto to cook. Braziwa would be head tracker, and in the event that a shot be heard, then Gauto and Hennery should come to help carry.

The day was hot, the sun high in the sky. Brett settled back to attend to his rifles. His passion for sheen finish on gun-blue and stock-shine on the butt of his rifle was evident as he smoothed a thin film of oil, and worked the action of the Mauser. The precision with which he assembled the weapon indicated an emotion of kind and compassion towards his rifles. They were, after all, his life-blood providers and protectors. The .318 had been carried and cared for over several thousand miles of footslogging terrain by his grandfather, his father and hopefully his grandchildren too. The .318 had saved life on many occasions, and provided food for thousands of hungry bellies. With the gun action good, click-clocking, slotting with precision into place, barrel shine glistening a craftsman's pleasure, and the internal rifling bore of both weapons spiralling, shining, with neither dust nor slight imperfection, Brett gathered his sheath knife and charged both rifle magazines to capacity. Braziwa had sharpened his axe to a bone cutting perfection and his knife was as sharp as a razor. Together they stood, Brett with the .318, Braziwa taking the .22. They moved up the steep climb above, taking some 15 minutes to reach the top, just 40 feet above the camp. It was more of an ape type climb than a lady-like park stroll. The mood was set for a short, sharp, quick hunt to fill the pot for the night. There was a long afternoon ahead, and no need for haste.

When they reached the crest of the river bank, it had been more a cliff climb than a river bank exercise; more arm than leg, more lift than carry, more pull than push, and they laughed.

The plains were vast open spaces to the south. Trees and hills and valleys and river tributaries stretched north to the horizon. The terrain was beautiful. The midday heat penetrated both men as they stepped out into the open plain. The odd lone tree scattered pods and provided intermittent shade and respite for the eagle during his search.

The pace was slow with particular attention to wind approach, scent, tracks and terrain. As they approached the crest of the first undulation they were attracted to a series of equally spaced, tall, shining people bobbing along a small ridge. It was a group of top naked women, with various shaped containers on their heads, and each had a child strapped to her back. They were talking, laughing and splashed with water carrying containers balancing on each mother's head. Braziwa suggested Brett remain distant while he skirted the ridge, approaching the women from the front. He moved quickly, and then slowed down with their approach so as not to alarm them into a water-abandoning flight of fear. He sat on a rock and awaited their arrival. They were startled to see him; laughing, giggling in nervous surprise, stopping to debate between themselves. There was a language problem between them which was soon overcome when Braziwa detected their dialect, recalling what he could of his times amongst the Shangaan people, and blending this with his m'Kore-kore and M'swina credentials.

The women were elegant; tall with loose hanging skirts woven in various materials, ranging from reed-grass, to tanned hide and some were wearing well worn cotton fabric. One pulled her crying child, by his wrist from her back and held it to a suckling position. Both she and her child seemed oblivious to the flies circling and landing on her nipples. The child used both hands to direct her wrinkled, elongated sausage-like breast into his mouth. It was lubricated into position by the yellow nasal excrement clinging from inside his nostril to well down and then over his upper lip, swinging, hanging like a well established stalactite. Flies settled content to challenge the risk of being squashed between the face of the child and the chest of the mother.

Braziwa explained that he was passing through the area, in the company of a white man who had great skills and strength. They were intrigued, friendly and offered generous hospitality at their village some half a day walk from here. They had experienced problems with a man-eating leopard that was also destroying their goats. Braziwa agreed that he may visit their village the following day as this appeared to be on the route of their journey.

One of the women sat atop her ankles, balancing her weight on her toes, and requested assurance that Braziwa was truly accompanied by a white man, "Nkos" which means "God". Braziwa assured that he was, and the separate parties continued on their way. The women were excited and hurriedly moved off towards their village. The shrieks and joviality, laughter and loudness of their departure indicated great excitement amongst them.

Braziwa met up with Brett who had stopped so as not to intrude on the meeting. He was watching two Nyala antelope stride in regal sophistication on a parallel but reversed direction of the women – making their way to water. Although these animals are gentle, timid and small amongst antelope, they were too big an animal to be shot for the pot. Brett let them continue undisturbed. Braziwa shared news of the village and the problem being experienced with the leopard.

They continued on a slow westerly bearing, receiving a gentle wind against their back. This was directly advising a presence to animals downwind, but was in plan. The return walk would be to the north, facing the easterly breeze, which would increase towards late afternoon, covering a wider segment of the kingdom broadcasting system, but to their track rather than their forward route. The afternoon became reasonably cool, at least to walk without heat-retarding progress. As the shadows lengthened animals seemed to crawl from their shaded afternoon hibernation, into the world of feed, flies, fear and freedom. Below overhanging branches of an acacia thorn tree, at some 50 paces distant, they saw a steenbok ewe with her pygmy rabbit-size progeny kneeling and suckling and butting her udder in frustration. The ewe was content with her tongue twisting around shoots of new weed, slicing sections of fine leaf of new acacia thorn undergrowth. Her quick-jaw movement at chewing the cud was eternally sharpening teeth. Occasionally a back leg lifted over and scooped the kid away from persistent teat sucking.

As the sun sped towards the west and shadows elongated Brett decided their food need to be priority over emotions, and he would shoot anything edible that was reasonably small. Within minutes a reedbuck whistled from across the vlei, and leapt high, slowly springing away. His whistle carried far with each leap through the air. A reedbuck sound is mistakenly thought to be “blown” through the nostrils; such is the nature of sound. Actually it can only be actioned during movement. It is formed through a pouch in the groin situated between belly and back leg which fills with air when opened, and is expelled through restricting muscle action, much as a bag-pipe blows air to the reed.

As soon as the decision was made to take the reedbuck, it seemed as if spirit was poured under its tail. With sudden energized movement it sped off, as if being whipped to the finishing post. Mental telepathy, thought Braziwa, as he refocused for return to the camp. Their walk out had achieved distance, and the return would take long. They would need to walk quick to return in daylight. As they turned into the gentle easterly breeze Braziwa picked up tracks of a big pride of lion walking in single file. He signalled Brett, and they studied the spoor together. The spoor was within recent minutes, possibly half an hour. There were seven lion in this pride; one exceptionally big male. It may be the pride that had been on the hunt through the night. The big male had implanted his paws, with exaggerated favour, not using his left front pad. He was leaving traces of blood in the sand, an indication that his foot was oozing blood. His gait was awkward, but there was occasional indication that every twenty paces or so he would stop and spread-even his weight over all paws, and they had now detected a place where this mighty king had laid down. He had lain on his side to embalm his foot-pad with the strong medicinal cure of his tongue-lick to the wound of his pad. The rock splinters had penetrated deep into his pad, rendering him of little value to any immediate hunt, but instilling an anger; frustration and aggression that is not advisable to cross.

Brett realized they were in competition for an evening meal. Instinctively he moved off their tracks, skirting a wide north bound curve, before homing in towards the camp.

Meanwhile, back at the camp, Hennery, Peleele-Pasi and Gauto had been surrounded by a troop of about 20 baboons on their way to the water, and then by a group of monkeys. They had green reeds from the riverbed and pliable clay piled on the rock near the fire. This was their fun-sport to fill in the hours while sitting in camp. It was to form "bullets" of clay on the end of the reed then whip-lash these golf ball size pieces of wet clay so to sting the baboon or monkey on the rump to scream speedily treetop away from the camp. They had devised score systems and stories of artistic and accurate sling-shot variation; had laughed and enjoyed keeping good guard on the camp. All three were highly skilled and incredibly accurate over distances of 15 to 30 paces. Each of them could reliably sting the other on the buttock at 30 paces with every attempt, and this teen-sport of Africa always created a yodelling scream, punctuated with stinging laughter and determined response. This was light hearted joviality – but it stung – and they yodelled with wide open mouths, echoing off cliff-faces and through the canyons.

They approached the camp from the top of the cliffs; the same undulating platform onto which they arrived for the beginning of the walk. The terrain had been open grassland with interspersed outgrowth of acacia thorn, teak, leadwood, panga-panga and occasional shaded area of mukwa trees. Rocky outcrops abounded everywhere. The area had been teeming with an abundance of animals, such that no worthy hunter should miss a course of a meal. Brett was concerned that this day had presented much opportunity but it looked like they may sleep hungry tonight. The sun was reasonably high and the return had happened very quickly.

Braziwa stopped in his track looking over a shallow valley. His gaze attracted the attention of Brett to five men with spears swung low, running a steady fast pace slightly towards them; more toward the camp. After lengthy introductions and respectful holding of distance it transpired that these men had been sent by the village elder. The water-bearing mothers had returned in a hurry to explain to their chief that they had met with an Impi of Shaka – who was walking the plains with God.

The problems that had befallen the village with the intrusion of a man-eating leopard and now the kraal being regularly depleted of livestock at night, the chief was urgent in request for help of a Saviour. The five warriors had been dispatched and ran immediately they heard of the wandering God in the area. They were led to the place by high pitched yodelling and canyon scream-sounds and now they were looking for the God they had been told of. Brett had sat in the shade of a tree, camouflaged, leaning against the trunk, while Braziwa presented himself some 80 paces away, to the running warriors, who kept their spears slung low. Brett observed the meeting from a distance, with his .318 bridging on top of his knees; his arms relaxed over the top. He had heard most words of the meeting; had grappled with a multitude of linguistic dialects. He decided at the conclusion that these men were not of the same origin as the women Braziwa met earlier in the day. They spoke with tongue and mouth movement; vibrating a deep throat resonance, more like the Xhosa people of South Africa's Venda region, the approximate area of chief Thoyandau. They broached on weather greetings, good hunting, and a cool wind. They spoke with a reverence; a plea that this god be brought to their village soon. A man of predictions in the village had forecast horrendous illusions of the area being again taken over by beasts of the wild, and that the people would be replaced on the plains and the valleys by sharp clawed, big toothed roaming predators. The village was desperate. Please would this god throw his skins of protection over this peace-loving people?

Braziwa told them to remain seated and sprang to his feet, leaning swiftly into his stride toward Brett, who had not yet been seen by any of the warriors. Braziwa quickly positioned himself, as always, at a lower level than Brett and advised him of the plea of the chief. The five young men had observed the entire approach of Braziwa, and now looked in awe as Brett stood, dismissing Braziwa to return to the men to assure them he would meet with their chief on the following day. As he turned to return to his camp the five young men lay flat, face down on the ground in certain belief they had now seen God with their very own eyes. None of them had ever seen a white man before. On advice from Braziwa, two agreed to return with the news to the chief and the others would be at this very place in the morning to escort the god to their chief.

Braziwa and Brett returned without meat to the camp and arrived to a pot of hot coffee. In the n'Debele language of Hennery and Gauto and Peleele, Brett and Braziwa absorbed the ridicule of a monkey that could not swim for his life. Brett contemplated the situation, with a hungry village to feed and decided that there was sufficient time before dark to go out on a short meat patrol along the river. With proviso that all meat could be carried by six men in the morning, he would shoot whatever crossed his path. He climbed with Hennery down to the water quietly observing upstream and down. They moved slowly downstream with the cool breeze touching over their faces. At a bend in the river, not 100 paces from camp stood a proud bull kudu with a full three curves to his horns. This glistening pride of his life shone brightly in the fading light of the day. He was old and alone, sent out from his herd. He was listening with his huge megaphone-type ears, and using his upturned face to the wind for any indication of threat. The majestic bull searched the wind directly away from Brett as he lifted his .318 and took aim to the shoulder, then moved slightly back, taking perfect sight on the exact position of the heart. The proud big bull turned his head to face forward, parted his front legs and elegantly bent forward and down to drink water. This close-up sight of magnificent pride sent a spine-chilling respect through Brett's marrow. He squeezed the Mauser trigger with articulate precision. Bang! The thunderous sound of the high powered rifle bounced, echoed, returned to the heavens and played the same sounds over and over again. The river acoustics were expanding explosion and the sounds reverberated again, again and again. Then like a retreating herd of rubber booted jackass rabbits the sound tapered off down stream. Silence! The kudu had taken the bullet central in the heart, which exploded on impact. The huge bull lunged upward and forward, leaping high through the shallow water, bounding over the pool, and onto the far side river sand. He crashed like a fallen gladiator, and his three spirals of glorious headgear rammed hard, one buried deep in the sand. His legs remained active in death-throes an instant, and then he lay motionless, dead. Brett and Hennery ran across the streambed, and Hennery hurriedly sliced his razor sharp knife through the jugular, oesophagus and the rest of the neck flesh, to the bone. The destroyed heart-muscle was pumping in determined but rudderless effort, helping to clean out the blood. Brett slit the tight belly skin from the sternum through the naval, past the sheath skin, through to the tail. He skilfully sliced through the muscular outer casing of the bowels and removed the huge, overfilled stomach, unbroken, rolled out and onto the sand. Brett removed the lungs and the liver, the heart and the kidneys and placed them on branches of green-leaf hanging nearby. Timing had been perfect, as the sun was now down, and the day was cool. Not a single fly settled on the meat, a miracle in itself. Removing the skin was a privileged task, with the object being to neither slice through nor leave flesh on the skin. Hennery was well skilled at this and had begun with the front legs at the hock. The skinning was well under way, ensuring that no meat could touch any sand.

The thunderous sound of the gunshot had woken and alerted the senses of everything. Within very short moments Gauto, Peleele-Pasi and Braziwa leapt from the camp and sprung down to the scene. All had knives and axes and expertly scrambled to action. The mood was alive, and the joy-song of the hunter rose from deep in the gut of the men.

Before darkness the moon floated high above. Braziwa lit a fire nearby and the carcass was expertly dismembered into manageable sections. The back leg of the kudu was excessively heavy, so shoulder poles were cut for the haul up to camp. Each back leg was skinned and the shoulder poles threaded through tendons and hung, straddling branches, gripped in the fork-cleft of low trees.

Up on the plain three village youths had been awaiting the morning so as to escort god to their chief. They had a small fire burning, and each held his spear in his hand. They were all astounded that they had each seen god and this day would never be forgotten. They were comfortable and were settling down for a night near god, each contemplating his own evaluation of the experience. Each one knew the story was excessive in profoundness to be believed in isolation. Each one knew that they needed the unconditional backup of the other that they had all experienced the same thing. A cool evening cloudless sky was ending the excitement of the day. They were ecstatic to be escorting this white spirit god to their chief, and they were talking in low voice, a deep throat sound. They were sitting enjoying the glow of coals and flickering flame when their beliefs changed forever.

As one they froze at the sound of a low growl, a rumble then crackle of dry-stick broken. They looked out to the most feared of sights in Africa – a low lying bunched up pride of hungry lion all looking them straight in the eye. Suddenly as a whip-lash of lightning, flashed a glimpse of his mane. The male was down to one side, lying in readiness to command out his roar of instruction. As he pulled up his gaze and opened his jaw to expend a full blooded roar, the sound of the canyon erupted. With perfect precision and at the speed of light …..It happened.

The heavens erupted with a sound of thunder on thunder on thunder, sounding like mountains collapsing and smashing, like two worlds beating and smashing and bashing together. Reverberations echoed, and the crack seemed to mount up, and recharge and volume itself to the heavens. Explosions magnified the circumstances. This majestic king of the wild had heard the identical sound before, and his foot had been agony since. His brow seemed to split as his eye slit closed and he sprinted into the setting sun. He never looked over his shoulder, nor gave thought to the rest of his pride. He sprinted at speed keeping his body close to the ground and was very closely followed by six other lions all moving at similar speed.

These confident and God fearing warriors of the wild had seen the "white spirit" in flesh – and were anxious. They were waiting to be in his presence in the morning. They were calm and quiet, assembled in good conduct and anxious in contemplation of this real white spirit. And now, with the white spirit real and in their midst, the horrendous sound shatters tranquillity; splits the heavens in half; is a frightening, ear splitting, nerve racking experience not possible to describe nor explain. The echo and acoustics expanded the sound, but the mood of the men enriched their now certain knowledge that this spirit is power, white, strong and in total command. They jumped at the sound and fell to the ground. This moment was certain confirmation to them all. With command over thunder, He had saved them from the lion and would meet with their chief in the morning.

They were in fear as the day turned to dark. They prayed in their fashion, yodelling, asking, pleading, surrendering to the spirit, rolling on the ground, and screeching into the air. Then they decided to follow Brett down to the canyon; be closer to the spirit than the hungry, now angry and shamed big king and his six followers. The tallest of the men developed speed greater than a trot in the direction taken by Brett and Braziwa. They were agile and talented trackers. They followed the track to the crest of the cliffs and peered down to two men skinning a kudu. They discarded their spears to the ground at the top, then clambered down in vertical descent and swung arm over arm as they expertly descended the slope. They arrived near the bottom of the river, and observed from behind bush that Hennery and Braziwa were loading the shoulder pole onto Gauto and Peleele-Pasi, with a full back leg of the kudu. They were amazed that such provision of food was presented to this white spirit, right on the door of his overnight stay. Could the thunder have been the white spirit's bellow for food? … Yes, it was, they decided.

Just then Hennery noticed their presence and alerted both Braziwa and Gauto. Together Hennery and Braziwa jumped across the shallow water and hurriedly crossed to the men hiding behind bushes. They became terrified but remained motionless, holding their breath. "Umfaan" commanded Braziwa as a centurion may speak to his slave. "What are you doing spying on us? Come like men and be seen." The men came from behind the bushes, looking like rats rescued from drowning. Braziwa spoke harshly to these trembling, fearful men. They had understood little he said, but his intoned language, body language and attitude said it all. They were terrified and tried to explain. Hennery listened well and so did Braziwa, but the "click, clicking" of the Xhosa mouth-sounds were too different. These men had been competent in dialogue when requesting the privilege of the white spirit, but in terrified uncertainty they challenged the language barrier too distant from good comprehension. There was a breakdown in trust, and this needed good clarification. Hennery moved over to one of the men, the biggest, who was probably 15 years old, the eldest, and secured his wrist with a very tight grip. It was painful and he winced. "Yes, they understand *this* language," thought Hennery. A few short moments, and an understanding was established. These were merely terrified men who had never experienced the sound of a rifle, and now they were making some story about lions and thunder. Shame on them, but no harm done! He offered them whatever meat they could use, and assured that the meat was for use of their chief. Gratitude could not adequately be expressed, and the men accepted the back leg on the shoulder-pole and hurried away, up-stream. They assured they would be present the following morning. It transpired that they moved on only 100 paces and lit a huge bonfire of driftwood and hardwoods. Their firelight lit up Brett's camp through the night. It was not a problem but a surprise that these men had stayed so close. They knew the reason to be fearful of the lion, but neither Brett nor any of his bearers understood the complex issues at play. Brett was their god who had rescued them from the jaws of the lion, and he would be revered forever.

The night was a privilege with everything perfect and fun. Not a worry nor care in the world. It was cool and they had all had a good wash in the shallow clean water. They had an abundance of meat, and Gauto had prepared a huge pot of sadza and a thick well salted gravy. The fire was glowing a glint and glitter that only the hardwoods of low lying terrain can achieve. There was not a cloud in the sky, and the moon was exceptionally bright, lighting the cliffs and reflecting off wavelets and ripples in the water. The sounds of occasional owl-hoots and batwings and nightjars and crickets were tuned in for the night. The gut-smells of full-grass antelope belly were sweet in the air downstream of the camp, wafting an occasional reminder to Brett. This was certain to call in some dog sounds or predators, possibly even the big cats – leopard or lion. The previous night had been long and everyone was now ready to take on the challenge of a good night in deep sleep. The camp was unlikely to disrupt any prowling hyena or jackal or lion, but it could possibly be in suitable place for the retreat of a leopard or serval cat. Hennery and Gauto placed three big, gut sized deadwood of hardwood central onto the fire and these were certain to burn good flame through the night. The campfire of the other three men from the village was central in the bed of the river, well stoked with an overabundance of hardwood and driftwood and dry bark and small wood. The light-glow reflected brighter than moonlight on the cliff faces and the men straddled the fire and kept talking and singing and dancing and eating and re-stoking the fire. They were chanting away the spirit of predators, and giving thanks to their ancestors for the white spirit that had saved their life from the jaw of the lion. They had mysteriously been blessed with the rib cage and rump and forelegs of the kudu, and their life had taken a turn. Lacking the planning when sleeping between cliff-faces and ledges in the bed of a river, these men had positioned themselves down-wind of the discarded belly and offal of the kudu carcass. Any incoming tracker following the direction of scent would certainly be forced right into their camp. Brett instructed Gauto and Peleele-Pasi to go tell them to expect intrusion of hyena or leopard. They were all over-bloated in excesses of grilled meat, with unaccustomed over-full bellies. They assured that the spirit was closely protecting, and no harm could intrude them this night. Brett and his bearers lay quiet for a short time and then faded out, into deep sleep. They all slept unmoving, through the cool of the early night, holding tight to their warmth and the fire. The chanting below continued unabated while Brett's camp journeyed distant places in dreams. The moon traversed high to the vertical standard of central day or central night. The cliffs were floodlit, and the stars were bright light as well. Still not a cloud in the sky, when the lower camp quieted to a low drone of deep voices and then passed silently to sleep. The moon panned over from a mid setting angle, having seen the lower camp men adopt vertical positions surrounding the huge fire. Silence in both camps except for the night-sounds.

Brett and his men slept most of the night. They awoke quickly to the sound of the lower camp in crisis. A hyena had unwittingly ventured too close to the vertical riverbank in an attempt to outflank the bright-flame perimeter of the fire light. It was en route to the scent of the degutted belly that had permeated westwards, hanging on the all night easterly breeze. She was being followed by three cubs that became nervous at the sight of the fire. They stalled in effort to by-pass the camp, forcing the leader to continue alone. Behind in the dark they were followed by a huge male hyena and two younger adults. The elder female realized she had been separated from her young and bellowed a blood curdling laugh that carries to distant places on the gentle breezes of night. Her holler was immediately followed by another blood curdling laugh and a bark from the male at the rear of the group. The wimpish young messengers woke to the first sound, and sat bolt upright in panic, alert, observing nothing in the darkness. They were all facing eastward into the breeze, the direction from where the first sound had come, when the male let out his bellow. The younger one screamed at the top of his voice and his echo reverberated as a cathedral organ may sound through the steeple. The other two were stunned into silence, riveted close to the warmth of the fire. They were trapped between two hyena with pups, with steep banks on either side. They were terrified. The huge male hyena was standing, lurching from side to side, heavy breathing, walking slowly towards the fire. His eyes glowed alternate yellow and red from the flames, and saliva dribbled from his mouth, hanging down to the ground as he swayed closer. Brett had his .318 pulled into his shoulder and stood observing from his elevated position. He eased a round into the chamber of the Mauser, squeezed the trigger, and closed the bolt action. It was loaded but could not fire until bolt action primed.

Hennery drew close, observing over Brett's shoulder and Gauto and Braziwa stayed low. Peleele-Pasi listened intently, but lay flat in a sleeping position. He could hear the panting and aggressive hyena and the fear emanating up from the men. Then his focus encompassed the flame-lit perimeter as the huge male entered the challenge of the well lit arena. Brett charged the bolt action, and this smooth sound of metal and lubricant attracted the glare of the male. Brett had him in the sights, but did not need to kill him unless danger overtook the situation. With a sudden loud growl and bark, the hyena lunged at the men just five paces in front. The lumbering, lurching ungainly movement built into his structure was aggressive. His oversized head swung from his right to his left, and then he stood solidly observing the fire. An agonized scream from the fireside alerted Brett to the fear and tension these men were suffering and he loaded, pulled the trigger of his big rifle once more. The eruption and confusion, repeat echo and deep sounds of the explosion again jerked the men into reverence. They had witnessed this huge vice-like set of jaws, could inhale the vile breath of this most fearful of bone-crushing predators slowly descending upon them. Their spears had been discarded at the crest of the cliff, and they had no protection, save the flame and the coal. The kudu meat was suspended on the shoulder-pole in two tree forks adjacent the camp fire and this too had attracted the aggression of the hyena. These three men would now claim having been in the gullet of god as he barked out death to a hyena. It fell heavily without any forward movement, and lay bad smelling slump-meat in the river sand. The pups and their mother vanished in opposite directions, and at very high speed. They were fast to vanish upstream and downstream, with the mother not stopping at the site of the kudu gut belly, for now.

The three men had been utterly dismayed. Now this second event of the Saviour was true, and beyond any dispute. They were certain beyond reproach that this white spirit was truly the god above all gods. It was not possible that man could create such powerful sound, nor rescue from distance any person in such fearful circumstance as to be surrounded by predators, unable to escape, then the animal drop dead with the sound of thunder. Yes, this white spirit, with straight hair had to be God. One of the men insisted on leaving at the first sign of light, to be bearer to the chief of news of the night's events. His fear and articulate gesticulation and expression convinced the chief and the people in the village that the presence of God was near, and coming to visit today.

Brett turned to the fire, and pulled the three legged pot onto a hotspot to brew. With Braziwa, Gauto, Hennery, and Peleele-Pasi they sat full bellied, well rested and ready, with the orange glow of flame in their face, awaiting signs of dawn.

The clanking pots and tin mugs swung tied to straps of bedding as they erected themselves from the camp fire. The routine of dowsing the coals was repeated, and they followed Brett and Braziwa up and onto the crest of the river bank. The relief of being on level ground worked its way through them all, as they fell in single file towards the meeting place scheduled the previous afternoon. When they arrived they were greeted by the most reverent and fearful people that they had ever seen. Brett felt a sympathy for the ignorance and misplaced attitude of these young men. He had not understood that they had never heard such a power sound as his .318 rifle being fired in a canyon. He had not realized that the sound had twice saved them from the ravages of hungry predators. He had not realized that none of them had ever seen a white man before. This situation led to two sided misinterpretations of the same situation. The gravity of division in spiritual depth and comprehension of the same circumstance was unique and profound. The three young boys shared the shoulder weight of the swinging meat with Peleele-Pasi. The leading eldest had both horns. He carried them sternly in protective determination. Braziwa and Hennery stretched the skin between them, hammock like, suspending bundles of hacked rib and offal. Gauto clutched a bundle of hacked ribs. The eldest took the lead, walking very fast in the hope of being the introducing hero at the seat of their chief. The walk was long, unbroken and at persistent pace. The route was along easy terrain, skirting fringes of densely populated trees and open grassland. Occasionally they would enter through trees then out again into vast open plains. Having started on the walk well before sunrise, using the early dawn light to escape the river-bank slope, it had been a long hard, fast walk. The midday sun was now directly overhead.

There had been an abundance of game throughout the day. Brett could easily have selected almost anything from the plains for the pot, but they had an abundance of back leg and offal and rib cage of kudu. There was no need of more meat for the day.

Slowly there developed signs of the village. Incoming paths became frequent as they walked. Then the distinct aroma of the African village. Smoke and livestock, manure and poultry, with occasional over-flying pigeons and now the sounds. A rooster calling the midday rest; smoke stack climbing high from close quarters. As this pungency developed, the walk pace reduced and the three men leading were vying for a lead roll in the introduction ceremony. They were all anchored to the speed of everyone by the shoulder carrying connection of swinging meat, now buzzing with flies, like bees at honey.

They turned a corner around a boulder of granite and stepped into thick wooded terrain. It was then just a short walk when the village unfolded from the edge of gentle sloping ground. At the sight of the first man entering the cleared space an eruption of high pitch ululating permeated the air. The path had been clean-swept by the youth and the women using brushwood. Strong smelling fires were burning outside many huts. The third young escort stopped, turned and humbly suggested to Hennery that all of the visitors remain in the shade of the trees. He indicated a well used, huge trunk of very old hardwood, fallen, now lying in the shade of several m'Chakata trees. It had probably served as a bench seat for hundreds of years, for thousands of buttocks. There was no grass covering the sand, indicating a playground for goats, chickens, children and cattle. Brett was relieved to sit, leaning both rifles against the tree trunk, one either side of him. Hennery, Braziwa, and Gauto joined him, but Peleele-Pasi made directly away towards dense leafy undergrowth. His need was urgent to be alone and behind cover.

The three village messengers disappeared down into the village, and became swallowed into the anxiety of the dancing, singing, ululating people. They entered as heroes, meat swinging between them, concentrating on self expressed importance written on their forehead. They were ushered directly to the door of the chief, where they were relieved of the meat. There they sat upon low log-seats off to the side. An elder women, blind in one eye with what looked like a pus-infected hollow cavernous void, dressed only in loin cloth and feathery headdress adopted a humble, submissive posture and entered the hut of the chief. An aura permeated the crowd. Silence overtook the village. Even the goats and the livestock and every creature of the wild observed this moment as sacred. The greatness of the white spirit would be explained by the three messengers, and then the headmen and elders would lead a procession to the trees.

Brett relaxed, having no knowledge of the reverence being imposed on him. It had become beyond dispute that he could control thunder and command death by his thoughts.

The village was an ensemble of a variety of tribesmen and women brought together through different circumstances. Travellers from Portuguese East Africa had climbed to the west in search of high ground, to escape the violent floodwaters that destroyed their plains, homes and crops. M'Kore-kore and M'swina tribesman from the highlands of the eastern districts of Southern Rhodesia had resettled in this comparatively low lying region in an attempt to escape the cold and continual rain as experienced in past years. n'Debele men and women from the area of sub-chief n'Tabazinduna had moved east to improved hunting grounds. Some had moved north from the Venda valley of South Africa, and from other locations of varying geographical and seasonal climate and culture. All these tribesmen had been united under one village in defence against marauding lion, leopard and elephant. They had all been accepted into the area of self appointed Chief Gono, in the interests of security through unity. Each little group of residents maintained self imposed isolation within the village, according to his original area and dialect. Occasional social or 'council' gatherings involving all villagers were attended, and inter tribal courting relationships occurred, thereby creating a blend of various language and cultural integration. All villagers learned the combo of language, but each retained his original roots as the chosen communication within his own house. The common language was unique in creation, but such integration has occurred throughout Africa from the beginning of time. Each wave of migration change be it seasonal, political, developmental or survival has resulted in cultural adaptation. The African is well accomplished in culture variety, social and survival adaptation. He is also ripe for persuasion into spiritual and religious re-direction, although reverence for his ancestors will seldom falter.

Seven young bare-chest maidens ushered in by a wrinkled elder women arrived into the shaded confines where Brett was waiting. They carried gourds of fresh milk, sour milk, a platter of uncut cheeses, clean wooden bowls filled with a variety of fruit; football size paw-paw, mangoes, marula fruit, m'Chakata, avocado pears, oranges and a coconut. One bowl contained clean honeycomb filled with golden rich pure honey. It was covered with an inverted bowl. They sat silently on their heels in a semi-circle at Brett's feet, peeling and slicing the cheese and fruit into manageable portions. Somewhat bewildered, Brett observed in silence.

It was traditional that this 'preparation' routine was carried out in the presence of the invited guest as a token of assurance that food and fruit had not been mistreated in any way. They were silent and did not at any time attempt eye contact with any of their guests. They looked either at the ground, the gourds, the cheese or the fruit. When the cleaning, cutting and peeling was completed they placed all the bowls in a semi-circle at Brett's feet. They passed a gourd full of water from maiden to maiden, offering to pour over the cupped hands of the guests, who all washed and dried their hands. The water was placed on the ground, to one side, adjacent the bowls of food.

In military unison they stretched their hands high then lay face down on the sand indicating a worshipful reverence. They stood, curtsied low, maintaining concerted visual contact at Brett's feet. Brett and his team sat silently throughout the procedure. The girls turned and departed in single file. This ceremony atmosphere was dignified, serious and appreciated.

The bowls were lifted by Gauto and Peleele-Pasi, for Brett to partake. He selected a slice of paw-paw. It was over-ripe and sweet. He selected a section of cheese and of orange. It was sweet, tasted good. He had another handful and left the rest for the others. He drank a mouthful of fresh milk. It was still warm from the cow. The mixture of orange, cheese and milk would curdle and digest quickly and efficiently. He would not become bloated or uncomfortable.

He watched the others enjoying the delicacies, and then smiled. His thoughts were with Peleele-Pasi, Gauto, Hennery and Braziwa who thought they were not about to gluttonously consume as before. But they did. To them the fruit was sweet and the milk was health. Cheese and honey was served to dignify and revere guests, should be totally consumed. This overabundance of kingly food was never about to take ill effect, because the intake was a balance that would nourish the body and clean the soul. This introductory presentation had been planned and reaped during the night. It was not often in the course of a lifetime that we actually meet and eat a meal with god. This circumstance had been wisely forecast by many ancestors of varying origins, and when all suggestions were brought together the result was this magnificent spread of nourishment as the beginning of a reverent celebration.

Brett stood, stretched his arms, legs, and walked a small circle. Some bowls were still overflowing and he knew that everything had to be consumed. "Makomana, let's see what you are made of" he challenged. Hennery retorted that it was Brett's doing and now required men amongst men to pass the test. "He with the pointing nose and long straight hair could not come up to the expectations of the village." Brett absorbed the jibe with a smile, in sympathy with the after-effects of the honey. He was well aware that fruit has similar laxative qualities as honey. "Now, fruit and honey are contained, held, with the binding influence of cheese and soured milk and goat milk. Beware the time when the river bursts a bank, or the lake flows over the top!" They all laughed, but continued with the task of finishing everything.

From the village there began sounds of ululating, high pitch singing and slow deep beating drums. Brett looked out across the village to see a huge mass gathering around the fires. Men were regaled in headgear and arm bands, clutching shields formed from cowhide. One word amongst many continually echoed out and seemed to hang in the air. "Nkos" – "God" in all the dialects of the region. But then, this was not of major significance because all the farm workers referred to Southey as "Nkos." To Brett it simply meant "Boss" or "Employer." To the masses it meant a very reverent God.

It took time to complete the meal. Hennery and Gauto had been a little cautious on food intake. Braziwa and Peleele-Pasi had excelled themselves. They were all full bellied, but not bloated. This meal would be well digested soon. They all stood, moved about, shook up and intoned leg muscle and flexed their arms as they spoke. Gauto accidentally kicked sand onto the .22 rifle butt and quickly took a cloth to dust it clean. Brett glared at the irresponsibility of such an accident and Gauto felt shamed.

Suddenly the mood of the village rang out. Beating drums and deep harmonious melody replaced the high pitch shrill that had started a jubilation. Brett looked out again, attracted to the magnificence of deep baritone harmonizing; drumbeat and traditional foot-stamping; shield bearing rotations blending with deep vibration of joyous men and women at the commencement of celebrating something very important. He was eager to move on, agitating his gun bearers to ready themselves and go. Hennery explained that they were compelled, having accepted food and hospitality, to leave this place only under escort.

Then it happened. The drumbeat developed a crescendo, the high pitch song-sound harmonized with the bass and the deep baritone voices reached out, booming. "Nkos, Nkos, sekelela, iAfrica. Buya, Nkos, bulala lo satan-nyoka, aaah,

Nkos, Nkos Buya katess Nkos. God, God, save our land, come God, kill the Satan snake, aaah, God, God come now God."

The chilling appeal and plea of the village penetrated deep into the marrow of Brett. He witnessed a desperate people, determined in seeking God for their problems, pleading His solutions. Brett had no idea they were referring to him as God. A group of men emerged through the door of the big hut. In the centre was an elderly man, strong on his feet and quick in movement, respected, shown humble regard, obviously in command. He had come out into the sunlight and lifted his right hand to silence the crowd. Then he removed the headdress from his head and placed it at the entrance to his hut. All dancing warriors with spears lifted them high in the air and walked in procession to the front of the hut. Every spear was leant against the wall, tip down in the sand. The man in command faced forward, outward and held his chin high, looking upward directly towards Brett. Then he lifted both arms to the sky, with flat open palms of his hands wide open, all fingers as apart as he could. On this gesture began another procession of men carrying axes, short ones, long ones, small ones and big ones. They were placed at the door of the hut of the chief, and solemn procession continued in silence. Then a drum beat began and the chief moved up the slope towards Brett, with his bare-headed men surrounding him. As they approached Brett peered out of the undergrowth. Hennery and Braziwa pleaded that he should not be seen by the incoming people until they arrived close up. As the chief drew closer youthful Brett instructed Hennery and Braziwa to bring his rifles and he stepped out to be in clear view. The chief moved in solemn procession up the slope, still enclosed in the circle of his men. Brett watched as they approached to a distance of 20 paces, where the chief halted and his men fell into line behind him, to his left and his right. Brett lifted his open palm hand in gesture of goodwill and friendship. The chief came closer, and the village remained in total silence, spellbound. Observing the spiritual relevance of their leader meeting God was an awesome experience for everyone. Many of the village residents had never seen a white man, or a person with straight long hair. This was a spine chilling moment that would never be forgotten especially amongst the youth of the village.

Brett examined the village, seeing a mass of men, women and children, motionless in breathtaking silence, framed in wisps of village smoke and huge hardwood trees. He thought quickly how Moses must have filled with emotion, holding two slabs of burned rock in his hands, overlooking the people from his elevated position on the mountain. Somehow, there was an element of reverence in this moment of reality in which Brett had come to help sort a problem with a leopard.

The chief approached closer and the men surrounding him stopped, except one. Together they moved within five paces of Brett and the chief lifted both arms high in respectful submission. The palms of his hands faced Brett indicating openness and friendship. Brett lifted his hand. The deep baritone voice of the chief boomed out. "Sakgabonani, Nkos."

Brett responded in the dialect of the chief, that dialect of the one time king of Monomatapa, Lobengula. "Sakgabonani Sekuru, Kunjaani, wena?" "Greetings, chief, how are you?" In contrast to the deep tone of the chief, Brett in his youth, spoke with the newly breaking voice of a young teenager

The chief was awestruck with the directness of this young man. His humble submission had been occasioned by the repeated deliberations of the women the previous day, and the excited lip-clicking tongue-splashing explanations of the men that had returned the previous day. All activities, imitations and explanations had supported the extreme power, competence and thunder control at the whim of this youthful, power perfect, white spirit. The chief had seen white men but many of his village had not. His experience of white men had been to witness assertive leadership; men and women who had vast knowledge and decision making ability. He had never seen a white man dependent on others, except for labour. He had never seen a white man unable to make quick decisions and issue concise instructions. But now he was before a white warrior who could command thunder, dismiss lion and hyena and have fresh meat delivered almost into his parlour. Chief Gono had not seen a rifle in action; had no understanding how the thunder is created nor what destroyed the hyena. He was totally submerged and swimming in an aura of being in the presence of God.

Brett noticed the respect, admiration and humble manner in which this well respected man of the people had presented himself. He invited him to come into the shade and commune. This too was accepted as an honour, even though it was on his turf.

Together they moved back into the shade and Brett took a seat on the log. The chief sat on his heels and looked up at Brett in reverence. Hennery, Braziwa, Gauto and Peleele-Pasi approached the chief with grand respect and dutiful fear. They cupped their hands and approached at a subservient low level, clapping loudly in the time honoured manner known to the n'Debele people. Chief Gono returned the gesture then realigned his concentration to Brett. Brett's boys sat some ten paces distant, behind Brett, observing, listening intensely. The discussion was all in n'Debele dialect.

They panned on the hunt that brought in the meat this day; the hyena death and the vanishing pride of lion. Brett had not been aware of the stories that had preceded him to the village, contaminating the mind of the chief in an undiluted form. He sat absorbing the adoration in quiet disbelief. The problem of the leopard was presented and Brett said he would look into the situation with urgency. He called Hennery and Braziwa instructing that they go now down to the village and question anyone who may assist in destroying the killer leopard. Establish the where, how, why, when and strategy of what has been done to prevent further deaths of livestock. The Chief told them who to see, and summoned one of his lieutenants to accompany them back into the village.

The meeting continued on matters of weather, wild fruits, and the hazards of life as conceived by this learned scholar of tribal survival and tradition. They laughed and each listened with intensity to the other, until they exhausted common ground. Then the chief stood erect and moved to a low log, a place of improved comfort. Two elderly women entered followed by three nubile young maidens, probably 12 or 14 years of age, all carrying gourds of brown, frothy millet beer. First Brett was handed an overfull gourd and then the chief took his. Brett had tried this brew on occasions, but had not acquired the taste. He filled his mouth full with the surprisingly cool liquid that had to be as much eaten as drunk. This intake out of politeness gave Brett the opportunity to cut through the lengthy irrelevant small talk and jump to his feet.

"That little taste of your good strong beer has given me the strength to go find this leopard. I must go quickly." The chief agreed, grinned widely then his wrinkled skin stretched tight over his face as he laughed out loud. "Thank you, Nkos. Hamba Gashle, Nkos. Tina bonana kuseni" – "Thank you, God, go carefully, God. We will meet in the morning" The elder man stood back for Brett to depart and proceed down the slope into the village. The men who had been in waiting for the chief all stood, and one lifted his right arm high. At that moment a drum-roll began in the village. Ululating went up to the sky, the men all walked with a reverence behind the chief, who was directly behind Brett. As they neared the people lining the path a group of about 30 young men started with a deep hymn type harmonious hum. The drums beat louder and then the soprano sounds of the virgin girls climbed high and spilled in, blending with the baritone and base of the Impi, the warriors and the elders. The foot stamping, toe shuffling, dust scuffing men were in regal jovial action; permeating a spiritual reverence. The young maidens were turning, gyrating and thumping the ground with their feet, skirts swirling and arms waving, flapping and clapping. The song sound was incredible; in tune and harmonious, but words were from a multitude of African dialects. Voices from a thousand mouths boomed out to the valley below. The dust swirled and the drums beat louder.

There were no elder women in evidence. They were behind the scenes tending to turning an ox, a sheep and two goats over the coals. They were stirring the barrel shape burnt clay containers of brewed beer, skimming the flotsam off the top. It was cooling, almost cold, needing final hygiene before the evening. They were preparing an exceptional feast for that evening in celebration of the presence of the white spirit.

Brett walked between people lining the pathway, and as he passed, so they expressed their reverence; some in tears; some by hiding their faces and some simply staring open mouthed in disbelief. None approached closely. They kept several paces distance between themselves and this great white spirit. Amongst the immediate followers was Peleele-Pasi carrying both rifles, now wrapped in his bedding to protect them from the dust of the dancing people. He was waving at the crowd, had already singled out a pair of huge doe shape eyes that caught his attention, and he looked longingly in the hope of closer scrutiny sometime later.

A clearing directed Brett towards the door of the chief's hut, but he needed to get away from this place. Too many people, too much dust, sweat and dancing and too much noise. He stopped, pausing for the chief to catch up. He leaned his arm on the chief's shoulder and the sound of the drums and the vocal harmony cut, dead. Silence. He spoke close to the chief's ear, and the old man listened attentively. Then bellowed loud an indiscernible sound and was answered by a whistle and shout from some distance away. He burst out laughing at the appearance of his most trusted tracker, hunter and aid, as he broke through the barrier of dancing, singing onlookers. "Of course, of course" he said, and used a hand signal to clear a way for Brett past the hut. The drum beat erupted and the singing continued; the dancing unsettled the dust once again.

Brett moved past the entrance to the hut and the chief was followed by his aides through the door. Hennery stood beside the head tracker, and indicated that they would leave in search of the leopard immediately. Wide way cleared for their passage, and they moved out of the village with the tracker leading the way. When they were some 1,000 paces from the village Brett stopped and sat on a rock in the shade. Everyone gathered around him and sat on the ground. He turned to the tracker and asked him the plan. The tracker knew vaguely where the leopard was and hoped to locate it quickly. It was an old animal, a little thin with many deep scars. He had seen it many times, once close enough to lunge at with his spear. It had retreated into dense dry undergrowth, and the tracker was wise not to follow.

The leopard had killed a suckling goat in the early hours of this morning, and the tracker had found the carcass well hidden, high in the fork of a tree. Brett needed to observe this and instructed his bearers to wait. Hennery and the tracker should accompany him to the hidden goat.

They arrived at a place within 3,000 paces of the village, where the tracker pointed, observing down the sloped edge of the hill on which they were stalking. His movement was deliberate, slow, well controlled. He breathed rather than spoke. His elevated position provided good vantage and the little red kid carcass remained high in the tree in the valley below. Flies were swarming around this pitiful sight. Apart from two very deep claw scratches in the trunk of the tree, there was no sign of the leopard. Brett scanned the terrain and the three men took up comfortable concealed positions from where to observe and contemplate. Between the three of them they had a .22 and a .318 rifle, two axes, a spear, three sharp knives and a shield. They would sit it out right here for a few hours. Observe in silence. They were downwind of the carcass and this elevated view of the valley below gave them every advantage. Then Brett thought deeper. If he was the leopard this is exactly where he would develop his appetite through the day, and then collect his meal in the afternoon. What better place to observe from? He scanned the closest trees, rocks and stumps. His vision widened to the middle distance. He was looking back, away from the carcass, seeing smoke and the village in the opposite valley. He turned to look back at the kid and slid his finger over the bolt and hammer of the rifle. The rifle was loaded, but the Mauser was closed. He felt uneasy. Slowly, quietly he lifted the bolt handle and checked the bullet in the chamber. The brass glistened in the sun. He closed the chamber, not pressing the trigger. The rifle was now loaded and ready. His thumb eased the safety catch on and he laid the rifle bridging both knees, pointing towards the tree.

The distance to the tree was further than ideal, but he knew he would easily hit an egg size target at the distance. He relaxed a few moments rejuvenating, re-gathering muscle strength and mental focus. His mind spanned the vast open spaces in front and he felt as an eagle observing from between wide spread wings suspended amongst the clouds. He took in the haze on the horizons and the tall cliff face in the valley below. The snaking river meandering deep into the haze seemed to work its way off the edge of the world. The open brown grassland areas seemed dry and thirsty; the wooded savannah interspersed with tall, steeple like spikes of deadwood saluting the plains, casting a liberty over all of nature.

Time passed slowly. The heat of the midday sun abated as the sun lowered itself to the western horizon. Brett momentarily stood, shouldering the rifle butt into the ready position, aimed at the treed carcass in boredom, moved to realign his seat-bond, giving change to his stance. "Yes, much better," he thought. The move had alerted a pennant-winged nightjar to flush from his well camouflaged roost amongst dry leaves on the floor, midway between him and Hennery. Hennery reacted. The tension of lying in wait for a leopard! He shuddered! Tracker lay chest down, motionless, undisturbed, retaining focus on the tree with the carcass.

Brett was suddenly alerted from the corner of his eye. With a speed of lightning the leopard was running full stretch, with his chest close to ground and his tail erect, pointing directly behind, aimed straight into the setting sun. This was his final lunge, having spent most of the afternoon observing these intruders into his territory.

He was moving behind a truck sized rock just paces behind Hennery, between the tracker and Brett. A well selected position from where to launch final thrust onto Brett. The tracker had not seen this movement until the leopard flew directly past like a slither of flashlight. Brett reacted, every tension in his body alert to the danger. This animal may be thin, and it may move with scars, but it was fast! It was agile and deathly silent. It had crossed an expanse of 50 big paces inside of two seconds, and slid behind the rock, all in absolute silence. Brett was advantaged in knowledge of the battle plan, but when the lightning flashed, he would not know which side of the rock it would appear. His rifle at ready, he now lay flat on his belly; elbows propping his shoulders; hands clenching, hard thrusting the shoulder and rifle butt at one with his body, held strong as a marksman at range. He panned the sight from right to left, taking in the prospect of being attacked from over the top.

The rock was about five paces from Brett and the leopard was immediately behind it. Hennery may have sight of the animal, but he was now behind, more distant, probably eight paces from the rock, unable to communicate except through movement. Hennery sat on his haunches with his axe held tight in his right hand and his knife firmly clasped, unsheathed, in his left. He could see the shadow movement of the point of the tail, twitching, sweeping the flat rock behind the boulder. The indication was that the pounce would come from the right. He managed to communicate this through to Brett, who aligned to the right of the rock. Lightning speed flashed. The left side erupted like a triggered puff-adder as Brett swung his aim to the left. The leopard was determined and agile as he sprung outstretched forepaws, trailing back legs trying to run through the air. In unfolding slow motion precision, Brett swung into action his instant clockwork experience, with jawbone tightly clenched; he squeezed the trigger and held the moment with wide open eyes. Flying through the air directly towards him with two inch needle sharp fore-teeth and sharp penetrating outstretched claws like a vampire came as a bullet, this enraged creature of extreme hunting prowess. But from his left, flying at equal height with a back swung axe, equal in grace and determination, the streamlined body of Hennery on collision course with the most aggressive of big cats of the African bush.

The bullet struck deep in the back of the wide open snarling mouth, ripping deep into throat-flesh, then shattering spine-bone and snapping the neck. Hennery swung hard with the axe, and this moment was planted in Brett's mind forever. The axe sliced deep into a turning neck bone, but the animal was already stone dead. The leopard had seen the flying, lunging Hennery an instant before the rifle shot crack and had twisted mid flight as only a cat can do. It turned on its side retracting its flight feet into aggressive claw-scratch intentions on Hennery. The movement was actioned; the bullet struck death but the flight action continued, until Hennery hit hard on the chest of this missile of spotted cat-flesh. They smashed into the rock, Hennery protected from the rock by the body of the leopard. Together they fell to the ground. Hennery was instantly on his feet, stabbing his knife to the body, but the animal was motionless, bleeding from a wide open mouth that was broken, smashed and dead.

The tracker was aghast. He had never heard the sound of a rifle before, and had not seen man challenge beast with the speed and aggression he had witnessed Hennery perform today. The vision he had, or the picture he painted, was that of an angel flying to the defence of his master, slicing death to the aggressor, and then standing blood-soaked, triumphant with his sword in his hand. That is the legend that followed, and remains as a campfire tale. Among the people of chief Gono today, this story is told with multiplied detail and definition, plying grand honour and reverence on the white spirit and his black angels.

The silent tracker was a hero when he returned to the village that evening. Carrying the leopard slung over his shoulders he yodelled loudly to the enchanted gallery, and took centre stage in presenting the smashed and broken cat carcass to the feet of the enthroned chief sitting on his well aged trunk of deadwood, from where he had been observing an exceptional bronze coloured sunset. Seven topless maidens surrounded him, seated on the sand, longingly awaiting his beck ‘n call for another gourd of cool beer to chew.

It was dusk, but not dark, and the village erupted in celebration. The elaborate preparations arranged for the white spirit were ready, but the spirit had sent a message that he had moved on toward a rising sun. But he will return!

Even the white spirit did not know that he would return, but this time from the sky! The next time Brett was in the area he was a 2nd Lieutenant in the SAS, fighting a bush war based on terrorising the very easily manipulated masses.

On his way back to the village, with the leopard carcass over his shoulders, feet clasped in front, two in each hand; the tracker had met Braziwa, Gauto and Peleele-Pasi, who were responding to the call of the rifle, searching for Brett and Hennery. They exchanged greetings with the tracker, and agreed to meet later in the evening. Peleele-Pasi had been magnetised by a magnificent pair of oversize doe eyes radiating out, above high cheek bones and the elongated neck structure normally unique to royalty. The tracker returned to the village and the bearers moved off to find Brett.

They set camp for the night some 2000 paces from where the leopard had died. Peleele-Pasi asked Brett if he could return to the village. He had met a maiden who needed his service. Brett smiled, excused him and told him they would be leaving very early the next morning. Peleele-Pasi heard most of what Brett said, but vanished hurriedly into the dark. There were powerful forces at play, well understood by young men.

Brett gazed, concentrating on Hennery, who was slitting his eyes to the smoke, boiling the water. He was mesmerised. Thoughts wafted like soft smoke on a windless day, drifting through his mind. Looking deep into the thoughts of Hennery, Brett could see a sincere, unique devotion. This boy had shown a courage today that was seldom confirmed or quantified. Hennery had distinctly demonstrated that he was prepared to shed his own life to save Brett, his friend and his master. He had voluntarily sliced the air between Brett and death, with his own body. He knew the minimal prospects of surviving such an event yet, when opportunity presented, without hesitation he threw his body to the defence of his master; in full confrontation with an enraged leopard. Brett found himself evaluating varying degrees of emotion.

"To like is to enjoy. To hate is to be cursed, repelled by something. What is to love? Love must be that element of emotion that expands or contracts through varying degrees, the ultimate of which is to be prepared to volunteer your own life for the sake of saving another. Like a thermometer measurement of boiling water. The other end of the love scale is probably to joyfully observe destruction. No. I have observed the destruction of much that I respected and enjoyed. I have observed in awe, a charging Bull Elephant, detesting the sight of his death, but very relieved that it was him, not me, that died.

Maybe that is love! The degree to which we expose our own safety in the protection of another. Yes. And I think Hennery has demonstrated his commitment. What a man! What a privilege to know such a person. Such valour and honour is buried, sealed in Africa. Other places try so gallantly to expose it, but this people merely pass on, go forward to other events. Probably because they place no value in honour. It is simply routine, expected. Conversely, dishonour amongst man or beast is relegated to the crushing jaws of a hyena, to be eradicated forever. Never repeated, never mentioned. If mankind would understand what constitutes honour amongst differing cultures there may be great understanding of individual responses to differing circumstances. "Yes." thought Brett. "Some world leaders are great people; some mere mortals are even greater. The difference? Some get acknowledged. Some don't. Tonight I sleep in the aura of an exceptional man of gallantry."

The night was cool and they awoke in the morning, refreshed.

Peleele-Pasi quietly returned amidst the early morning sounds of night; the hooting owl, flapping batwings, crickets and night-jars. He had a joyous night, treated as the representative of the white spirit, a slayer of leopard. Treated as an angel from heaven, a warrior and an associate of god. The village warriors, youth and elders were all celebrating, prancing around the bonfire, sitting consuming beer, and singing, talking and celebrating. The chief was seated on his throne of well smooth deadwood, the leopard carcass suspended in a tree behind him. Peleele-Pasi had been seated at the same throne.

He had enjoyed being treated like a prince, and had especially enjoyed the warmth and energised body of the doe eyed, long necked, virginal maiden who had eagerly responded to mutual desires. He had eaten on the lavish preparations of a village in celebration. He had been hosted by a select group of talented women and maidens. He had thrust hard, vibrating his body, blending an abundance of his seed, deep within the warm, cream filled loins of the regal, elegant maiden of his dreams. He lay on top of her feeling totally spent, exhausted. Multiple blends of mutual fluids flowed out from within them, down, between her thighs, buttocks and dribbled onto the sand. His mind recalled! The last time this sensation had overtaken him in such uncontrollable, emotional height, the pleasure had been when he accidentally broke an egg, fresh from under the hen, the warm white fluid sliding over his hand. Youthful manly instinct had driven his hand to his very erect and pulsating, sensational nerve endings that seemed to be screaming out. He instinctively massaged the egg white over himself, his manhood, using both hands, barring no parts of his body, arching his back, gyrating bending, thrusting achieving pleasure, and an ecstasy that redirected his life. He had been near his home, his parents, his brothers and sisters. He felt shamed!

Now, lying on the maiden of his dreams, feeling her warmth and slow movements he lifted himself onto his elbow. Then he stood, covering his nakedness, moving psychologically proud and physically weakened, into a pre-dawn horizon, in remorseful sorrow, bidding her silent but fond farewell.

The night passed quickly, too quickly for Brett and Hennery, Gauto and Braziwa. Peleele-Pasi hoped the night would last forever. His bonding was more than physical entwinement. It was a heart-searing emotional bond that would never be forgotten, and no amount of egg producing chickens could ever repeat the sensation of this night.

Brett woke early and stoked the fire, pulling the three legged pot over heat to boil the water. He made strong black coffee and poured some into his mug.

"Hey, vuka, madoda, handei, handei, handei" – "Hey, wake up, men, let's go, let's go, let's go." Within 60 seconds the camp had changed from quiet sleepy rest-place to "ready to go" action filled men, waiting to leave. Brett took the lead and again set a hard pace. The dawn was cool with isolated cloud cover. Good distance was required today. The group had water to last to the river, but not sufficient for the next day. Necessity demanded suitable and adequate water be available at the river. There was a gentle downward slope passing the tree-line and the grass was cropped short, having been traversed by big herds, resident waterbuck, kudu, sable and other plains game. Evidence of animals was everywhere. The terrain was an easy walk. The river should well be behind them by mid morning. Brett walked shoulder to shoulder with Peleele-Pasi who had exhausted his manhood the previous night, all night. He wanted to share his enjoyment with the boss. He explained his emotional crescendos and physical completion. Brett listened but offered little else. Then quiet banter reflected on old times. Old "finish". (Peleele translates to 'Finish)

Brett told Peleele-Pasi of the values to be inherited, and how these would benefit future generations. They discussed some of the hardships experienced during the life of the old man, "Peleele", and discussion returned to the roots of Peleele-Pasi in the flatlands of Somabula. Brett learned today that his grandfather and Peleele had crossed riverbeds and cool streams; had eaten from the same flesh and had common purpose in the advent of survival for a silver bearded traveller some 80 years before. They both knew the story, through campfire moments, but it had never come together as it did this day, through the living spirit of old Peleele, his grandson, Peleele-Pasi spoke of those olden day events. Today a kinship tightened an extra turn.

They walked at a reduced pace through the heavily wooded area in anticipation of an unsuspecting steenbok or duiker or other small animal for the pot. They were no longer talking, but searching. Interspersed throughout the trees were areas of grass, some denuded of tree cover about the area of a playing field, others the size of a tennis court. The ground was soft under foot, and easy to walk. Brett wished he had left his boots on the truck, but thought he would be grateful later. The area of trees was the resting-place of grassland animals and evidence was everywhere of this being their habitat. Animals would return here during the heat of the day, and go back to their sun splashed pastures in later cool hours. The sun had risen high and was being warded off by the bright green leaves of the Msasa trees, the Teak, the Mukwa and the occasional giant stemmed Panga-panga. There were regular outcrops of the Kaffir Orange tree, with fruit at varying stages of ripeness. An abundance of red and black berries that were palatable and nourishing alerted Brett to the absence of baboons and monkeys. This indicated that the river was probably further than anticipated. Braziwa confirmed this suspicion by retaining his water bottle full; foregoing desire to refresh.

Brett slowed to a gentle stroll, giving opportunity for muscle to relax, recharging the physical gears, extracting the bush-craft concentration of a hungry man. Teamwork was well practiced, and brought into immediate action. Hennery swung out to the right to peripheral vision from Brett. Braziwa moved left the same distance. Gauto and Peleele-Pasi flanked either side of Brett, mid-way between the men on the extremities. The pace was reduced as they scanned minimal undergrowth below the tall leafy canopies of Msasa and Mfuti trees. They searched left and right, forward and upward in slow, focused deliberation.

The lowveld is agronomic paradise to the dreaded buffalo bean that could drive a man to insanity, merely touch-passing the itch-bearing out-skin of the seed pod. At certain times in the year the pod housing the beans is a delicacy to certain animals. Baboon and monkey thrive on chewing the entire pod, swallowing the bean, sometimes discarding the outer skin when it is too dry. There comes a time when the pod is no longer edible to smaller, man-like animals, requiring the tough outer lip skin of the giraffe, rhino, buffalo or elephant to consume this bean. The outer skin develops sharp, needle-like fine hairs with microscopic barbs, and a sweet but very toxic, almost citric acid flavour, much sought after at certain times of growth. The dry growth cycle leaves a pod that creates unbearable itch and debilitating skin eruptions, causing uncontrollable unpleasantness to any unsuspecting intrusion into the lower leaves and small lower branches. Peleele-Pasi had been concentrating into the lower branches of surrounding

Msasa, totally absorbed, failing to detect the much dreaded shrub, full clustered with well dried dark bean pods. His inner thigh skirted the leaves, and he put spring in his gait to pass over the shrub. He looked down, noticed the beans and screamed, "Maiwe, Baas." (This has no translation, other than traumatic expletive in surrender to desperation. This word is never used lightly, use always interpreting desperate urgency.) Peleele-Pasi had seen the beans and sprung, attempting to 'over the top'. He had risen and landed wrong, in the heart of the driest and most prolific section of bunches of dark dry bean pods. One pod was sufficient to cause excruciating pain and severe itch. He landed amongst bunches, like grapes in full growth. The fire-like sensation tore through his inner thigh on both legs. The pods had been thrust into the sleeve of his very short shorts, infecting itch and fire-type pain from his knees to his crotch; between his back buttock cheeks, onto his most sensitive areas. He lay screaming, in the full knowledge that what he had so far experienced was but a fraction of what was to come. Brett had sympathetic observation, and then moved out of the heavy wood area to the outskirt, seeking rock area, searching for aloe leaves. Hennery and Braziwa had the same purpose and the three crossed paths in anxious search. Brett located a small outcrop of aloe, ripped off several fat, well juiced leaves and ran back to Peleele-Pasi. He was in agony, rolling on the ground, screaming, feeling that his legs were covered in coals, and itching. Gauto had made a fire nearby, and was blowing, billowing, in attempt to hasten heating a pot of water. Brett handed him some leaves, and stripped the outer skin from one. He handed a leaf to Peleele-Pasi who grasped it urgently, and bit through the foul tasting skin, exposing steak-like slices of white jelly-type inner flesh. He rubbed this onto his upper thigh, between his legs, and through to the cheeks of his buttocks. Brett handed him a well peeled fresh leaf. He grabbed this and scraped out the flesh with his fingers. Holding it in cupped fingers he gently massaged the cool flesh over his entire manhood. Then using both hands he applied more onto his entire back rump area, penetrating cleavage and more. Tears had been cascading from his chin but had now dried; leaving moistened salt stains trailing down his face. The burn was subsiding but the itch was not. His skin had turned an ash grey colour, and his lips were quivering uncontrollably. The agony of a burn sensation had depleted his energy; the itch was excruciating and the humble humiliation had not started. All those present had experienced this trauma at some stage of youth. Few ever experienced it twice. Articulate eye action and astute judgement seldom permitted a repeat of such experience. This man would not be allowed to forget the experience. He would be mocked, ridiculed and laughed at for weeks. This was part of the tribal system, the roots of survival that would assure keen awareness of the strength of the buffalo bean forever.

The violent body thrashing and screaming and tears had subsided. Peleele-Pasi lay exhausted and debilitated and very itchy, with the inner thighs having been hand scratched to a raw meat. Sensitivities do not allow such extremes to be enacted closer to more delicate body parts, so his crotch and back were comparatively less harmed, but just as itchy.

Brett suggested that Gauto remain with Peleele-Pasi, while Braziwa return to the village and seek the assistance of the medicine man and any young maiden of Peleele-Pasi's choice. This was an introductory jibe, designed to level the type of ridicule he was about to encounter. Such humiliation would be beyond his physical endurance and Peleele-Pasi abandoned mental memories of his agony, now concentrating on prevention of his young love becoming aware of this humiliation.

Final decisions were made. Gauto returned to the village and requested help from the chief. The medicine man was elderly, but able to walk quite fast. 15 young men in their later teens were summoned and an additional ten volunteered to return and help the young messenger of white spirit to full recovery. It was deemed as spiritual intervention that Peleele-Pasi was the person struck down by the buffalo beans, especially that his crotch had been severely attacked. This was considered justice in view of his activities the previous night, in cohabiting with the most regal of virginal maidens in the village. She had not been punished in consideration of having surrendered herself only to this messenger of the white spirit. In contrast, she had received honour and praise for her good conduct, and invited to assist the medicine man in care for Peleele-Pasi when he returned to the village.

Brett left instruction with Peleele-Pasi that Gauto remain and care for him, or continue into the east and catch Brett. In any event, the lack of water necessitated that the walk would have to continue. They bade farewell to Peleele-Pasi and started on the journey east. Braziwa remained, having received instruction from Brett as to where to locate him when Gauto returned, when help arrived. The scorpion sting and the puff-adder venom are preferable experiences to the agonizing itch of the buffalo's choice of culinary delight. The dreaded Buffalo Bean.

Southey was a caring parent, having played mother and father, playmate, mentor and student as well as very best friend to Brett, from birth. They had done so many sports together, camps and hunting expeditions; they had made a raft and travelled the Zambezi River from Chirundu to the 30 mile wide flood plains north of Beira, and they had ventured the entire length of the Zambezi River where Lake Kariba is situated today. They had laughed, hungered and thirsted. They had been encouragement for each other and they had been dependent on each other but they both retained very independent, individual identities. And bonded in knowledge, admiration and love for wildest Africa.

Southey knew that Brett had everything necessary to handle all adversity, but there was slight wariness, more acceptable in a mother than a father. He would never discuss such effeminate concern, but he would have to live in the knowledge of having experienced it. He drove his vehicle hard, fast, and was back at the ranch before the cattle had arrived at the dip-tank. His stock whip was hanging in the forked branch as always, and flicked out the full length of his 22 foot leather crack-and-sting machine. This was his only toy, but it was his work-lever in managing his 5,000 head of cattle. With precision he could flick an engorged parasite off the forehead of a charging bull on every attempt. He had often cracked a 2,000lb bull-charge into instant immobilization by that sting of the end-whip, breaking the sound barrier, as it sliced, vacuuming air at the instant of impacting those delicate nerve endings at the point of the bull's nose. He was a master stockman; animal husbandry was a passion. The well-being of his herd was his great pleasure. His thoughts now faded from his tiring, thirsty son walking in the dry and dusty mosquito infested buffalo and elephant country, being stalked and preyed upon by lion and leopard, by the deadly cobra and the fat, docile puff-adder whose fangs will defend to the deadly detriment of anything.

Southey had guests arriving later in the day. They were all men commanding influential station in politics and national leadership. They were all friends, and knew each other well. They were all sportsmen, hard working community leaders. His mind panned memories of Arthur, his father, comforting a lonely glass of scotch whiskey while facing the setting sun, overlooking his 2,000 acres of irrigated crops, lamenting, "What a magnificent world our Lord has created. How long can it last? Will our children experience this magnificence through their lives? Peace, happiness, satisfaction, beauty and comfort. Perfect contentment, but for how long?"

His guests arrived at intervals of around ten minutes, giving time for dust from the forward vehicle to settle. The lead vehicle was a new Chevrolet, kitted with an external sun visor for improved comfort. It was a luxurious vehicle, still bearing the aroma of factory-polished leather. Sir Humphrey Gibbs, governor of Rhodesia, climbed out from behind the driver's wheel. Brigadier Andrew Dunlop, the local member of Parliament and Minister of Transport, had been a passenger and escort. Other vehicles arrived, Des Burke, Jock McDonald, Lord Angus Graham, David Smith and Adam Savory.

Slowly they all assembled in the Porte couchere, everyone jovial, relaxed, permeating an atmosphere of humour, tranquillity and positive future. These were men well informed on matters of Rhodesian political direction. They were respected leaders, each with very opposing views as to the future course for the country. Des and Jock jointly owned a legal practice in Gwelo. Andrew, Humphrey and Southey owned ranch land. Humphrey was also governor of Rhodesia, a position representing Her Majesty, observing, reporting to her and conveying her messages to the Rhodesian people.

The men were enjoying the cool of the setting sun. Southey was the overnight host. Discussion reflected on rugby in South Africa; the combined school cricket tour of Somerset, Essex and Wiltshire in England; the winds of change permeating Africa, now breathing unpleasant odour over Rhodesia.

Humphrey listened intently as Des and Jock debated the spreading riots; calls by worker groups to strike, South Africa and the system of separate development.

The queen had appointed a man of exceptional wisdom in nominating Humphrey Gibbs to be her eyes and ears over this colony during the troubled times of "the winds of change." This astute diplomat was amongst friends of great wisdom with intricate comprehension of world affairs; played good rugby and cricket in their day, were men of honour, impeccable integrity and respected community leaders. "If only they could comprehend that there is another world surrounding their cocoon!" he thought.

Humphrey slopped his whiskey around in the glass, blending it with ice and then knitted the events of the evening into coherent perspective. "The world is changing. Leaders are losing authority. Decision making ability is being overridden by sheer numbers, most of whom have limited overview of world events. Good decisions review all relevant information and circumstance, and then action is implemented. Today the privilege of assessing every pertinent view is no longer available. There is a raging sea of hysteria and every individual wants to put his voice to every international decision. The strength of America's president remains in his supreme command of the military. That will soon be removed. Britain has systems of 'consensus' that support or hinder the Prime Minister. He has controlled limitations to his authority." The Brigadier smiled, revealing an opposing interest. Humphrey continued, "Des, you cannot change the systems. Reality has imposed the winds of change. The hard fact is that Rhodesia will become Zimbabwe. None of us want that. We all know that for the masses we need to retain good governance. World leaders everywhere know that. Reality is that you can resist the winds of change as hard as you like, but good governance will crumble. Men of only self-interest will replace it. This reality will materialize through mass action galvanized and prompted by impossible promises."

Humphrey sipped on his whiskey, retaining the concerted attention of everyone. He let his statement mature in their minds, whilst savouring his whiskey. Then he saddened at the realisation that solidarity was entrenched between them. He sympathized, but understood. He too, had played in an opposing cricket team. He knew the grit of winning and of not winning.

He continued, "Joshua Nkomo is making impossible promises, his followers unquestioningly swallowing everything. James Chikerema, Ndabaningi Sithole, and even members of the clergy are promising a land of milk and honey in exchange for civil unrest. Mob rule, hysterical action and continual erosion of solid structures will destroy the ideals that we all aspire to. Gentlemen, we are of single mind for the desires of this land. Sadly, there is no prospect of retaining any part of Africa in systems of good governance. Black leaders know how to manipulate their own people. They can be relentless in establishing themselves in authority. The difference within leaders is that some lead to benefit themselves. Others seek authority so as to establish improvements for their people. British gallantry is based on extreme service and demands, within objectives of goodwill, as a parent cares for a child. The developing new system in Africa is based on individuals promoting and empowering themselves for their own interests. This is the new direction. This is the policy of future leadership. No guns or bombs can prevent it. Civil unrest will continue, probably unabated, until the demise of good government."

Humphrey had struck deep into the clear-thinking minds of his audience. He did not enjoy what he was saying in the knowledge of being a bearer of bad news. Reality seeds had to be carefully sown and nurtured in this delicate situation, especially because he was in the company of exceptional men of leadership.

His oratorical skills and global political understanding assured silence; keen attention from an audience absorbing reality. Although the mood was sombre, moments were necessary for Humphrey's words to ripen and mature. The words had been carefully selected, every one being harsh but true. Brett listened in silence, his mind working a global net of political quiz. Sauros, Hennery, UDI. The Ranch. Territorial call-up. Hunting Friends and Polo partners. What future course for all?

UNFOLDING GENERATIONS

BROTHERS: HENNERY – ETERNAL FRIEND SAUROS - TERRORIZING ENEMY

Naison had worked with Southey in the formative adolescent years of Ceres; was 5 years older than Southey; presently had three wives, two of whom had given him five children each, and the third had given him another 2. He had inherited a sub-chieftainship in the Silobela district of lower Gwelo, verging on the Zambezi valley, into Binga regional district overlooking the Zambezi River. His hereditary birth-root was of harsh terrain, his people surviving off the land; hunter, trapper, stalker and fisherman. Mental focus was primarily survival, secondly, as an afterthought of necessity, procreation.

His eldest son, Sauros, was born in 1949, to his senior first-wife. He became a studious academic, class captain at the farm school and developed commanding leadership qualities. Hennery was the second son born to the second wife. His year of birth was also 1949. His youngest brother, Gauto, was born in 1953.

Through the fifties and sixties Sauros, Hennery and Gauto were very loyal friends to each other and the De La Harp family, to Yvette, Norman and Brett. All shared special times together and in isolation, individually. All five boys knew each other from deep inner understanding, through intimate events of childhood, boyhood and young manhood. All had shameful secrets on each other. All had experienced parental, emotional and physical hardship together, and tested their physical prowess to extremes of speed, pain, emotion and endurance. They teased and bullied each other: they fought with sticks and ran through fire-flame and swam swift streams in support of each other. They laughed, they cried, they fished and they hunted. They protected against the stalking leopard, the charging bull and the venomous striking pain of scorpions and adders. They all had occasion to render assistance to each other and had shared fresh-fruit and fat meat of roast rump. They had all been reprimanded and chastised, individually and communally.

Hennery, Sauros's younger brother was born on "Twin Streams" ranch, in the hut, with Southey and very pregnant Sybil present for the duration of the birth. Brett was born soon afterwards. Socially and mentally Hennery bonded well with Brett, together experiencing the learning curve and sharing the craft skills of clay moulding, wild fruit and berry selection, clubbing rabbits, stalking guinea fowl, sharing catfish and water-slugs for survival. They walked the vleis and the hills, the river-beds and enjoyed the tree-shade and the granite boulders – together. They laughed and they cried, they played and they sulked, they fought and they comforted each other. They talked, argued, debated and screamed at each other, but always in close understanding, with anger and hate directed at the subject in debate, never against each other. It was inevitable that every togetherness ended in the return of Brett to the comforts of the ranch house and Hennery to the smoke-filled hut in the village.

In 1965 Brett was conscripted into the army, returning to "Twin Streams" after the initial six week first phase of polishing boots and driven to the extremes of physical endurance, tested to a benchmark of all-round physical and mental challenge. Running 110 miles in fifteen hours, daily assault course, planning and tying rope for crossing rivers, climbing rock-face and steep hills, swimming cold streams and drinking from mud-brown pools, hiking the savannah and the forests, tested to the limit of hunger and body weariness. Fitness and strength were the benchmark of aspiration for every male of Africa. Brett had it all, bonded to a clear thinking mind as well. He was clearly Hennery's hero.

In 1962 Sauros left "Twin Streams" ranch to seek work in the big city, Bulawayo. His farewell was memorable for Norman and Brett. He called at the main ranch house, accompanied by Naison, his father, and Hennery and Gauto. Strangely, Peleele-Pasi was noticeable by absence, the complexities of which later unfolded. They sat in the shade of a tree behind the kitchen. His bag was self-made, using the un-shaven skin of a baboon, and he wore a narrow brim hat of the same material. This transpired with time, to be an indicator of membership or support for the banned Zimbabwe African Peoples Union. Norman, Brett and Sauros had been hunting a leopard when a huge troop of baboons had silently, mysteriously surrounded them and the leader had demonstrated a rabid aggression. This had motivated the troop, whose aggression necessitated Brett and Norman to kill two in self defence. Sauros and Hennery had skinned them with care, discarding the head-skin. The tail bone had been peeled out from the hide, inverting the skin, exposing a clean uncut hollow tail, wholly attached to the well skinned body. This was to become the shoulder strap of his carry-bag,

Together with Norman and Brett they laughed at events that had stung or brought tears, they laughed at the swaggering vultures with overfilled bellies, bloated too heavy to take off and fly, they laughed for over an hour and then settled into the future. Sauros explained that the country was on the verge of change. There was a spirit of darkness that had so far not established a presence on "Twin Streams." Sauros had visions and dreams. He was sad at departing, unsure of direction, but had to go through with traditional commitment that the eldest son should venture out, before shouldering the challenges of the chieftainship which would pass on to him at the death of his father.

Southey appeared and walked to the truck. He was clad in his town clothes of white safari suit, white socks, highly polished red/brown shoes and a white dust coat, which he wore while travelling. His green smart-hat sat aside on his head, and his briefcase was clenched in his hand. Sauros jumped and ran to the truck, and requested a lift to town. Southey obliged, telling him to climb on and hold tight. Naison handled the crank into action, and Southey spoke kindly as he bade everyone farewell. He would be gone for the rest of the week as he had business to attend on behalf of the Bulawayo Agricultural show. With his cases on front seat and Sauros well seated behind the cab, the long dust journey began. For Southey just another trip – for Sauros a new world – with baboon skin hat and his bag on his shoulders, he waved farewell to his blood brothers and playmates; his masters and his friends. They moved down the driveway, past the citrus orchard, through the entrance gate, and away, leaving a cloud of dust climbing high.

The journey to Bulawayo was monotonous, crossing the Somabula flats for hours. The welcome sight of the n'Tabazinduna hills on the right brought relief to the fact that they were close to the original home of that great King and warrior, Chief Lobengula; Southey's destination for a few days. The Town Hall, that throne from whence the city mayor efficiently commands the municipal tedium, has replaced the original site of his chieftainship village. The place known of old as guBulawayo, now Bulawayo. This had been the headquarters from where Lobengula had administered the land of Monomatapa. It was here that Cecil John Rhodes, on behalf of Her Majesty, Queen Victoria, had signed the entire nation into her name; formal agreement acknowledged through a document penned by Rhodes, typed at his residence in the Matopos hills, and explained to the King through elders and men of wisdom and good fortune. It was here that Sauros was to get off the security of the ranch truck and wander into the crocodile's jaw or fly the skies of circling eagles. Either way, he was opening new horizons.

There was a short discussion between them as Southey pulled out his wallet and handed Sauros two ten pound notes, both having portraits of the stunningly beautiful regal, crowned head of Queen Elizabeth ll. Sauros gratefully accepted this very sizeable gift, turned and disappeared across the street and round a corner.

Sauros had an amenable manner, a generous smile, an aura of efficiency and kindness. Southey was always disturbed by an excess of familiarity, lack of submission that Sauros could remonstrate from deep in his marrow and the blue-blood of chieftainship. Yes, thought Southey, Naison had done well in bringing up children. Sauros was good, a bit too clever, perhaps, and he should stop thinking he is white! Otherwise he's OK.

He was quickly employed as a clerk in a semi rural Shell petrol station on the outskirts of Bulawayo, the road towards the Victoria Falls. He learned typing skills and filing, cash counting and stock taking. His work made him privy to confidential business information, and his employer, Mrs. Hendrina van Tonder developed a trust and confidence in his loyalty. She allowed him to handle cash takings of the day, and discovered that he was honest and trustworthy. His responsibilities increased with experience. One morning Mrs. van Tonder arrived a few minutes later than normal and opened the shop. She called Sauros and explained that her husband, Baas Willem van Tonder, was unwell in hospital. "The madam will be spending the night at the hospital and Sauros needs to open the shop in the future." That means taking the keys to the township. Sauros had no problem with this. His reliability and trustworthiness impressed Mrs. Van and she rewarded Sauros with regular gifts of cabbage, a dozen eggs from time to time, and even some packets of boys meat from her farm. Sauros learned the management aspects of opening the shop, checking the till-float and doing the pump readings. When supplies became necessary he had learned the telephone system to re-order, and Mrs. Van developed and enjoyed her new life of late starting hours. Within weeks she had no need to go to the shop on a daily basis. She attended farm tasks that her husband was now not tending and would pop into the shop only once each week. Sauros was doing an excellent job. Despite several unannounced stock checks he had never been short by a single penny, biscuit, box of matches or roll of sweets.

His evenings were active amongst black peers and comrades in the overpopulated urban residential suburbs. He befriended sportsmen and orators; ironmongers, rail workers, craftsmen and clerks. In the meagre environs of densely populated, smoke filled dusty dry streets of Mpopoma Township they gathered for regular discussion about soccer and hunting; women, work, travel, politics and leadership. He was a persuasive orator and a committed listener. His work skills and social talents set him apart and above his compatriots. His earnings were better than average and he dressed in superior western style. His trade mark dark glasses and a bright guinea feather in his hat band were adopted from his idol and mentor, Baas Norman de La Harp.

He was being persuaded of the merits of establishing business; challenging within a competitive fuel trade amongst national decision making people. The local centre forward of the national football squad, Frederick Shava, was amongst his most determined supporters, and together they decided to explore possibilities. Frederick accompanied Sauros for the fifth time, to the local council office to hear the result of his third application to trade, this time on the Bulawayo road; to establish a black owned fuel and grocery outlet. They were well dressed, Sauros wearing his bright green suit, red tie, small brimmed hat with a guinea feather in the hatband. His dark glasses were positioned at the end of his nose so he could look through or over the darkness!

This attire was an affront to the white civil servant behind the desk at the council office. It was an affront to most of the white people, who preferred to see and experience humbleness in the black people. They should wear shoes made of discarded tyres, and wear shorts or loin cloth! The Council clerk looked Sauros up and down, then announced in a loud, jovial, mocking voice, "No Sauros your application has been refused, boy. Get back to your job, and accept that you are just a little black boy, man. You will never start business amongst the 'mzungu' – 'whites.' Forget it. Maybe in your Reserve, boy, but not here." Sauros requested the refusal document, which the clerk lifted between two fingers, and tore in half, folded it and tore it in half again, discarding it into the waste basket. "There's your paper, Sauros. Now voetsek back to your job, man." Sauros removed his hat in humble respect, "Yebo, Nkos, shlala gashle, Nkos" – "Yes, God, stay gently, God" and he turned and walked out of the room. Frederick was incensed at the arrogance of the clerk while Sauros was disappointed at this repeated official refusal. It was frustrating. The little tin god administrator had law on his side. The request had received objections from traders on either side of the intended place of business; had been refused on sound commercial recommendations. It would not have been approved even to Mrs. Van Tonder because it could not be viable for too many fuel outlets on this little used road. But the clerk had ignorantly rubbed salt into a political wound. This pained and disappointed Sauros; infuriated Frederick, effectively igniting flames of anger and hatred.

As they neared home Sauros developed deep anger, becoming enraged that this white "idiot" could contemptuously destroy his paper and discard it without explanation. He realized that being black had inhibited certain aspirations, but not expected his career to be so finally closed by some nitwit.

It was 1965. He had been with Mrs. van Tonder for nearly four years and had developed good communication with the suppliers of fuel and of groceries; men who read the electric and water yards, the local customers – mostly farmers, and even some hoteliers and police, district administrators and national parks wardens – people of all persuasions living anywhere from guBulawayo to Victoria Falls.

In 1944 Willem van Tonder had been offered a stockman's position on new land designated as ranching area. This land on the perimeters of the administrative district of Bulawayo was in the low rainfall, sweetveld area of Matabeleland. He had worked diligently, demonstrating passion and exceptional knowledge as a youthful, energetic learner stockman. His employers were Mr. Solly Rick and Mr. Isaac Phillipson, both partners in several trading business operations as well. They lived in Kumalo, an elite suburb on the eastern boundary of Bulawayo. Willem learned the challenges of stockmanship, and was reliable in supplying the butcher's outlets with meat requirements according to a year planner. Willem developed a well controlled system of pasture rotation, establishing increased livestock capacity per acre of grazing. He imported cattle breeding stock from the higher altitude areas of the eastern districts, and he crossed breeds with indigenous stock from the Limpopo area of sweet grass and hardiness. In 1947 Willem managed a herd of 2,000 cattle and 250 indigenous goats.

His social life was restricted through work obligation, but he did get to meet the neighbour's daughter, Hendrina van Biljoen, and they married after a six month courtship. Hendrina had been reared in the saddle of horses and cracked a whip as well as any man. She was thick set, well muscled and competently came to grips with any physical ranch activities amongst the workers. They made a good team, producing excellent results for Solly and Isaac. In 1948, on the death of Isaac Phillipson, Solly offered Willem an option to buy the ranch and all livestock on very generous terms. Willem rose to the challenge and with Hendrina constantly at his side they expanded. In 1953 they purchased a section of the adjoining van Biljoen estate and increased the stock numbers dramatically. In 1960 they built their ultimate Dutch gabled ranch house, surrounded with sprawling lawns and masses of well-planned rose gardens, bright coloured plants, shrubs and trees. The swimming pool was in close proximity to the tennis court, and Willem had laboriously threaded pipes and bolted planks to make a swing and seesaw area for visitors' children. The design and ambiance was luxurious, in keeping with well deserved very demanding personal aspirations, living excellence and high work standards.

Hendrina and Willem had lived in their dream home for almost six years. It was now winter, 1965, hunting season, biltong season and dry grass. Life involved long work days and very physical daily ranch routines. Willem and Hendrina lived comfortably. The ranch labourers were an obedient group of hard working black men, well rewarded for their reliability and skills. They looked to Willem and Hendrina as parents. Distinct bonds had developed, maturing with the passage of time. A mutual interdependence blended with individual independence.

A pink dawn came gently over the hills to the east and the smoke from cooking fires hovered in the air above the workers compound a quarter of a mile away. Hendrina and Sixpence, the supervisor, were standing near the corrugated iron roof of the farm workshop. The morning was cold. Very cold. A fire had been struck into action giving flame and warmth for the workers. Hendrina and Sixpence absorbed warmth into their hands, waving up-fingers at the flame.

A plough disc was suspended from a nearby tree and Sixpence struck it hard ten times with a two foot metal bar. Clear, resounding chimes rang out across the valley in the still morning calling the workers in the compound to work. The disc was struck to start and end the working day. It was also struck in an emergency to summon all within hearing.

"How is your new son, Sixpence?" Hendrina asked.

Sixpence's eyes shone and a grin split his black face, showing crooked but gleaming white teeth. "He is a lusty boy, Nkosikasi. He cries like a bull and drinks like a fish!"

"Has your wife recovered now?"

"Yes, but my second wife, she is now jealous, Nkosikasi. She has only four girls and wants a boy. They are fighting all the time and I am caught in the middle. I fear to go home sometimes. If I try to stop the bickering they both shout on me in common purpose! For sure, it is better to have only one wife," he said mournfully. He had seven children from two wives, the first wife having borne him three sons.

Hendrina laughed. "Have you heard from Hunsvi?" He was Sixpence's first born son from his first wife; a year ago at the age of sixteen he had been sent by his father to the Catholic Mission school 50 miles away to learn to read and write.

"He is progressing well, I think. He wrote me a letter to say he will be home soon for the school holidays. It is the first letter he has written." He said with pride. Sixpence himself had been taught to read and write by Willem when he was home from boarding school. They spent hours during the school holidays in the cool shade of a tree scratching; first letters and then words in the dust.

As they waited for the workers to arrive they discussed the work program for the day. At this time of year the landscape was brown and dry, and the ground hard and dusty. Small whirlwinds ranged over the sweltering countryside, swirling dust and dry vegetation into eyes and mouths. The rains would be here soon and then they would plant the crops. In the meantime, there were livestock to dose for parasites, roads to be maintained and contours to be repaired so that the torrential rain did not wash the precious topsoil from the lands.

The workers started arriving, each greeting Hendrina with a smile and "I see you, Nkosikasi" in Shona. Sixpence divided them into work gangs with a boss boy over each gang. Hendrina knew each worker well – she had delivered some of them in their huts in the dark midnight hours that labour pains seem to favour. Most were related, having been in the area and on farms for two or three generations.

After instructing each boss boy and issuing the workers with the appropriate tools required, Sixpence accompanied them to work. The sun was peeping over the horizon. They would only work until noon when the merciless sun drove them into shade, returning later in the afternoon when it cooled a little.

Hendrina entered the office, a large room attached to the workshop, containing two desks, four chairs and two walls of shelving packed with files and papers. All the farm accounts and administration was done here and she spent at least an hour or two every day keeping the paperwork in order.

She sat at the desk trying to concentrate on the tasks at hand but her mind kept straying to the discussion with Des Burke the previous day.

Some sort of confrontation with the British Government seemed likely. What form it would take was anyone's guess, but their lives would change. That was certain. Macmillan had blown his winds of change across the colonies, and Joshua Nkomo was agitating in the townships with riots.

Already there were rumours of young black men leaving the country for military training in Russia and China. There was talk of international sanctions against Rhodesia and armed confrontation with the African nationalist parties seemed imminent.

She laid down her pen and stood up. It was hopeless trying to work and worry at the same time. Locking the office door behind her she returned to the house and donned her wide-brimmed straw hat. She would work in her rose garden – it always eased her when she needed peace.

At 10:30 am Tadarera the cook brought a tray of tea and biscuits and set it down on a table on the wide veranda. Gratefully, she thanked him and sat down on a deep cushion in a cane chair. The cool shade of the veranda was a relief after the heat of the sun.

Her eye surveyed her peaceful garden with pride. In the 15 or so years she had been mistress of this home she had built a large greenhouse wherein she kept rare and exotic plants from all over the world, especially orchids; expanded the rose garden to include rare root stock; and kept a large plant nursery from where she freely donated propagated plants and trees to keen gardeners. Naturally, as she also supplied Willem the eucalyptus tree seedlings for his farm forestation she felt quite entitled to raid his fertilizer and chemical stores at regular intervals.

She sipped her tea and dark thoughts of the future returned.

The banned ZAPU and ZANU African nationalist parties had been inciting the rural populations to rise up against the white man. Not being well received, they had taken to organizing youth gangs who randomly killed the white farmer's cattle either with poison or hamstringing the animals during the night, setting alight precious grazing land and then melting back into the general population. Petrol bombs were thrown at homes of both black and white Rhodesians including the occasional hand grenade at a lonely police outpost.

The previous year a white factory worker and his family had been ambushed on a lonely road on his way home, the man stabbed repeatedly, the car with his wife and ten year old daughter doused with petrol and set alight. They were saved when another vehicle approached and the attackers ran. Sadly the man died, but his wife and child were saved albeit with extensive burns.

Worst of all, the gangs had turned upon their own people who would not support them. There were thousands of black police reservists, constables, rangers in the National Parks and general government staff accused of being informers and they and their families were easy targets for the youth gangs with no regard for gender, age, material or psychological impact.

The majority rural population had little or no concept of democracy. They had always been ruled by tribal chiefs – tribal decree or his word was law. Their tribal laws and traditions had stood the test of time and wealth was measured in livestock. They were a naïve people of happy innocence living contentedly in tribal villages as they had done for hundreds of years. Now, a few young upstarts, mostly with unremarkable origins, had proclaimed themselves "leaders of the black nation" and advocated "one man, one vote", recruiting young men and women of the villages – who should have been helping to bring in crops – to disappear for weeks on end to who knew where. The children would return from these absences arrogantly refusing to explain themselves and had become surly, disrespectful of parents and village elders. The very fabric of their society was being ripped apart. Village elders would meet under the tree at the centre of the village over gourds of beer to contemplate; and lament; for they knew a change was coming that would affect all their traditions, laws and way of life; something alien, something very dark. Many could sense an aura of great evil, powerless before the onslaught, as families were ripped apart by distrust, secrecy and fear.

The British government had rejected a proposal by the Rhodesian government for a transition of political authority to include an educated majority. Too many generations of white settlers had poured their blood, sweat and tears into carving a land of abundance and prosperity for all Rhodesians. Black and white, the masses had no intention of allowing the country they had built for 80 years to degenerate into mindless civil war. Amongst the natives economic collapse happened in newly independent countries throughout Africa. Newly empowered black politicians had stripped once prosperous countries of assets within a few years and millions of pounds found their way into Swiss bank accounts. In many of these countries the whole infrastructure had collapsed; there had been unchecked famine, minimal judicial system, no medical services, ruined ecology and rule by terror.

As Hendrina pondered these things she reflected that their ranch, "Silver Star" and the surrounding areas had not experienced any attacks – yet. Hopefully the police and army would keep things under control and stop the sporadic spread of rioting and civil unrest and domestic violence soon. But in her heart Hendrina knew it was only beginning.

Suddenly the air was filled with the rapid, loud ringing of the plough disc chimes, signalling an emergency. Hendrina jumped up, shaken from her reverie, and ran through the garden to the workshops 200 yards away. As she ran she was joined by others coming from all directions.

Reaching the workshops she discovered Sixpence still beating away at the disc. Only when he saw her did he stop.

"Sixpence, what's wrong!" she said breathlessly.

"Fire, Nkosikasi! Look there!" He pointed in the distance to an area bordering on Henk van Biljoen's farm. It was a paddock of 700 acres where 500 of Willem's pedigree breeding cows were grazing and she knew Henk had cattle on the other side of the fence as well.

Quickly she ordered trailers hitched to five tractors and machetes issued and the workers piled on to the trailers as they pulled away, transporting them to the blaze. Normally the truck would have been used but that had gone with Willem. It was at least three miles to the paddock and the cattle had been moved there only two days ago, so the grass was tall. She knew there would be a raging inferno by the time they got there.

"I'll meet you there, Sixpence. Get going!"

She ran to the house and jumped into the Landrover parked in the garage. All the household staff and gardeners piled in after her, some sitting on laps, others dangling out of the windows.

She drove furiously over bumpy dirt towards the fire, passing tractors and trailers piled dangerously high with workers. Those who could not find space on a trailer cut through the bush, running, and hacking branches with leaves from any shrub they passed.

Already the air was thick with smoke and whirling black ash as the tinder dry grass burst into flame, reaching 50 feet into the air creating vicious gusts which served to drive the flames at greater speed.

Hendrina screeched to a stop beside the stream which bordered one side of the paddock, deciding the vehicles would be safer there if the fire got excessively out of control. Everyone jumped out and ran to the nearest tree and shrub, hacking branches with leaves to beat out the flames. When everyone was armed with a branch she instructed two of her gardeners to remain and cut more branches while Hendrina and six workers ran toward the fire. By the time the trailers arrived there was a goodly pile of branches, but not enough. Sixpence instructed the tractors to return with full water bowsers and the men to grab a cut branch each; those left without were to continue cutting and follow to the fire. He sped off after Hendrina who had by now dispatched six men to herd the cattle out of the paddock to the other side of the stream.

The fire was now severely out of control, intense heat and smoke preventing any approach within 30 yards. The only plan was to attempt a controllable back-burn when the water bowsers arrived. While they waited the workers slashed grass in a long line across the fire path. The slashed, shorter grass would be more manageable when burning. This they set alight and controlled the burn towards the larger fire, beating until it met with the inferno and simply died. Short, small areas only.

Bowsers arrived and they set about burning the slashed grass with a beater every few yards to control the flames and send the burn towards the larger fire. The line was 400 yards long and every able man, woman and child on the farm was spread along the burn vigilantly preventing fire spreading towards them.

It was working. The inferno had nearly reached the back burn.

"Nkosikasi!! Nkosikasi!!" A man screamed from down the line. She turned towards the sound and there was a flicker at the corner of her eye.

She turned and in horror watched a wall of flame 30 feet high stretching laterally behind them only 200 yards away. It couldn't be possible. Even if a few sparks from the wildly dancing mountains of flame had been thrown into the air and managed to ignite somewhere else, it couldn't have started another fire so consistently along such a long line behind them! One hundred and fifty men, women and children were trapped between two roaring, out of control infernos hurtling towards each other; and the safety of the stream was on the other side of the new fire.

Frantically Hendrina searched for a way out. They had no escape.

"Sixpence!" she shouted as loud as she could above the roar of the flames.

All workers had seen the second wall of flame and were milling about in panic, shouting, screaming, looking to Hendrina for direction. Children ran to their mothers, clinging in terror.
"Everybody here to me!" Hendrina shouted again in n'Debele.

Those few who heard her above the roar and thunderous "vWhoosh" of the flame started herding the people towards her, dragging, pulling, screaming and shoving.

The heat was unbearable; eyes were burning and it became difficult to breathe. People were coughing, choking and inhaling burning smoke. “Cover your mouths and noses with your shirts!” Hendrina shouted again.

“Oh God, help us!” she breathed silently.

For a split second she thought she saw figures behind the back wall of flames but the width of fire was so thick and intense that she could see nothing on the other side.

Suddenly the flames seemed smaller near where she had parked the vehicle and there were figures moving about on the other side! They seemed to be pouring water on the flames and the flames were now only a few feet high.

And then through the flames jumped a huge blond man, a wet cloth wrapped around his head, dripping with water. Henk van Biljoen!

“Papa! What are you doing! Get back!” she yelled.

“Hendrina? What the hell are you doing here? Never mind! Just follow me through that gap. Jump the flames and run into the stream. OK? Come now!”

“Get the kids out first. They’ll have to be carried!”

The heat was intense. Eyes and lungs burned incessantly, the smoke so thick that visibility reduced to a few feet. Some children overcome by smoke, lay limp on their mother’s backs. Now totally surrounded, the flames bore down on them with incredible speed and the crackle and roar was deafening.

“Hendrina! Move!” Henk shouted angrily, grabbing her arm.

“Sixpence! Tell everyone to run through where the flames are lowest. Jump straight into the stream! Quickly!”

The terror on the faces of the women and children assured Hendrina there was no way they would follow. She pulled herself free from Henk and through tearing eyes grabbed the nearest child not tied to his mother's back that she could see.

"Sixpence! Move them, damn it! You'll all die in minutes if you stay here!" She screamed in frustration.

Suddenly galvanized, Sixpence grabbed two women with babies on their backs and propelled them rapidly towards the area of lower flame before they knew what happened. As they jumped through the flames their screams rose above the roar of the fire, but everyone saw them caught by helping hands on the other side. Now the flames were only 4 feet high in that area and not so thick. Suddenly everyone was stampeding through the gap. As they landed on the other side Henk's workers caught them and immediately dunked them in the stream to quench the flames and burning clothing and bodies. Hendrina and Henk were the last through. Hendrina choking, blinded by smoke, barely able to stand and still clinging to the child was physically carried over the flames by Henk and dunked in the stream.

Helping her out of the water Henk sat her down on the ground beside her Landrover, exhausted and unable to stand. Her beautiful hair, eyebrows and eyelashes were severely singed and she had bad burns on her arms, legs and hands.

"Hendrina, are you alright?" Henk said. She nodded, still unable to speak.

"Are you sure? I have to get this bloody fire under control. I've sent for Jo, she'll take you home. You stay there until I'm done."

She found her voice, except it was now a croak. "Thank you, Papa. Yes, I'm fine now. Did all my people come out safely?"

"I'll get Sixpence to do a roll call as best he can for the moment. I understand most of your labour was here. Including women with babies on their backs!"

Henk had sent a runner back to his homestead to summon Jo with medical aid for the injured. Within minutes, seeming like hours, she arrived with two household staff, food, drink and burn dressings.

She leapt, flying out of her car and ran to where Hendrina was shambling amongst the injured.

"Hendrina, are you alright? Gracious, what a sight you are! Sit down and have a cup of tea. Mind. Sit. I will check you over and tend to the injured"

"Thanks for coming, Mama. I'm fine, really. I just don't understand what happened."

"You're not alright! Now sit and let me get on with my work. When I'm done I'll take you home and you can tell me all about it. After a bath!"

Hendrina smiled gratefully as Jo handed her a cup of tea from the flask. She knew her mother's brusque manner was a cover for fright.

"My nerves! I must look appalling," she thought.

It was almost sunset before Hendrina and Jo had finished cleaning and dressing the wounds of the injured and they were transported back to the compound on trailers. Jo drove Hendrina home.

As they walked into the house Tadarera, who almost dropped his tray at the sight of her, met them at the front door.

"Nkosikasi! What happened, are you alright, madam? Aaaah, my Nkosikasi you look burned! What is the Nkos going to say? Aaaaah, Maiwe!"

"I'm fine, Cook. Just dirty. Mr. and Mrs. van Biljoen will be here for dinner. Please prepare the drinks tray now? I do believe I am ready for a glass of sherry a little earlier than normal this evening."

Jo relaxed in the lounge while Hendrina went upstairs for a bath. As she stood in front of the mirror she was shocked. She was covered in soot and dust; her clothes were scorched; she had no eyebrows or eyelashes; her hair had been singed to half its original length. Being covered in soot and dust it looked and felt like a chimney sweep's brush on top of her head.

She realized a shower would be a better option and when she returned to Jo half an hour later she was carrying a pair of hair scissors which Jo accepted without a word.

Henk and his workers together with Sixpence and other uninjured "Silver Star" workers continued to fight the fire long after sundown; the cattle had escaped but a huge area of grazing on both farms had been destroyed. Hendrina had also lost a tractor and water bowser caught between the two fires, completely burnt out.

When Henk arrived back at "Silver Star" at ten pm that night, exhausted and filthy, his face was grim and angry.

"Drink or shower, Papa?" asked Hendrina. "I've left some of Willem's clothes in the guest room for you."

"Beer, thank you." As he took the ice cold Lion Lager from Hendrina he said, "We talk when I've showered." He downed the beer without removing it from his lips, turned and went to the guest bathroom.

Jo raised her eyebrows but said nothing. Hendrina closed her eyes. She knew what was coming.

Fifteen minutes later Henk returned; clean and refreshed but still with the dark look in his eyes.

After he helped himself to another beer from the trolley, he seated himself in an easy chair facing the two women. He spoke quietly.

"That fire was deliberate. When you were all in position another was lit behind to trap you."

"I had that suspicion," said Hendrina.

No one asked whom they were discussing. Jo looked startled. "Why would they try to kill everyone?" she asked incredulously. When no one answered she whispered "Even their own people. The women and children?"

"Sixpence's youngest son is missing." Henk said quietly.

Hendrina sat up in alarm. "Was he at the fire? I don't remember seeing him."

"No one seems to know. They're still out looking for him."
Kalulu was a happy boy of twelve years old; and though not as bright as his brothers his happy go lucky attitude endeared him to everyone.

Hendrina rose and fetched her torch and jacket.

"What are you doing, Hendrina?" Henk said calmly.

"I'm going to help search, he may be hurt somewhere in the bush." She replied with a touch of annoyance.

Henk's face changed and became a mask of anger – she had never seen him this angry. She stopped in her track, suddenly unsure.

"You're going nowhere. Sit down and I'll explain a few facts."

She started to object and Jo started to say something.

"Now, Hendrina! I'm not asking, I'm ordering you!" Henk ordered with a cold, harsh authority neither woman had ever witnessed before. The mood changed from 'a hard days work' to 'cold, deathly politics.'

He was normally a calm, unflappable man. A deep thinker, he was not given to mindless chatter, he spoke seldom; but when he did it had message.

Suddenly frightened Hendrina sat down.

"This fire was deliberately started by someone. I also found ten of my cattle hamstrung. I'm certain it's that bastard, Sauros. He is too clever for his own good. He sent a bunch of terrorists; it's the way they work. Assuming I'm correct, the conflict has finally reached us, as we knew in our hearts that it one day would. And it's not going to go away. It's probably only a small band which is miles away by now, but we're not taking any chances. I don't know how many there are or how they're armed and I don't know if they will strike again tonight. It appears both farms are targets, so pack an overnight bag. You'll stay with us tonight. I'll call the police now to report this and ask them to put a watch on your house."

Henk's cold anger frightened the women and Hendrina thought better of objecting. Jo sat motionless, staring at the bowl of roses on the centre table. Both women knew Henk was right. With terrorists in the vicinity it would be foolish for a lone white woman to stay alone in a house where the nearest neighbour was ten miles away. She would be an irresistible target alone and defenceless. So far the terrorists had avoided any contacts where they were at risk, preferring to attack and run.

She was thankful Henk had taken charge of the situation, but suddenly aware that she couldn't contact Willem. She felt very lonely and vulnerable.

They dined while waiting for police to arrive, all three picking at their food. After Henk consulted with the white patrol officer and three black constables, they left for Uitsig, Henk's farm, taking two of Willem's high powered rifles with them.

They reached the homestead without incident and the ladies gratefully sank into bed at three a.m. Henk remained on watch with a loaded rifle in the shadows of the deep veranda.

The next morning the area swarmed with police personnel questioning most of the workers and investigating the surrounding area. Finally, at midday Henk and the police officer commanding the region, Derek Le Page, stepped onto the veranda where the ladies were waiting and sank down into the chairs. Both looked angry and disturbed.

As Jo poured the tea, Derek reported.

"Henk was right – they are terrorists. Six, from the tracks we picked up and we can't tell whether they're armed. We found the petrol cans they used to light the fires. They're headed north back to the Tribal Trust Lands, no doubt. We are on their tracks. I'll keep you informed. I think it's safe for you to return home Hendrina, but keep a pistol nearby at all times."

The two men exchanged uncomfortable glances.

"And…?" Hendrina asked. She knew there was more but neither man wanted to break the news.

Finally, Henk took her hand and gently said, "We found the burnt bodies of two children. Both unrecognizable."

Jo and Hendrina sat stunned. Finally Hendrina said, "Who?"

"They're unrecognizable but I think one is Sixpence's son, and the other could be the daughter of another worker, she has also been reported missing. I'm sorry, Hendrina."

She covered her face with her hands as tears ran down her cheeks. "Little Kalulu." She had delivered him into the world in his mother's hut 12 years ago in the dead of night. She watched as he grew into a well nourished, happy little boy – the apple of his mother's eye, and often sent him treats from the kitchen and the store. She felt a special bond with all the children she delivered on the farm, but Kalulu had always been her favourite; his brightest smile always reserved for her. Finally composing herself she looked up.

"Please take me home now, Papa," she said. "I must go to Sixpence and his family."

They drove along the dusty farm track and the land was blackened on both sides. The acrid smell of burnt bush was strong, as the breeze rotated black swirls around the passing vehicle. Hendrina could see that many hundreds of acres on both farms had been completely devastated by fire. An isolated tree or log still smouldered. There was not a soul seen all the way back to "Silver Star". Hendrina knew the entire compound would be mourning the loss of the little ones for a long time.

They drove straight to the compound and parked a little way off. When they stopped, they could hear the wailing and crying of mourners. The whole workforce with their families was seated on the ground around Sixpence's hut, all the women wailing at the top of their voices, tears streaming down their faces and clutching their heads or beating the ground with their flat hands. The din was deafening.

As Hendrina and Henk approached the wailing died down with just the occasional wail here and there. Everyone watched them walk through the throng in stony silence. The atmosphere became tense and Hendrina saw resentment and fear in their faces.

Her steps faltered in confusion as she looked into angry faces she had known for 20 years. Henk urged her forward with his hand gently on her back.

"Act normally." He whispered quietly.

She straightened and resumed walking confidently towards Sixpence. He alone stood up and regarded her approach with gratitude.

"Nkosikasi. Nkos." He said sorrowfully. His face was haggard from lack of sleep and he seemed to have aged 20 years. He was filthy from the fire fight and night-long search for his son.

“Sixpence, I’m so sorry.” Hendrina said with tears running down her face, taking his filthy hands in hers.

“I know you loved him too, Nkosikasi. Thank you for coming, but you must go now.”

“May I see your wife and the parents of the other child?” Hendrina asked, hurt.

“I will send them to you later. Please go now.” Sixpence said quietly.

Hendrina felt Henk’s hand close over her arm and gently pull her away. Confused and hurt she allowed him to lead her through the wall of silence and resentment back to the car. As they pulled away, her tears started again and she asked Henk, “What’s wrong, why did they look at me that way? What have I done?”

Henk looked worried. “I don’t know. There’s something not right. I’ll take you back to your house to get more clothes. You’re staying with us until Willem gets back.”

“I can’t! What about the farm? Someone has to be here!” She protested.

“These people will mourn for days and no one will pitch up for work anyway. I’ll instruct my people to send over the carcass of a hamstrung cow I had to shoot, for the funeral gathering. There’s no point in you staying here and I don’t like the attitude of those people. Something more than death has happened here. Those workers were angry. They’re also scared, Hendrina. We have to find out why.”

“Oh Papa! The way they looked at me was just awful,” Hendrina said in a shaky voice, “They’re my people. I always cared for them when they were sick, delivered their babies, and helped them when I could. I’ve loved them as if they were my own children and felt that they at least liked me! I feel like I’ve been kicked in the stomach.”

“I understand how you feel. I’m shocked myself. I’ll give Derek La Page a call when we get back.”

As always, they were met at the door to Hendrina’s house by Tadarera. He looked relieved, but tried to hide it.

“Taddy, what are you doing here? Why aren’t you at the funeral?” Surprised, Hendrina asked.

“I was concerned for you, Nkosikasi, and I am protecting the house.”

“Protecting the house? From what?” Once again Hendrina was confused.

Immediately Tadarera’s face became a blank mask and he said, “I heard there were strangers in the area, Nkosikasi.”

Henk stepped forward and gently put his huge hand on Tadarera’s arm. “Do you know who these strangers are, Taddy? Do you know anything else about them?” He asked urgently.

A flicker passed over his eyes and he pulled away. “I know nothing, Nkos. But I believe that Sauros from the garage has been talking strange things to the people. Shall I make tea?” he forced a smile.

“Taddy! Something terrible has happened here. Tell me what you know!” Henk said angrily. He had known Tadarera for many years. They were frequent visitors to "Silver Star" and he always had good rapport with this old cook who had been in the household before Willem met Hendrina.

Henk and Hendrina had often discussed Sauros. With the same 'gut feel' of Southey, Henk had an identical inclination. Sauros was too clever, too friendly and a little too sure of himself. He was a good man in many ways, but radiated arrogance, without verbally saying so. He walked tall, not humble!

Tadarera regarded Henk in stony silence. Finally, and after extended eye contact, devoid of tribal or traditional respect, Tadarera said, "I know nothing." Henk straightened, squared his jaw-bone, protruding his chin and his eyes hardened. "Very well, Tadarera. We will speak again."

A flicker of pain passed over the old man's face for a brief moment.

"Yebo, Nkos. Kabanga so" – "Yes, God. That may be so," he said. Sad, cold, angry and terrified, he nervously left the room.

It was in the later hours of a particularly hot evening Sauros and his close friend and ally, Josiah Tongogara were walking home after deep discussions and sober debate on the future of black nationalist leaders. They had been sitting in the Mpopoma hall at the end of an early evening of children's scripture studies. The children had left a hall scattered with sweet papers, dust, ice lolly wrappings, discards of crisps and coke bottle tops littered liberally.

Joshua Nkomo, Frederick Shava, Emmerson Munangagwa, James Chikerema, Moven Mahachi, John Nkomo, Kumbirai Kangai and Crispen Hunzvi had sat on the window sills or propped up against the walls, waiting, listening to the joyous words of the Catholic Padre, a magnanimous gentleman from a quiet village, Ashill, in Somerset, England. Padre knew all of them by face, and the names of some, like Joshua Nkomo, Fred Shava, Emmerson Munangagwa and James Chikerema. He knew them as family members of his scripture class, but had heard of some of their trade union and agitation activities from the press. This evening had not been an organized political meeting. It was an impromptu gathering of parents and relatives of the school children. The big man, Joshua Nkomo had been given a staff chair, and was sitting touching shoulders with Mahachi and Munangagwa on benches either side of him. The children had all left, and the padre had excused himself for presentation of a sermon to the city fathers in the town hall. He would get a meal, too, if he arrived there soon, he quipped. Everyone in the hall had good regard for Father Padre, and he for them. He smiled, waved and left.

Sauros followed him to his motor cycle. "Sir, Father Padre, please will you pray for an answer. We are discussing the prospects, like surrounding the city of Jericho. We have mere trumpets with which to fight the big guns and aircraft of this government, but our leaders are talking serious plans. There is rumour that Winston Field is being too lenient on Black Nationalism. We believe that someone more aggressive towards us will soon take control. Father, Padre, must I listen to the big man over there?" he thumb pointed over his shoulder to Joshua Nkomo, "must I listen to my white father on "Twin Rivers" ranch or must I survive as a servant for Mrs. Van forever? Help me, Father, Padre, Sir, please?"

Padre straddled his leg over the Matchless 500cc single cylinder motor cycle. Tongo joined them and listened. "The word of the Lord says you are to obey those in command of your land, for they have been placed in positions of authority by none other than God, Himself. Sauros, my son, your father named you after one of the greatest saints and messengers of God. You are named after Saul, also known as Paul, a man who committed his life and skills into the pages of the word of our Father God. My advice to you is to be obedient to your father and your leaders. You are a strong man, Sauros. You have good foundations and you are clever. You will convert; take many people in whatever direction you choose, my son. Now if I don't leave I will lose out on supper with the mayor. Will you excuse me? May God be with you, my son."

Tongo absorbed and digested the solemn concentration on Sauros' expression. "Hey, Shamwari, you are my friend for ever. I am going for this training thing in Tanzania. I want you to come. We will learn shooting a gun for hunting, and we can be clever like the white man. You and me we are together. Understand!" Each grabbed the right wrist of the other, turning it into the thumb holding bond; a traditional handshake of solidarity, and Sauros looked relieved. They walked back inside the hall and sat against the wall, on the floor, listening to the commanding baritone of Joshua Nkomo.

He was becoming very aggressive and dictatorial in explaining his view to the people. This is the language of Lobengula. It is the language understood by warriors and it is with pride that it is spoken, commanding, unquestioned, totally accepted.

Tongo lifted his hand to request the attention of the big man. "Excuse, sir! How many leaders are there in a land? And who is our leader?" He turned to face Sauros to observe his attitude during the response.

"This country is led by a few white men who are strong individuals, but have not been elected by the majority. There are supporters and defectors amongst them. This chap called Harper is good evidence of the poor bond between them. They are representatives of their home in England and they are not united. They don't know the meaning of unity. Even their own Big Ben, their Queen and their army back home have revolted against them. Their very own forces will shoot them in the foot if they do not hand power to me. I am your leader, and together we will govern this, the land of our forefathers. The handful of whites will spend their semen on the internal fighting between themselves and their queen, and when they are exhausted with every muscle in their buttocks free of all adrenalin, we will move in and cut their throats and use their women and daughters to till our fields and provide pleasures much needed by warriors. Makomana – (Gladiators) the white man is about to experience a wave from a nation of suppressed and very determined warriors. And we have half of their very own people on our side. Harold Macmillan has declared the structure crumbling, talking of "the winds blowing something or other – what he call it – 'the winds of change'" At this juncture the big man involuntarily exploded a deep-gut belch, and the people laughed. After a short pause, he continued. "Harold Wilson is making things very clear, too. He will not support these white people, even though they are the very semen, the seed of his country. He does not have unity as a benchmark in his culture. All his conquerors and gladiators and men of good courage died in two world wars. There are no British with balls remaining. There were and they developed this land. Now they are dead skeletons on desert battlefields, or as toothless bulldogs to nibble our ankles. One kick and they will yelp like scolded dogs. They are too busy injecting themselves with the cancer of self destruction – which they call debate – to know what they are doing. The British will talk themselves into and out of everything. They have lost that power of determination and unity; lost to 'dialogue and appeasement.' The mighty strengths of their Queen Victoria will remain in our land forever. It is the name of the most powerful natural force in the world today, the power and determination of the Zambezi River crashing and tumbling deep into the meat and bone of Africa. Yes, we can respect and admire the warriors she sent here, but the slime that she retained to look after her doorstep is spineless dregs. To answer your questions, Tongo, 'How many leaders are there in a land? And who is our leader?' Every person is his own leader according to his strength, and I am your leader. Is there any part you do not understand?" The group sat head-nodding, murmuring a deep-throat agreement. Tongo lifted his hand again. "Sauros and I are ready for the cause, sir, and we can die in the name of this land. I have just one problem, sir. My father is a herdsman on Gwenoro, the ranch of Mr. Ian Smith. I do not want harm to my family. Mr. Smith has looked after me from a very young age, shown me everything I know in the bush, and he is my father, too. His young son, Alec, has been my playmate – like a brother. We will commit our lives to freedom, but you must never allow harm to the family or employers of Sauros or me. I understand, Sir, that this Winston Field will not be the leader for long. I am told that Smith will soon be the Prime Minister of this country. I also understand that the winds have changed in England, too. Edward Heath is still a bachelor. Because of this the Queen will soon change him from power. Yes, Harold Wilson will become the next leader, and he is much the man that we can defeat. Sauros and me, we can leave tomorrow." Both Sauros and Tongo raised a clenched fist in salute of the cause of African Nationalism.

The big man smiled and turned to Emmerson Munangagwa. "That is the type of loyalty we know – commitment, unquestioning and total. Sauros, who is your employer? Where is your family?" Sauros was articulate in response, acknowledging the deep-rooted appreciation of loyalty and unity; acknowledging disunity as a cancer in the crumbling rule of Britannia. His family was in good employment with a good master on "Twin Streams" ranch near Que Que.

Joshua Nkomo took over. Acknowledging that he would not have to fight; his presence would adequately intimidate. His adversary is nothing more than a toothless bulldog – as seen in the non-inhaling, pipe biting Harold Wilson – little man; talks, talks, talks and more talks. Plenty bark, no bite, plenty threat, no muscle, no loyalty, no honour. Hang his seed out to dry, then crush it to powder, bottle it and sell it! That is his way!

The room was moved by the articulate contempt and disregard expressed by the big man towards Edward Heath the British Prime Minister. It was even more encouraged by the contempt he barked out over the likely next leader of England, Harold Wilson. The man who symbolised domination over this group of simple Africans. "The authority vested in such a pitiful squirm could be well reversed, like a snake eating its own tail. Yes," said Nkomo. "We will gain self determination and survival away from the jaws of this 'colonial crocodile' by developing on his own instinct. We will observe the dog as he returns to his vomit. We will see their queen consume her very leaders. Yes, her own white leaders in this land, Rhodesia, discard their bones as a tarantula does. We will use 'the winds of change' as the given signal that all spirit of that mighty Victoria has gone forever, dribbling down the shin-bones of Heath, Wilson, Field, Smith and the Queen Elizabeth herself. There is a single surviving man amongst them, but his great leadership is like a dying elephant. Yes, Churchill is old and his body is weak. Even Wilson has a quicker mind than him. But we will wait until he passes on before we mould the corridors of Whitehall to the shape of our visions. The spirit of Churchill will awaken; become anger at the sight of the ravenous snake that is eating itself. We can organize some local disturbance amongst ourselves. This will destabilize the authority of Winston Field, but it will not be effective for long. We have the spirit of Harold Wilson and Harold Macmillan trying to destroy their people and give us this nation. We have the strong spirit in Winston Churchill and Winston Field resisting. Two 'Harold' spirits, against two 'Winston' spirits. Yes, we will play one against the other. The spirit of the elephant, my spirit, and the spirit of Joshua will trample all."

Sauros and Tongo bade humble hand cup-clapping farewell to the elder men and were the first to leave. They walked slowly, deep in consideration and discussion. "Tell me, Tongo, you were brought up in the midlands like me. You were cared for and paid wages, and given employment and good medicines like me. You were taught in the farm school, with teachers and books and chalk and blackboards paid for by employers, the same as me. You know how to hunt and how to fight, how to listen and how to fix oxen to the plough. Why, then, must we go far away, to a place we do not know, to a place where the people are all white and they do not speak Shona or 'Ndebele or even English?"

"This "gurumende" – "government" is strong. Do you think a few of us will ever change this system, and improve it? Do you think the big man can support us to the standards of our employers, and look after our families as well as we do? Do you think there is anything in what they are talking and planning?" Sauros waited for Tongo who had knelt to tie his shoe lace.

"Yes" said Tongo. "Joshua Nkomo is a true leader. What he says about the British is true. They have no unity, not even within themselves, not even between their foot and their finger. Their united strength was smashed in the wars against Germany. They are a beaten bunch of pink faced, long nosed jelly-bellies, selfish and very argumentative. They have great strength in having just about ruled the world. But that is history. It is over and so are the British. A few are trying to cling to isolated pieces of property but we can have all that if we just play the plan according to Joshua! His strategy is to simply prompt the British into division amongst themselves. A few; Smith, Graham, van der Byl and Burke are strong, but they don't have the support of the British war machine, and they cannot resist against any ruling of the Queen. Wilson has to be the strongest weapon we have, but his followers, the whites, will divide opinion, then hand us everything on a plate. 'Shamwari' – 'Friend' this war will be easy. It is a simple plan. By connecting the strings that will ripen disloyalty and division within the very people of this government and the British, we will rule this country. The British trade union leaders will become our labourers. We will hardly have to fight anything, maybe a few red nosed jelly-bellies."

Sauros mumbled. "Mmm, Shamwari, this man PK van der Byl, he is a tiger. He will burn us and shoot us if we touch his farm, or that of his people. Lord Angus Graham, he is connected, maybe even related to the Queen. They drink tea together. He is cheeky and his connections are like the web of a spider straight to the boardrooms that make decisions over this land. We know that we have to do something, but the war plan must be properly worked out. It is like David and Goliath. But, Tongo, you and me are together. We will be united forever. Our differences will not allow broken loyalties. We must think very carefully, Shamwari."

Both Sauros and Tongo had good planning ability and leadership skills. They were both adventurous, filled with the muscle and spirit of youth, and neither had any development prospects beyond their present work status. They were ripe for leadership training. "OK, Sauros, we do it like this. Tomorrow we will meet with the big man, just the three of us. We will bring out all thoughts then decide a plan. OK?" With that Tongo turned and sprinted back to the school hall, arriving just in time to join a casual procession escorting Joshua Nkomo to his blue Ford Popular. The big man was in close concentration, listening to Emmerson Munangagwa, agreeably nodding. As the entourage arrived at the car the group surrounded him, all eager to be included in the friendship. Tongo elbowed his way through the elder men, disregarding the customary, humble respect. He whispered close to the big mans ear. A nod; handshake, a clenched fist salute from the passenger seat and the car rolled slowly away. A meeting had been arranged for the following evening, in this very hall.

A seed was about to be sown; a root cancer that would consume southern Africa, reducing it to a starving, desperate, very sick desert region. This meeting would impact many nations and millions of people. It would result in severing friendships and family bonds – and the demise of the nation of Rhodesia.

Joshua Nkomo arrived back at his home and his wife shuffled out to greet him. He was again in deep concentration, but acknowledged her humble affections with a smile. He moved heavily into the brightly painted blue and yellow sitting room, where he picked up the phone and cranked two short and three long rings, cranking the sequence through several times. The phone was picked up at the other end by his close confidante and reliable warrior, Dumiso Dabengwa. He had been out, returning home with his friend, Lookout Masuku, who would be staying the night. They spoke in deep, quiet tones and agreed on meeting the following evening. Unbeknown to Josiah Tongogara and Sauros Mphofu they had arranged a spearhead meeting that would destroy the entire fabric of the tradition and root of their ancestors' society. They were about to plant seed that would germinate in blood, be nourished with a fertilizer of heartache; produce fruit of misery – inedible, misshapen and growing out of control.

The meeting had not been assembled on a time schedule, merely 'after work.' Sauros and Lookout, and Tongo arrived within minutes of each other, all having travelled by bus from their various places of employment. Lookout Masuku was a pleasant surprise addition to the meeting. He explained that the big man had called Dabengwa, requesting the meeting. Sauros hoped that a personal discussion could be held. Not a political address! It turned out to be a series of instructions.

The three who arrived earlier had sat in the shade of a tree in the customary 'haunch on heels' style, discussing, drawing in the sand and laughing. Joshua Nkomo arrived in his car, together with Munangagwa, and George Nyandoro. As the car arrived they moved towards it. They all exchanged greetings, some humble and some superior, more aged. Now a group of six, they moved into the empty hall.

Still standing at the door, Joshua Nkomo started with a booming barrage of instructions. He moved slowly, towards the only chair in the room. The others sat on wooden benches, tables and an inverted dustbin. He reversed the chair and straddled his legs, sat, with his huge belly pushed up against the backrest. Distinctly, he was addressing the five. His instructions related briefly to recent riots in Salisbury and Bulawayo. He would like to see more similar incidents in other towns, notably Gwelo, Que Que and Sinoia. But this was minor. The object of this evening had been to assemble a military high command. Each member present was to carefully plan a future for the coming months.

"George Nyandoro, you are the wisest among us for buying. I want you to help me closely. We will travel together and you will negotiate. We will be relying heavily on your negotiating and strength of persuasion. Your task will be to procure the necessary weapons and ammunition to establish isolated attacks around the country. I have taken leave from the railways for six weeks, starting on Monday. Friday night you and I will leave the country. You must be discharged from your employer for reasons of insubordination, and collect your full pay. Any questions?" Without time for George to utter a word, Joshua continued. "Lookout, you Mphofu and Tongogara will travel with us also. Sauros and Tongo will be joining you to TANU camp in Tanzania. They are getting some instructors to teach how to shoot with guns, and how to run away. We will be leaving on the train, but will not travel together. We will meet up on the other side of the Victoria Falls Bridge. I will be at a house in Livingstone on the first road past the hotel, on the left. It is marked on the gatepost 'Naidoo Prakesh.' I have not met him, but he is a very good decoy for future military purpose. When you approach his house you must not mention my name. Even his servants will not know who I am. You should say you are travelling on your way to Lusaka, and you want accommodation. The servants will know what to do. I will wait for you all there. You should all be there by next week, Monday." Emmerson Munangagwa was writing notes throughout the evening. He knew his role. With Joshua it had been regularly discussed. His priorities were to complete his degree at Fort Hare, from where he would join forces in Lusaka with Herbert Chitepo. The big man joked with him "Yes, Munangagwa, one day I will be the man issuing degrees. At the rate you are going I'll probably be the one to issue it to you. Study quick my boy; otherwise I'll have to just give you honorary degree." And they laughed.

In 1965 Sauros returned from his training camp in Tanganyika to being the hero of his father and brothers for having taken the challenge of travel to the big city. He was mentally mature, focused, seldom smiling but happy. He had developed an exceptional body, with trim muscle, standing at six feet three inches and very strong. His family was not aware he had been trained in leadership, military strategy, in guerrilla bush craft and killing. Mind-games and the wheels of propaganda had reshaped his brotherly love into focused determination to lead others towards black empowerment. He had returned home to recruit trustworthy supporters to be trained in methods of destabilizing and disrupting civil society. Whites of English origin could not be recruited. Their loyalty was not even skin deep. Norman and Brett were the most loyal men Sauros had ever met, but he had been told that whites had no loyalty. This would be tested later by forcing each of them into decisions that would bring two opposing loyalties into confrontation. 'Yes' thought Sauros, 'they say in English about which side the bread is buttered. Their priorities are so soft, weak, buttermilk and whey. They cannot be trusted. Not yet, anyway.'

Hennery, his ardent admirer and hero worshipper was taken into his confidence. Sauros explained his military training; described the people he had met; the places he had seen; huge lakes in Tanganyika; the big sea, called Indian Ocean, and his relationship with the big man, Joshua Nkomo. He went on to advise "Hennery you are a determined and skilful survivor in African environment, and your abilities are many. Opportunity for the practical survivor is not the same for you as for the academic achiever. You, Hennery will not become a world leader developing an academic bias. Your potential is restricted to being a work foreman or possibly a mine captain. You are the blood son of Royalty, friend (almost family) of the De La Harp family, you can run, climb, swim, hunt, snare, and dream abreast every physical attribute of baas Brett. Baas Brett will own the ranch one day, and drive big cars. You will own a bicycle and be a herdsman forever. Through De La Harp connections you may become a Foreman. Through me, Sauros, your brother, your blood, you will become a warrior and a leader of national significance. Join me and we go forward together."

Harold Wilson was Prime Minister of Britain and Ian Smith now leader of Rhodesia. Winston Field had all but retired, sulking and bitter, on his Karimba Farm in Marandellas, producing pigs, tobacco and cattle. These were strong men, all of them. Wilson was strong in favour of Black Nationalism. Smith opposed it, but could not toy with the military machine controlled by Wilson.

Sauros went on to explain the small war strategy of disrupting the 'gurumende' and manipulating Harold Wilson into submission and surrender. He explained the power of vehicle land mines, adding a carrot that every fighter will have his very own rifle, .762 calibre AK47, made in Russia. He explained a brief outline of the strategic planning. Isolated, vastly scattered 'incidents' carefully put into action at strategic places throughout the country, thereby mobilizing huge government resources. Thinly spread throughout the land, government defences would be easy targets. The ultimate objective being that Harold Wilson would dismiss Ian Smith from authority, attracting European investment, funding black Empowerment.

Hennery could not accept that the white man in England would turn against the white man in Rhodesia. No society in history had demonstrated dishonour to that degree. Surely baas Brett and baas Norman could not originate from blood of such diluted loyalty. Sauros was suggesting Harold Wilson and his cabinet would demonstrate disloyalty at the ultimate extreme. This could, surely, not be true.

"I will be here for a few more days. In that time you must decide, but tell nobody. Do you understand?"

Hennery was devastated. His loyalties were being ripped asunder. His emotions lay hard toward fulfilling national duty, and supporting his brother. This would be deep erosion into the world of "Twin Rivers" ranch, his life, his father, his family, Baas Brett, Baas Norman and Nkos Southey, too.

He sat, like The Thinker, his dark purple lips bouncing, huge, rubbery, nervously together. Sauros put his hand on Hennery's shoulder and said "see me on Tuesday, when we will leave for a new world, new beginnings and a big future with big brother."

Hennery watched Sauros move down the path, disappearing into the long grass like a stalking leopard.

The train snaked itself over the web of rail intersections, clacking the track, out of Bulawayo towards Botswana and South Africa. Brett was on his final trip returning to school after another wonderful and very varied school holiday. This was his final term at St. Andrews College in Grahamstown, South Africa. The journey would last three days and three nights.

Fellow students, friends from Zambia, Malawi and throughout Rhodesia were in excited banter discussing holiday experiences. Some had been to the Mozambique coast, fishing, camping on deserted beaches amongst palm trees. Others had hunted the Zambezi valley, and a group of seniors had toured Kenya, representing their district cricket team. Brett was amongst a group of Matric students, debating and evaluating a diverse range of examination holiday projects. The train brakes screeched, gently bringing them to a halt at Mpopoma siding. Brett needed refreshment, walked briskly, accompanied by several of his group, to the railway kiosk. He was amazed, pleased, and joyful to see Sauros, whom he had not seen these holidays. Sauros was equally surprised, and they greeted each other warmly. Sauros had developed unexpected physical strength; peak body fitness. They had not seen each other for an extended time, and like any friends in that position they exchanged jovial banter. The train was not due to remain long, so Sauros had to assess and decide quickly. He indicated Brett to one side, away from other ears. "Brett, I consider you as my brother. Our world and the life we live is about to change. I am now going on a journey to Zambia, and meeting with Joshua Nkomo. I have many things to resolve, but importantly you and me must decide which side of the waterfall we swim. Shamwari, you have heard of the riots! Yes? Well you must think carefully. Things are changing very fast. It is only a matter of a few months. Whatever happens, it must never divide us. You and me, we are 'brothers' Shamwari. Don't betray me. I will never betray you." The shrill train whistle penetrated loudly, simultaneous to a slow 'chuffing' departure, powerful thrust and a cloud of black smoke from the chimney of the steam engine. Brett looked into Sauros's eyes as if to bid a brother farewell to the gallows – not knowing who would be executed.

"Sauros, what the hell are you saying? Are you a bloody terrorist, or what?"

"No, my brother, I am your friend. I am a realist not a terrorist. You are wise, but very young. Do not betray me. I will help you and you must help me. We will meet next holidays, Hennery will guide you. Your train is leaving. 'Hamba Mushle' – 'Go Well.' And good luck with your exams this term. You better pass, Shamwari, otherwise I will be cleverer than you!"

Brett returned to the train, having to accelerate to catch a handle and pull himself onto the step at the door. Sauros ran swiftly next to him, and slapped him on the back, then waved an open hand farewell as Brett disappeared into the carriage. The train clacked on the rails disappearing into the distance.

Brett excluded himself from his friends, selected an empty compartment, and closed the door. He sat staring out of the window, observing a dry and barren landscape. The Mopani trees were leafless, seemingly dead, devoid of undergrowth, everything having been consumed by browsing livestock. Isolated goats stood on their hind legs trying to reach the odd remaining leaf. "That encounter should not have occurred. Why did that bastard have to do this? What is he saying? What are the terrorists up to? Does he know something I don't? Is he a terrorist? Dad always said he was 'too big for his boots.' Dad always said he wore the baboon skin hat and dark glasses to taunt us! What's he mean? Who here will know the answers? With whom can I discuss this? Should I phone home? Should

I tell Naison and Hennery about Sauros? Should I tell the police? What do I tell the police? No! Let sleeping dogs lie!"

He redirected his concentration onto exceptional experiences of the holiday. With Norman, Hennery and Braziwa, Southey had accompanied them on a raft down the Zambezi River, from Chirundu River crossing to Kanyemba on the Portuguese border. They had camped every night on the banks of the river, and the trip had no time limitations. They could camp long or restrict their time as the mood arose. They had been surrounded by elephant, and experienced a very aggressive pride of lion in confrontation with another pride. They had witnessed crocodiles in a feeding frenzy; had been pestered by fearless hyena attempting to steal from the camp. They had caught fish, bathed in the river and holed a drum on the raft. This drum was removed and discarded, now superfluous.

The environment of natural Africa had warmed their emotions, deepened that inner bond amongst people who share the wild amongst the rulers of the wild. The raft was equipped with two freezers, both filled to capacity with frozen supplies. The cuisine on the trip was comparable in variety and quality to anything available in a well starred hospitality resort. The leisure of being carried by the current down the river made for an enjoyable and relaxed school holiday. The ranch vehicles had been driven from Chirundu to Kanyemba and the drivers were equipped to last several weeks on arrival, camped at Kanyemba. The entire expedition had been eventful, informative, very peaceful, but stimulating for the adventurous minds of everyone. These men all had many experiences in every bush circumstance. Being alert was routine, even in time of rest.

Brett returned to reality; the present; prospects of riots; conflict amongst brothers and friends; his young vision was being stretched to challenging depths. He permitted himself the comfort of "knowing his enemy" should it ever occur that uprising result in racial confrontation. He could not accept such conflict would materialize. The bonds between the black and white Rhodesian were too deep for divide. Harmony was entrenched deep into the aspirations of everyone. What could Sauros have been referring to? He must be dreaming nonsense! Although he did seem serious, well focused, authoritative and self assured!

During the school term Brett had devoted more than average time to his studies. He was head-boy of his House, and deputy head of the school. He was senior student officer of the Cadet Corps, and represented the school in squash, tennis and athletics. His long distance achievements had established cross country records at each age level since his early years at the Prep School. He had an enjoyable very busy final term. In the November, his second last month of schooling the news highlight had been of the Unilateral Declaration of Independence in Rhodesia. He had listened to several repeat radio broadcasts in the common room, by Mr. Ian Smith – who he knew well as a good family friend and regular visitor to "Twin Rivers" ranch. He sat listening, in deep concentration, disturbed on one occasion by a fellow student using him as a case study in pencil portrait, titled "the thinker." The words of the speech were spoken with articulate deliberation, emphasizing loyalties and high-spirited national pride. Brett was moved by the proud emotions and determination expressed by his little "David" nation challenging the "Goliath" Harold Wilson, Westminster and socialism. The words were momentous, challenging his thoughts; reverting to the meeting with Sauros at the Mpopoma rail siding outside Bulawayo.

When Brett returned in December, having sat his final exams at Post-Matric, he arrived home to warm greetings from his Rhodesian friends and especially from his father and elder brother, Norman. He had not expected any fanfare for his homecoming. The Que Que railway station was teaming with well-wishers, messages of congratulations and groups of school leaving girls and boys, his friends, brother and father. His territorial call-up papers had arrived. He was to report to the railway station to collect his concession rail pass for a journey to Llewellyn Barracks on 25th January 1966. His military number, PR 62061, Rfn De La Harp B, were included in the registered envelope with instructions that the enclosed 'neck tags' were to be secured with a string and worn at all times. He was to report for territorial service, 92nd Intake, Royal Rhodesia Regiment. He had planned a university course but this would have to wait. His military status afforded him 'hero' status on his homecoming. He was amongst the first after the Declaration of Independence to receive call up papers.

On the long journey back to the ranch Southey congratulated, spoke with pride and respect to his youngest child; having finished Post Matric; significant sport achievements and volunteered for the call of duty in support of his country. Southey had achieved the rank of Colonel, commanding in Abyssinian desert during the second Great War. It was now a privilege for him to guide his youngest son into combat with an experience and sincere commitment to support the national call of duty.

The family had exceptional celebrations during the festive times of Christmas. The ranch received good rains, the pastures were green, vibrant in palatable growth, the cattle were in very good condition, the dams were all full and the rivers were flowing swiftly.

The following morning, early, Norman was in the ranch study, working on his new grazing theories. Southey had prepared for a meeting with the local intensive conservation group, and would later be receiving Sir Humphrey Gibbs as an overnight guest, together with his delightful lady, Molly Gibbs. Brett took control of the ranch, saddling his horse, Petit, and riding out to the gathered herdsmen. He met with Naison en route and dismounted for short greetings and "welcome home" message.

He held the reins in his hand and sat on a rock, whilst Naison sat on his heels and spoke quietly. After formalities of kind greetings, wide smiles and a quick summary of the position with the cowherd, Naison and Brett agreed the work plan for the week. Brett inquired individually after each member of the Mphofu family. "How are Sauros, Hennery, Gauto, your wives? Everybody well?"

Naison shook his head, holding his gaze to the ground. Brett stood to mount his horse, but the old head foreman remained on his haunches. "Sir, we have much to discuss. There have been many dark clouds over the land since you went to school in 'Soctemper'." His eyes looked to the sand between his feet. His head hung low; the cool morning breeze could not prevent perspiration droplets forming on his forehead. He looked unwell, concerned and in dire need of time with Brett.

"Set the men off to the camp. Collect those calves and young steers into the kraal, and then I will come with you to see everyone. Then we can talk."

"No, Sir. There is trouble in my bones. The work is fine. The men are well, the cattle are looking better than they have ever been. I want you to remain. I will put the men to the task. Can we meet at the river under the big Msasa tree that has the big nest of 'uThekwane' – Ndebele – 'Hammerkop.'" They had often resolved intricate management matters in the shade of this tree on the banks of the Matura River, overlooking the major stock watering reservoir on the ranch, the river now fast flowing, almost torrential.

I will be at the river when the sun is there, and Brett indicated an 8:00 am sun position. Naison was pleased, agreed the plan, indicated with a broad smile and, despite his advanced age, a set of teeth that a man in his teens could be well proud of.

Naison had insisted on keeping Brett apart from the workers. They had somehow been alerted to politics and civil unrest. They did not agree with the idea, but had wanted to discuss events with Brett. Naison was not ready for confrontation of this nature. Surprise was not his system. Brett must be warned, not alarmed. This will be done under the nest of 'uThekwane' on the banks of the river.

Brett rode up at a steady canter, reining Petit to a trot as he neared the tree. Naison was sitting at the base, leaning against the tree trunk. He stood, removed his axe from his shoulder and dropped it on the ground. "NKosana, shlala mushle, lapa." – "Little god, sit comfortably, there," indicating the regular bench, an old dead tree trunk straddling a huge flat granite rock lying flat to the ground. Brett sat, observing desperation in the physical and facial expression he was looking at. 'Good old Naison. He does have a problem. This must be that renegade son of his' thought Brett.

In unusual directness Naison came to the point. "Sir, a spirit of confusion has blown over the ranch. The youth, that is half of the stockmen, are talking of leaving. They seem united in their plan to go. I don't know where they want to go, but they are talking of training with guns."

"When did you last see Sauros?" Brett inquired.

"I have not seen my eldest boy for a long time, but this is the problem. I have heard that he has visited here, but not been to see me. He has slept in the bush, avoiding his mother too. I am told he is big, strong, his voice now deep, like a bull Buffalo. But he will not present himself to my eyes. This is a sign. Please, my boss, you can help us? He is my son. He is your friend. He will talk with you; he will not come to me. I think he has been struck by the spirit of Rinkaals, planning to coil himself around us all. I fear for our safety because I fear he may have been overtaken by the meat of Satan?" With this the old man looked physically exhausted, drawn to the outer limits of physical tolerance. He was losing his eldest son to a dark force. Not normal! It would be a matter to be proud of if he was losing him to some well rounded pair of jet black virginal buttocks, or even to the goring horns of an enraged bull buffalo. But, no. Naison was certain that Sauros was deep in the grip of Satan, working on captivating the entire youth of the district. His control over the people was powerful, more so than could normally be expected, unless he was in the grip of evil, filled with many strong spirits that blind by their blackness. There was desperation in the face of Naison who seemed to have aged 20 years since Brett saw him in September.

"Sekuru, I am soon to leave the ranch. I will be going end of January. I must talk with the 'Makomana' and see what is happening. Satan will not win here. We have the strong spirit of God amongst us. I will meet with Hennery, Braziwa and Gauto after the calves have dipped. I would like to see Peleele-Pasi later in the afternoon."

"Aah, Sir, I have not told you! Peleele-Pasi left us soon after you went back to school. He disappeared with all his pay and that of Hennery as well. He vanished in the night. We hear rumours that he has been called by the spirit of his son. We hear that he has good spirit guiding his future. Hennery is behaving strange. He does not look into my eyes as he should. Braziwa and Gauto are also not walking with the head high. They seem to be hiding something. My power is being strangled, through my very own son, Sauros."

Brett had a concise memorized vision of the hard facial features of Sauros at the rail kiosk in September. His mind bounced from that to the radio speech on 11th November; ID Smith declaring UDI, then to riverside fishing camps, laughing with Sauros and Hennery and Gauto and Braziwa and Peleele-Pasi. What had penetrated so deeply as to slice such deep scars, effectively breaking old Naison and eroding everything that history had engraved in his soul? When Brett left in September Naison had stood tall, walked erect, been proud, and commanded from solid foundational authority. Now desperate, destroyed, weak. The great strength of his tribal roots had been to uphold dignity in the face of all adversity. Naison had been overburdened with emotional excesses, surmising that the venom of Satan was overtaking his world.

The calves arrived at the dip-tank and a messenger arrived to call Brett from his office. All heads had been counted and all animals were on hand, none missing. He jumped in the Fargo, and free-wheeled down the driveway in front of the ranch homestead. He jump-started the engine into life and travelled the two mile straight road down to the dip tank. All the herdsmen were huddled in the shade of an Mfuti tree with its brightly coloured velvet type leaves gently waving in the breeze. They all stood, in acknowledgement of Brett arriving, indicating a respect and pleasure at seeing him again. Hennery skipped across to where the Fargo was parked and humbly cup-clapped his hands together, beaming his broad smile as he lowered himself to customary submission. Brett greeted him with a smile, whereupon he stood tall, accepted a friendly back slap, and then returned to the others. Braziwa and Gauto waved friendly welcome to their master and friend, which Brett acknowledged with a wave and a smile. He called for a stock count at the gate, confirming that all 1,847 calves and steers were accounted for. They were dipped and returned to their grazing. Hennery peeled away from the other herders, making his way toward Brett.

"It is good to see you, Sir. How were your exams?" Banter was jovial, light hearted for a while, and then Hennery changed his expression to a focused concentration. "Sir, there are very dark clouds over our land. I hear that the riots in the cities are going to become serious. Joshua Nkomo is talking many things that are not good. My problem, Sir, is not simple. Someone can offer me very good employment. Says I will live off the land, have a gun and plenty bullets."

"Come on, man, how can a gun help you, Hennery? You can't even hit a sack at fifty paces. You are looking deep in the mouth of a charging lion if you think you will get a better life with Joshua Nkomo. He's all bad, bad, bad!! How is Sauros? Have you seen him this term? What is he doing with his life?

We must talk, Shamwari! Tell me how everyone is. What is everyone up to these days?"

Brett stood with one foot on the running board of the Fargo. Hennery jumped on the back, sat on the mud guard. Worried.

Hennery spoke in his favoured tongue, n'Debele. "Life is about to change, Sir. What I tell you has been revealed to me in darkness and in secret. According to my custom I must never disclose the source of information! Tokoloshi is moving over the houses, over the trees, over the grass lands and over all the animals in the trees. The spirit of Tokoloshi is blowing winds of change over all the land, over all the people. You will experience Tokoloshi in a secret way and in a dark place, Sir. He will show you what will happen in this land."

"Come on, Hennery, you are not going to believe that nonsense, are you? Tokoloshi is just a harmless fable. He is certainly not carrying messages of doom."

"Sir, you are not understanding. The dark cloud is building into a black storm. At the moment it is only a cloud. It may take many seasons but it will be gathering a violent storm over our land. I think you must listen on your radio. Even Harold Wilson has said 'it will take days, rather than weeks' for the 'gurumende' — government of Baas Ian Smith to be finish. We have to believe the radio, Sir, especially when they quote Britain's Prime Minister, in his very voice."

Brett reflected over many personal incidents, confirming a series of events suggesting waves of turmoil, increasing civil unrest. "Where are Peleele-Pasi and Sauros? Are they together?"

Hennery looked perplexed. Why had Brett questioned this? What relevance did Sauros have? Why should they be together? Did he know something about my meeting with my brother? Yes! This white man knows everything! No good trying to keep the truth from him, but what for anyway? Better tell him the whole story. "Sir, it is like this.........." and he expanded on all meetings with Sauros, with Simon Muzenda, the local Ox cart mechanic and carpenter from Umvuma, illustrating each memorable detail as accurately as possible.

Brett appreciated Hennery sharing this information, expected nothing less! He understood the reasons for "beating about the bush" and the enormous responsibilities being shouldered by Hennery, and Naison.

Brett had been reluctant to accept reality, but the harsh facts imposed it on him. There was unrest, civil disobedience, there was dissatisfaction amongst certain groups, political vibes spread dark news and there was a leadership structure that was about to guide revolutionary change.

BRETT AND SAUROS

Brett went into his military training with determination. He was selected to go for officer training at the School of Infantry officer training camp in Gwelo. He was fit, strong; an exceptional master of bush-craft and his school debating society gave him an oratorical edge over his corporal and sergeant instructors. He was quickly detected by the other training officers as being a man with outstanding leadership qualities. He represented the officer training school in Rugby, Cricket, Squash, Tennis and Athletics. His athletic forte was long distance running.

The training involved Hard Square Parade and shining Boots, ridiculous bed and personal cupboard packing and square folded pillows and sheets. Floors had to reflect almost mirror quality shine; barrack room door and window handles and latch brass were expected to shine, radiating a diamond reflection off dull brass! Lectures on Mapping, Bush Survival, St Johns Ambulance emergency procedures and Fitzsimmons snake bite instructions. Rifle stripping, cleaning and range practice were daily events, and officer cadets had no idea which day of the week it was. It made no difference. The initial 8 weeks training involved long hours, being deprived of sleep for up to 20 hours a day. The canteen food was good, never sufficient for the youthful appetites, but healthy, providing energy and stamina. After $4^1/_2$ months of training the passing out parade was a moment of exceptional pride for all parents and invited guests. The occasion was used to boost morale, always presided over by men in high office. The State President was Clifford DuPont, who on this occasion presented the Sword of Honour to 2nd Lieutenant PR 62061 Officer Cadet Brett De La Harp.

This was a moment of marrow-deep pride in the De La Harp family, as Brett led the march past, and commanded the Battalion to the salute of the State President as the Band of the KAR – (Kings African Rifles) struck up "Oh, when the Saints go marching in……." The battalion marched out of the parade ground, to be dismissed outside the Marquee where parents, invited guests, camp training staff and all Officer Cadets mixed as equals in this once only occasion of social celebration and equality. Brett accepted proud salutes from men who had been his team players, and they now formally acknowledged him as their superior officer.

Brett assumed 2i/c of 1st Independent Company based in the Zambezi Valley, tasked to search and destroy any subversive activity by any insurgency emanating from the Zambian side of the mighty Zambezi River. This was his terrain of preference, within an environment of search and destroy, simultaneous to being surrounded by every conceivable predator of Africa. Command of this unit had been an exceptional privilege and the time passed all too quickly for Brett. On completion of his first uneventful 6 week stint on patrol, the unit was returned to base for a five day period of R&R (rest and recreation.) It was during this time that Captain Coventry was recruiting from within already trained soldiers for new recruits to join the elite corps of 'C' Rhodesia Squadron, SAS. Within an hour Brett had committed himself to a three year stint in the regular army. If he were to fail the selection course for the SAS he would become automatically enlisted in the Rhodesia Light Infantry. He was relieved of the 2i/c command of 1st Independent Company and instructed to report to the RLI barracks in Braeside, Salisbury in ten days. He was granted a leave pass for that time and returned home to the ranch.

Over the next few years Sauros distanced himself from Brett, the ranch, and his family. He never left a contactable address. Hennery seldom heard from him, but did receive occasional mail via a neighbouring farm worker. The mail was always sealed, confidential, secretive. This system of communication could take two months from post date to receipt.

Ranch work continued, usually with jovial, refreshing work atmosphere; sometimes, though, shrouded in dark moods. Meetings and social gatherings amongst national players continued, generally culminating in topics of nation unity, subversive activity, employer loyalty and policy direction. Diverse political aspirations continued to dominate social events in most sectors of all communities. The black leaders and their youth met often, impromptu gatherings, developing in communal circumstance; after school parent groupings, Beer Hall joviality and afternoon soccer events.

The white leaders continued to meet in atmosphere of weekend tennis tournaments, evening squash challenge, sometimes polo, la-Crosse, school cricket or national rugby events. Every event was well flavoured with liberal political banter.

There was a grand divide now in formation.

The black leadership used conference facilities of long dead hardwood benches; boardrooms of sand floors, décor of seasonal leaves shedding or budding, conditioned with sunset breeze amid musical sounds of birdsong and leaf rustle. From these facilities they assembled and stimulated energized brigades of youth leaders in promotion of civil unrest. Aggressive. Disruptive. Attacking. Violent! But it was youthful fun well garnished with impractical promises; every perpetrator deeply sealing his own self-interest.

The white leaders within Rhodesia were assessing circumstances, imbibing Gin and Tonic, cucumber sandwiches and Scotch whisky on ice. They sat on folding canvass deck chairs, shaded and served; serving and surviving. Their work responsibilities and family obligations were highly organized. Together with their youth they expounded academic development, sport, hobbies, bush-craft, global events and challenging survival. Sessions in Whitehall were deliberating how to retract the self governing authority and assurances being practiced by the Rhodesian Front government. Typed volumes of constitutional amendments, opinions and impractical suggestions were being passed across well polished boardroom tables, amidst the clinking of tea cups and crystal brandy tumblers.

The country was like a deep, fast flowing river powerfully moving towards rapids, turmoil, then over the precipice, into the chasm of a seemingly boiling pot of instability. Like calm but determined waters above Victoria's Falls, about to be splashed, broken, separated, droplets and mist plunging hundreds of feet, crashing, exhausting its power and might against rocks and precipices on a journey deep into the jowls of eternal affliction. This determined commitment was set on course in the ornate marble and gold, wood panelled boardrooms and arches, by ink-splashed confirmation of the winds of change.

Lines were drawn, the game plan about to commence.

The teams were established, with many of the ever seeking players remaining sidelined. The field was undulating, having no goal posts. The scenario was basic, involving the rugby-playing Rhodesian Cabinet, captained by Ian Douglas Smith.

The football playing team of Joshua Nkomo comprised a majority of his kith and kin from Matabeleland, with a few Shona people clinging on for glory. The mediator of the game was part Cricket referee, Football and Polo umpire assisted by a team of whistle blowers. The portly front of the Judging muscle was represented by Harold Wilson, who announced the score before agreeing to the start whistle.

The general principal for SAS training included tests of outer limitations of endurance, strength, survival, loyalty, obedience and team spirit. The highlight of combat training was in the obligatory parachute training course, folding, landing, packing, embarking and static line jumping from aircraft. Brett was an exceptional soldier and multi-talented leader. As a commissioned officer in the Territorial Army he retained his commission through SAS pre-selection, selection course and final training. His instructors referred to him as "Sir," but treated him as a recruit in training. His perks as a commissioned officer were minimal. His advice, council and direction were on constant call. Brett was a man amongst men, an exceptional leader, a fine soldier and a loyal servant. He had cautiously evaluated all options presented during the course of his young life and settled on defending his country against any adversity. The aspect of becoming a trained killer was juggled in his mind for a while. He based resolve on the alternative, living amongst a dishonourable society determined to undermine authority, bedevilling progress and development. If he had to kill to prevent an undesirable society, then, yes, he would kill.

His training required duplication of some of his School of Infantry Officer training, weapon handling, rifle range procedures and marksmanship competence. He was trained in instant action and reaction with SLR, FN and Uzi weapons as well as the bipod assisted MAG. His achievements exceeded anything ever recorded on the RLI rifle range. The multi disciplinary competence in situations of alarm, emergency, compassion and other aspects of human tolerance were tested to extremes. Initial demands and tests were heavily accented towards individual ability, individual skills, reactions and tolerance. Brett had no equal competitor in stamina, determination, resilience, endurance and alert reaction.

Team-work was challenged in the selection aspect known as "All In." Teams of three were dropped from Military transport at 15 mile intervals, on the Golden Sands road between Sinoia and Hartley. Each team was left with comprehensive maps, a two man canoe, three machetes, three ex 2nd world war .303 service rifles, including barrel Woodstock, but drilled, barrel filled and welded into "ornamental" status. The Bolt action mechanism and firing pin were dysfunctional but had to be retained clean, well lubricated as if inspection and serviceability would be tested at any time. The group had three back-packs each containing six bricks in sewn green canvass containers. Each recruit had a full water-bottle and a total of 60lbs that had to be carried. In addition they had to share the dead weight of a non functioning military radio, a rowing paddle and the canoe. The object of "All-In" was to challenge team skills and grass root events as and when situations arose. Careful pre-briefing was given by the instructors. Everyone had ten days to get to the shores of Lake Kariba, at the base of the Matusadona escarpment. A point was marked on the map indicating the pick-up point. All recruits should anticipate prospects of being captured by an enemy, possibly tortured for information.

Each group was body searched at the discharge location, and all matches, hidden food, pen knives and cash confiscated. The walk was set in challenging terrain, descending from an altitude of 4,500 ft to the low lying Zambezi River; heat; Tsetse flies, wild animals and isolated village outposts. A truly appropriate test of communal effort, bush-craft and survival.

Brett observed the convoy of vehicles move off, around the corner, dust clouds developing in their wake. He opened the maps, assessing the objective and the terrain. The canoe was cumbersome, having limited value as it could only take two people with minimal luggage. The heavy immobilized .303 rifles were strapless, so Brett and his team each made a strap from the inner bark of Msasa shrub, so as to sling the rifle over the shoulder, leaving hands free to attend to other challenges. After evaluation and discussion it was agreed to walk 28 miles south and take advantage of the Umfuli River, which was known to be flowing well. Because the canoe could carry only two people, it would be used by one as a transporter, leaving the others to move fast, uninhibited by parasitical weight. All rifles would slide inside the canoe, with the radio and packs of canvass covered bricks. The journey began in agreement and finished 138 miles later, almost without incident. Lack of food had posed a problem. Brett negotiated transaction with a village elder to exchange a pen-knife for two roosters. Both parties were delighted with the transaction, and one rooster was cooked on the fire with the village approval. The people volunteered a full pot of boiled beans and another pot of the staple, Sadza – Maize meal cooked to a thick porridge. The other chicken was carried and cared for so as to become a meal in a few days. The group arrived at their destination on the sixth day, two days ahead of the advance party of instructors, who flew in by helicopter. They were amazed to see Brett and his two men, washed, clothes washed and looking relaxed. This distance had never been achieved in less than nine days.

The time in SAS training had honed fine skills; in combat techniques, capture and escape practices, health, bush medicine and medical knowledge, hijack and hostage rescue, navigation, tracking, leadership and personnel motivation. With a lifetime of practical experience he was now thoroughly versed in theory, practice and physical competence.

Brett passed into "C" Squadron, with the fastest and highest recorded achievements. The youthful looking Prime Minister, at an elaborate parade presentation ceremony presented, after a congratulatory speech, the Beret and Blue belt to all successful candidates. Brett wore his fawn beret and SAS insignia with a pride almost equalled by being awarded the sword of honour at the School of Infantry. This sword was now paraded, fixed as the medal of proud attainment that it represented, to Brett's belt.

After the presentation, there was a formal reception for all successful SAS recruits; free-flowing beer and cocktails, enjoyed amongst invited guests, parents and the Prime Minister. Southey stood with Brett, admiring his bright shoulder lapel 'pips' confirming his youngest son as an officer amongst an elite fighting unit, one of the most respected in the world. Ian Smith joined them, and again congratulated Brett, using his rank, and calling him "Sir" in recognition of the brass on his lapel. Then he focused on Southey.

The meeting at the Bulawayo agriculture show had been a success. The Prime Minister had imported stock semen from America to upgrade his already outstanding herd of Brahman breeding cows. They discussed the Currie Cup results and briefly debated the game. Then they turned to current affairs. There was general banter including selected press articles, the riots in the townships; in Bulawayo, Salisbury and now Gwelo. "I have a darn good team on Gwenoro. One of my senior herdsmen Phineas Tongogara, worked for my old man, and now, still in his prime, is working for me. But, man, he has a son, Josiah! This blighter is giving old Phineas a serious run for his money. I believe he has got in cahoots with one, Sauros Mphofu. They are causing havoc everywhere they go. I am told they are burning grazing from Bulawayo to Plumtree, from Tjolotjo to Binga in the Zambezi valley. Yes, they tell me its old Phineas's son. I have known Josiah Tongogara since his birth. This chap Sauros Mphofu, I believe is also from the Midlands."

Southey looked at Brett, who looked straight at Ian Smith. "Sir, I know a Sauros Mphofu. He is my age. His father works for us on the ranch. Could our stockmen have something in common? The name Sauros is not common. In fact I don't know another Sauros. Ours is definitely up to no good, but what? I don't know! He has become secretive, elusive, seemingly turning his back on his family."

Ian Smith hooked his eye over his lower lid, clenching his jaw bone, concentrating on Brett, permitting extended silence. Inviting. Brett turned to Southey. "Dad, I think we must get Naison and Hennery into action. They will tell us where Sauros is. They must know, surely.

The Prime Minister was alerted, by a member of his entourage, to the time. He had to catch a flight from the air base, so he excused himself. He requested Southey and Brett accompany him to his vehicle. As he moved through the crowds he greeted everyone honoured this day, affording special tribute to the men with Fawn Berets in their lapel and blue belts.

As they approached the green Peugeot he suggested another afternoon croquet and "sundowners" evening at the Ngezi ranch house of Clifford DuPont. They agreed a date from Ian Smiths diary, shook hands and the Prime Minister entered the passenger seat of his car. They pulled out of the RLI barracks, turning left towards the airport, disappearing into traffic.

Brett had signed a commitment into 'C' Squadron for 3 years. This was active from the date of his territorial enlistment in January. His wage was built up to accommodate the resultant short pay for the previous five months, and 2nd Lieutenant 62061, De La Harp, BB was granted another ten day military pass, with an overfilled wallet in his back pocket.

Southey returned to the clink of glasses, cocktails and social joviality. He circulated among the guests. He spoke briefly with his school friend, Des Burke, now minister of Law and Order. They agreed to dinner later in the week, in Gwelo at the home of the Minister, and in the company of Jock McDonald.

Brett arrived with his good friend, 2nd Lieutenant Jeremy Calder, who would be accompanying him and Southey to the ranch for a few days. Jeremy and Brett had been at St Andrews College, travelling the train trip together for five years. Jeremy's father had been a senior commissioner in the British South Africa Police, and Jeremy was obsessed with a legal career. Known throughout his school days as 'Judge' Calder, he had also received the sword of honour from the intake following Brett. They had much in common, and their time of rest and recreation had been planned to coincide on this occasion.

With Brett behind the wheel, the three men moved out of the barracks, through the security boom, acknowledging several saluting military police. In just two hours they passed the ranch home of the State President, their neighbour and friend, and arrived in the port-couchere at "Twin Rivers" ranch homestead.

The whereabouts and activities of Sauros was about to unfold.

That afternoon and into the evening, Jeremy and Brett patrolled the main ranch dam, casting, spinning, willing fish to take the lure and feeling the anglers' pleasure. Facing westward into a panoramic sunset which reflected off the water, they stood apart, just within talking distance. It was cold, but they were dressed for the occasion. There were no mosquitoes and the mood was tranquil. Brett had arranged for Hennery and Gauto to meet them at the dam.

When they arrived they greeted Brett and Jeremy well; humble, in traditional submission. They were pleased to see their boss, their friend and mentor. They were pleased to see Jeremy, who they knew well from many ranch visits through the years of College.

Fishing rods were laid aside and the group sat amongst long reeds, some flattened, carpeting the lower edge of an anthill. The setting sun was awesome. Herons glided low overhead, and frogs had struck up their orchestral symphonies. Orange breasted waxbills flocked through reeds, to roost atop the tall dry grass. Isolated ducks flew past, some landing nearby water, others flying in 'V' formation to more distant places of roost.

Brett passed out three beers from the cooler bag, demonstrated delight that the four of them were again together. Talk started on light-hearted insignificance, quickly turned to Hennery and Gauto volunteering the latest information on Sauros. Brotherly confidentialities were no longer sealed. Sauros had attempted to persuade neighbours to burn livestock and pastures in the district. This had infuriated the herdsmen who indirectly depended heavily on grazing for their livelihood. Sauros had been banished from the area. Naison was relieved that Sauros had been discovered as a subversive operative. His inner strengths had been restored at the expense of his family emotions. He would not tolerate insubordination and now there was no longer need. Hennery and Gauto had been severely threatened with emotional blackmail by Sauros. Their decision was tipped in favour of loyalties to their father, ranch employees and employer.

Brett could see relief in the attitude of the two brothers. They had been subjected to extreme psychological pressure, potentially splitting the family and destroying the ranch; the very core of their life. Sauros had used terrifying tactics to get them to "eat their own tail."

Jeremy detected a fear that Brett assessed as relief. "What is Sauros doing now? Where is he living? When will you see him next?" Jeremy directed this at Gauto. Hennery replied. "We never know! When he left he behaved like a cobra, leaving with a look of death fixed to whoever he focused on. His words hang heavy as smoke that will not move. 'Brother, the future is open sky. You can make it rain, shine or wind. If you join me we will make thunder and control the lightning. You decide. I will return with much power, and you better be ready.' We have not seen him since, but he will return."

Brett and Jeremy detected an open sincerity, mingled with fear. They were not going to get additional information from either Gauto or Hennery, probably because they had no more to offer.

The beer tasted good as a small flock of whistler ducks passed overhead, paddling their wings in urgent effort to over-fly. The sun had disappeared below the horizon. Frogs croaked and fish splashed, a pair of Spurwing geese landed in the water, proceeding to walk along the nearby bank in search of slugs.

Brett asked after Peleele-Pasi. Why the sudden departure? Gauto assured that this was purely a man thing. Pressure of women! Peleele-Pasi had become a father, needed the company of his 'wife.' Word had arrived that he was settled in a very distant village, surviving on wild fruits, occasional hunting and herding a few goats. Gauto interjected, holding eye contact with Brett. "We are scattered as a family. Peleele-Pasi moved in a natural way. Dark clouds have blown Sauros in the wrong direction. He is being taught things that demonstrate strong desire for ownership of property. He has turned against mother and father, against all brothers, and you as well, Sir. He is not under good shade. His spirit is poisoned by the venom of vipers. He has grown fangs and will strangle his own flesh if we are not obedient to his instructions." Hennery interrupted his little brother.

"Our position is difficult. We are under threat from Sauros. He will return in the night, unobserved. Gauto and me have to follow him into darkness. If we do as he instructs we will own big herds and vast plains. If we do not he says we are dividing the family. We need your help, Sir." His eye contact bounced pleadingly between Brett and Jeremy. The four men reflected in silence, sipping beer, contemplating the degree of the problem. Each had varied assessment agreeing the complexities, severity and consequences as seen through individual circumstances.

Brett visualized burning cattle, charred pastures, dust and war.

Jeremy had courtroom visions, wigged Judges, gallows, over-crowded Prisons and an exhausted police force.

Gauto contemplated hunger, disunity, and loneliness.

Hennery's visions included rifle ownership, becoming an exceptional marksman, feeding his family and sitting in shade, being family provider and revered by his family.

Jointly, they all experienced horrific visions of drought, desert, starvation, denuded terrain, destruction and devastation.

Despair was not permitted to mature. Euphoria surrounded them. The night-sounds were tranquil, sufficiently pitched to be invigorating. The night colours splashed vivid sentiment, now punctuated with the bright evening star twinkling high on the western horizon. Jeremy grabbed the cooler bag, removed another four beers, circumcised the top off each and passed three on.

Brett stood stretching a leg, and then peered down at the others. "This issue has developed too far, maturing into a rotten, sour spirit between everyone. I saw Sauros at Mpopoma siding in September. It was a hurried meeting. He assured me he is not a 'terrorist,' but a 'realist.' A big picture is developing over the whole country. Sauros is a small cog in a big wheel. He is clever, may become a bigger cog in the wheel if we allow more civil unrest. To prevent spread of unrest we need to understand all arguments in the confrontation. What is Sauros trying to achieve? Who are his leaders? What does he want from life? Does he have a plan to achieve his aspirations? Is he prepared to break regulations to achieve his goals? Who are the other players in confrontation? What are their aspirations? You two guys must get this information. Hennery, you are the cleverest man I know. Gauto, you must help. You guys must find your brother and ask him these questions! You understand the relationship between him and me. I will meet him as soon as he is ready. We are all together in an attempt to fix our problems."

"Gauto, I want you to go in the morning. You must find Sauros and return with him here as soon as possible. Bring him, whatever it costs. Tell him whatever you have to, but just bring him here. We must all sit by the campfire, breathe the same smoke and chew on one issue at a time. There is chance that between us we can prevent things from becoming violent. The sooner we all meet together, the better for us, but especially, the better for our land and our future. The solution is that we 'nip it in the bud' now, before things get out of control." Brett raised his bottle towards the evening star. "Cheers, guys, here's to a wonderful few days break."

Gauto tried to interject that he was being sent on an impossible task. Hennery assured him that Sauros would be contacted, and everything would be arranged, but probably a week away.

When Sauros arrived as per plan the five met under the tree, the nest of 'Uthekwane' – Hammerkop, having the huge flat rock – 'ruware' as their floor; several logs of fallen deadwood as benches. Brett brought a lavish hamper of sliced back leg of buffalo, pots, pans, maize meal and a crate of 24 Lion lager.

Sauros adopted aggressive body language and attitude toward Brett and Jeremy. His attempt at stamping authority and supremacy over the meeting was determined and then dropped. He quickly realized that the leadership qualities of both Brett and Jeremy were supported by a lifetime of commanding experience. Brett handed everyone a beer, which act prompted very relaxed joviality and light-hearted, friendly banter.

The principle of Sauros having contravened unwritten bonds, heart-searing activity against his parents was 'wafting in the breeze,' but not mentioned. His guilt radiated, penetrating the mood. Brett and Jeremy determined not to open discussion on the topic of 'subversion' until the beer acted to mellow the mood, temper any aggression.

Sauros lay outstretched, leaning his head on his hand, propped up on his elbow, taking in a mouthful of beer and chewing a succulent stem of green grass. Although now facially passive, he remained challenging, dogmatic in posture, sure of his plan, certain to win. Past subservience had totally vanished, speaking as if commanding instructions, debating nothing. Jeremy sensed a no win situation. Brett could not allow this picnic occasion, this casual meeting to terminate now. Ian Smith had needed solutions. The country could be balancing on this moment.

"Hey, Shamwari, remember when we were chased by that hyena?" About 12 years before, Brett had been waiting for Sauros on a river bank, casting his line into pools hoping to entice a fish or two. Sauros arrived shouting, exhausted, perspiring and panting heavily. He had been scared by the aggressive appearance of a Hyena swinging heavy udders under her belly.

"The one that had rabies?" smiled Sauros.

"Not rabies, you twit. It had babies. If you just listened properly sometimes, maybe you would be clever by now!" Everyone laughed. "I am sure you said rabies" retorted Sauros. He smiled, his mind certainly having returned to their youth. For the first time in recent times he changed his attitude and his address to Brett, referring to him as 'Boss' or 'Sir.' "That bloody dog, bitch, followed me all the way, you know, Sir. I have never run so fast in my life. She seemed to be walking, swaying her head from side to side. No matter my speed, she stayed just behind me. Then you wouldn't believe me, remember, boss?"

"Yes, I remember seeing her puppies scampering around, yapping and jumping to suckle. You were just hell bent on getting away. Do you remember when I picked up the rifle and they ran off into the bush? You were screaming, 'shoot, shoot' and I said she has babies."

"Okay, I can understand now. I thought you said 'she has rabies.' I never understood why you not kill that bitch. I have never been so afraid in my life. I was only 12 years old, you know, boss."

Brett mused, allowing mellow moments to flow light spirit over the people. This ambiance was exactly right. The answers would flow. Be patient, he thought. Don't get serious yet.

Jeremy stood to stretch muscle, flex legs and pee into a bush. This broke the topic, keeping matters light, permitting a slight regain of confidence for Sauros from his puppy humiliation. Brett led Hennery to elaborate on a very intimate embarrassment experienced by both brothers.

"Aah," said Sauros, humiliated, unable to prevent an embarrassing revelation from his little brother. "Don't tell me. Aaah, don't tell me. Puleez. There are people here who do not know these things, my brother." His humility was complete. More ammunition was kept in reserve. Brett was a master at making the mood, and he knew this people from deep within. He understood the exact moments to expand on a multitude of strengths or weaknesses. He knew too much about Sauros and his culture to be brought into social or personal submission. He handed another lager to each person

"You told me you are not a terrorist. I hear you. Are you trying to undermine authority in the land believing you are a realist? You are too clever to believe in rubbish. Even if

Joshua is promising you all these things, why are you turning on your friends, your family, and your own father? Do you move with spirit of a Buffalo, the spirit of a hyena, or the spirit of Rinkaals? Sauros, look into my eye. Tell me if I am your friend, or tell me that you slide with Rinkaals. Sauros, my friend, in the presence of your very own flesh, your brothers, friends and all you know as good, have you turned on your father, on us and on honour? Are you sliding with Rinkaals?"

"Now look here, Brett. Listen. Stop talking! Hear from deep. I tell the truth. This land is finished under the present government. Joshua Nkomo is our leader. He will take power from Boss Ian Smith. Even you white guys are saying that we must rule ourselves. Look at Harper, Clutton-Brock, Garfield Todd, even Harold Wilson. Hear what they say. Listen, man. Just listen to what they say. If I stick with you, we" pointing to signal Hennery and Gauto, "will perish as paupers. You, Baas Brett and you Baas Jeremy will become rulers and we will remain labourers." He went on to explain his anger at being refused a business license, frustration at not being able to play a role as a leader in business. He had to surrender against prospects of business success in favour of developing the land for his children. The only way to do this is join the chimurenga and terrorize the people, all people, to surrender some leadership responsibility.

Brett was visibly passive, but seething inside. He could not comprehend any destruction for Honourable ends. This indicated self seeking disgrace. He had heard this debate, had deliberated the living circumstances of Sauros, Hennery and everyone he knew, but reality and further debate were futile. Body language and attitude had implanted volumes of reality.

Jeremy looked straight at Brett, sending an unspoken message of hopelessness. Brett understood. The remainder of the time under this tree, the nest of uThekwane – the

Hammerkop was pointless socializing, incorporating opposite and tangential views that could be resolved through amicable discussion if all sides would listen less than talk, receive less than impose, hear widely and talk less.

Extensive talks and discussions; think tanks and business meetings received publicity throughout the world. The British Prime Minister, Her Majesty's government, the American President and congress had all become involved. Harold Wilson met Ian Smith on board British battleships, supposedly on 'neutral ground.' Various delegations by-passed as delegates flew across the globe in pursuit of resolving differences between a few conflicting groups. Joshua Nkomo, Robert Mugabe, Ian Smith and many other representatives crossed global paths and some met in wide corridors in New York, London, Brisbane, Geneva, Pretoria, Paris and Salisbury. Representatives were dispatched by every authority and ilk of international business. World leaders imposed 'guidance' and 'advice' onto the people of Rhodesia. Decisions were concluded on boardroom tables throughout the world. In 1966 Harold Wilson assured the world that it would take days rather than weeks to get the Rhodesian people to surrender……...

Isolated incidents of national significance increased slowly. A white farming family was shot at the front door of their home when responding to a request for supposed medical assistance. Remote incidents of suspected 'criminal' activity occurred at strategic places, generally confined to isolated rural areas. Enemy modus operandi appeared disjointed. In return for killing a village headman, or ambushing a farmer en route to market, young men became in conflict with the might and military expertise of the Rhodesian people. The majority trained in military action was from the Rhodesian African Rifles, predominantly black Rhodesians that made up approximately 80% of the fighting strength of the country. A war was developing between opposing interests, inaccurately termed as a black / white war of racial conflict. In reality the conflict related to a very few, usually black, frustrated leaders motivating support to overthrow the government in return for promises of material privilege, and life in retirement! These leaders gathered initial support from better-educated urban blacks whose aspirations were in business ownership.

Conflict developed based on the Rhodesian government claiming terrorist aggression against the people of Rhodesia, whilst distant leaders turned wheels of propaganda based on racial divide. The perpetrators of bush war in Rhodesia became well financed, personally supported by eastern powers, mainly Russia and China. The defenders of the bush war, the government, were placed on a financial back foot, having to fight fire with brushwood. The world responded to a call from Harold Wilson to sanction trade with Rhodesia. Restricted fuel and armaments should bring the country to its knees. Typically, under guidance from Ian Smith the country determined psychological resolve to defeat any aggressor. The government portrayed optimism maintaining a spirit of certain victory. This optimism was kept afloat well after the eleventh hour, in fact up to the very last minute. National motivation was maintained through a spirit of honesty, honour, and decency, which spirit usually flowed gently on most congregations.

It was a reality in the living rooms of every Rhodesian that daily news broadcasts included "The Ministry of Defence announces with regret the death in action of……."

The terrorizing bush fighters supporting the Zimbabwe African Peoples Union – ZAPU – Joshua Nkomo, were motivated by improbable promises, and access to guns for killing. They had matured from hard-working labourers to self-supporting touters of AK47 rifles. The resultant village respect and admiration for these young men generated certain tribal privilege and awe.

Sauros was particularly active in recruiting and training his fellow rural herdsmen and scholars, in exchange for an AK47 rifle and 200 rounds of ammunition. He set up a training camp on the upper slopes of the Zambezi Escarpment, west of his parent's chieftainship in the Silobela district. Here he trained just 20 cadets at a time. He taught weapon handling skills, and exhorted his students to extremely demanding physical trials. He was a competent instructor in physical education, keeping himself as strong and fit as any of his students. He led every run, walk, mountain climb or river crossing expedition. He carried equal or additional added ballast weights so as to complement his own muscle development.

He invented a system using a cigarette; expressing the tobacco, placing the head of a match against the filter, and replacing the tobacco. When burning dry pastures, his trainees could light a primed cigarette, place it under dry tinder-grass, and leave the scene, having about 12 minutes lead time before the match would ignite, turning the tinder to very hot flame. This system could effectively destroy the agricultural backbone of the country.

He instructed well, selecting only the upper half of any classroom of students. His recruitment was not particular about student age or sex, believing an alert mind to be more important than an inactive one.

Sauros had to make regular return trips to Lusaka, crossing the Zambezi River, walking 30 miles per day for three days. He returned with 25 rifles, and 10,000 rounds of ammunition, usually carried by new recruits. His training system was simple, turning his men into physically strong, very athletic porters and thinkers. With their AK rifle as a reward for satisfactory completion of training and additional ammunition from each terrorist activity undertaken, his men penetrated the entire western and southern sections of the country. They were under instructions to bury their rifles and resume routine work habits, becoming known to employers as reliable and hardworking.

Josiah Tongogara had a similar strategy. He created a training base camp 50 miles inside Mozambique, using buildings, roads, bridges and other facilities abandoned by the Portuguese owners. His weapons were delivered to him on a monthly basis and his camp had running water, pumped from an old farm borehole. His monthly intake of new recruits was dependent on the success or failure of previous internees. Many of his recruits were collected involuntarily, from rural schools in Rhodesia. His regional responsibility was from the confluence of borders, Rhodesia, Mozambique, South Africa, northward then westward to Mana Pools on the Zambezi River.

Boardrooms in Rhodesian bush, in Russia, in China and in Lusaka determined new strategy. Agreement between ZAPU, led by Joshua Nkomo and ZANU led by Robert Mugabe stipulated that two armies would split the country. Each segment of terrain would come under individual command, slicing the country along that range known as the Great Dyke. The eastern segment would be under the overall command of Robert Mugabe, a member of the majority Mashona tribe. Joshua Nkomo, the self-elected leader of the warrior descendents of King Lobengula, would command the western segment.

This resulted in two friends, Josiah Tongogara and Sauros Mphofu, being dealt different, potentially confrontational command structures, one loyal to the Mashona tribe, the other loyal to the n'Debele tribe.

Both achieved high rank. Both were incorporated within their individual High Command. Mugabe was financed by the

Chinese and ZAPU funded by the Russians. Similar systems of strategic command were established. The chief procurement officer for ZAPU was the youthful and energetic George Nyandoro. The procurement responsibilities for ZANU were headed by Combo Moyana, whose severe speech impediment excluded him from achieving active military rank. His astute business acumen, however, gave him beneficial advantage when negotiating arms procurement through Chinese translators.

Crocodile Pools

The men who came to see; to toil, teach and aid
The men who came to mine and the men who came to
Trade,
They came in wagons to live and die, to help, protect and
work.
They never did accept an end – the land was not a quirk.

The land was vast and free, with many open spaces,
Every type of dream unrolled in all those many places.
Hills well treed, vales well grassed, and many flowing
streams.
The men they formed their groups and set out on their
dreams.

With sparsely scattered rural folk – it was almost void of
people.
In desperate need of the word of God beaming from His
steeple.
They learned the clicks, a twist of tongue, were shown
Victoria's falls.
Gallant men they were, and attended to her calls.

The land had people few and far but carved a life for all.
Black magic some time rose to laugh, amid that smell of
Gall.
Her prodigal son brought in a calf and he made a nation tall.
The white man came and shared his skill, giving muscle to
Her call.

The spear, the shield and the warrior's axe
were not quite right for developing man.
They must be replaced by a government Tax
So Her Majesty's empire fulfil the plan.

They rallied around in defence of her lands
With muscle and gristle and sweat from their glands.
In two world wars they honoured her call to stand or be
killed
But her government assured that they must be stilled.
Then her leaders, both Harold, signed the wind in their hand
Imposing Dictator and Killer by wave of a wand.
He controls and devours his progeny too, as they slither and
squirm on sand.
His name is a legend in the crocodile pond
As he splashes and shatters their every bond.

This Garden of Eden, now a megalomaniac's dream
Has fading visions of sunrise as attacking hyenas scream.
This mind-scheming dictatorial son of Satan
Can only function with his master's baton.

Ruler, Dictator, self seeking tyrant of evil,
This man is certainly a son of the devil
Whose plan is a terror of unruly bands.
Because two Harolds and Maggie had to wash their hands.

The land was ripe and ready to tame.
Oh, so active with an abundance of game.

The skin and bone of ancient times used skills from short and tall.
Her Majesty will surely grieve to know that all her men now fall.

The reason Britannia had to throw in the towel
Was that Russia and China and the Muslims as well
Were determined, not united, to erode to the bowel
To assure that good leaders all fell.
They implanted a cancer in the anal tract.
This Mugabe cancer is a deadly fact.

Disguised as soldiers with skill, in the pay of men of self will
They enact only cowardly kill; are truly not men of goodwill.
With funding and friends from mainly the east
Their system and leader is surely the beast.
He cannot look you in the eye without seeing a feast
The smile is so dry as he contemplates a meal.
He winks and smiles and rests as he plots what next to steal.

Brett was summoned to attend a meeting with 'ComOps,' the government controlling authority of combined operations. This was a unifying committee that determined overall activities of the Police, Air force, Army and Civilians. The meeting was at King George VI Barracks in the Officers mess.

Brett was escorted, marched into the Billiard room, where his escort saluted him and departed, closing the door behind. A very casual group of men was seated at one end of the room, around two joined coffee tables. Sleeves were rolled up, some were smoking, tea cups were arranged on the table with several huge platters of fresh sandwiches, covered by fly netting. Several regional and national maps had been spread over the billiard table and others had been opened, suspended on the wall.

Brett stopped at attention, noticing General Peter Walls, the commander of the Rhodesian forces standing to acknowledge Brett, smiling. The Prime Minister, Ian Smith stood quickly. Brett directed a salute at the Prime Minister. "Good morning, Sirs." Ian Smith walked over to Brett and shook his hand in warm welcome, "Hullo Brett. Good to see you again. How are you?" then formally introduced him to everyone in the room. Peter Walls was wearing a brown sheepskin jacket, open to the navel. The room contained the most powerful decision-making men in the Rhodesian government. The ambiance was informal and friendly.

Brett was directed to the only unoccupied chair, central against the coffee tables. Ian Smith was at one end and the General at the other. PK van der Byl, Jack Howman and Lord

Graham lined the one side. Brigadier Andrew Dunlop sat next to Brett.

"Ok gentlemen, let's begin." Ian Smith was in command. "Things have spread further than intelligence had indicated. We have additional subversive activity strongly perpetrated against the village people in the lowveld, between the Limpopo and the Sabi rivers, against the Mozambique border. We have had shots fired at wardens in the game park, and hundreds of animals have been wounded. Resources are being stretched from Kanyemba to Beit Bridge, from Umtali to Kariba. General Walls will inform you of his action plan. Broad planning is to decentralize all regions to people familiar with the area. Not all local residents have good understanding of the customs and traditions of local people. Regional command will be among regional roots. General Walls will elaborate in a moment."

"Gentlemen, we have the resources, expertise, infrastructure and determination to rout evil from our land. Intelligence advise me that the enemy are mounting a surge. When they are soundly beaten from this round they will retreat into oblivion."

"As you all know I am in regular communication with Wilson, Andrew Young, Kissinger, Carter, Vorster, now Kaunda, Seretse Khama and even Banda. Things are coming to a head. We are strong. Our military is well trained and morale is high. Keep it that way. Our every action has been honest, exemplary morals being forefront in justification. We will overcome this thuggery. Now please excuse me. The General has things to say. Goodbye and good luck." He looked at Lord Graham and Andrew Dunlop, reminded them of the lunch meeting, turned and departed. Brett stood, respectful, followed by the others.

Prime Minister gone, everyone seated respectfully after the General. Peter Walls shuffled a file of papers, removed a single sheet and spoke in a commanding style, quiet, articulate, concise. He used a swagger stick to indicate areas and events on the wall map. His talk was mostly on the military front, but he interjected with snippet information gleaned from several recent discussions he had with various world leaders. PK van der Byl listened behind closed eyes, arms folded, dismissing all references to the maps.

"Brett, you are being sent to an area that I understand you know. You will be stationed on the crest of some cliffs overlooking the Lundi River. Here." Indicating the red cliffs Brett enjoyed in younger days. "The problem here is not so much terrorist activity against people, because there are few. It is being used as an area for rest and recreation prior to these bastards ambushing the road to South Africa. They are established at several camps in small numbers. We understand that Chief Gono is supportive of their activities. Do you know the chief, Brett?"

"Yes, Sir." Brett responded. "I have not seen him in years and he was old when I last saw him. He must be very old, probably a cripple by now. He is a darn good guy, Sir. I shot a leopard that had been disturbing the village. He was very grateful. How did you think I may know him, Sir?"

The General replied, "We have detained some of the villagers suspected of feeding terrorists. This was a police action, not army. One gave your name as his employer, but this was refuted by others under interrogation. They indicate he is a terrorist leader, foreign to the village, but has a whore in the village that he visits regularly. His name is," and the general referred to some papers, "Peleele-Pasi. He is amongst a group of vicious bastards under a section leader code named Hitler Hunzvi. This Hitler apparently trained him in the Binga district, but escaped when we got onto him. Some of his recruits have signed on with RAR, and are becoming properly trained soldiers. We have information that Hitler is now permanently resident in the area. He is a bad bastard, Brett. Be forewarned."

"The point, Brett, is that you are needed in the area to stop further butchery of the wildlife, and to seek out any terrorist in the area. Your mission, 'seek and destroy,' will leave from New Serum Air Force base next week. You will report only to me. You will select 12 of your troopers and advise Major Coventry what you require to fulfil your mission. He is already aware you will be going. You will have an Alouette helicopter based at your camp, which will be under your command, but used also by Major Ted Cutter, based in Chipinga and Major Buster Johnson, a territorial, from Tarantellas, who is based on the Bubi River, near Beit Bridge. I expect you to penetrate the villages and hunt for isolated camps. You will fly in 'scatter' formation with three helicopters to transport your men and supplies. One will remain with you for the duration of the exercise. You will be in regular radio contact with both Majors Cutter and Johnson."

"This pre briefing is in the presence of ministers because you will encounter variable circumstances that will cross ministries. The Department of National Parks is active in the area. The police continue routine patrols. Internal Affairs, that is Minister Howman, are in continual search on animal health and welfare matters. We do not want you seen, but you will be active over hundreds of square miles. Daily contact will be connected between you and my office. The sensitivity of inter-departmental responsibilities is clear. Do you have any questions?"

Brett looked at Lord Graham. This man is huge; his forehead is like a buffalo bull. "Sir, you are Minister of Agriculture. What is your role?"

PK opened his eyes and boomed out in his articulate Oxford accent, "Never you mind, my boy. Just you get out there and shoot those bloody terrorists. We will run the country. You run your bush war. Kill every black bastard that is out of line. Angus is here at my invitation. We are wondering why Minister Howman has to retain his men in the area. I believe they should all be pulled out. Clean the area of terrorists, and then Lord Graham and minister Howman can return their people to continue farming a clean place. Agreed! Well, what are your thoughts, boy?"

"Sir, if everybody suddenly vacates the area then the Terrs will have a free range. They will also be alerted that something is happening. They may even think they are winning the war. We would not benefit from such a morale booster, but they would! For my part, Sir, I will respond to your decisions. I would like to take one of my farm workers. He can penetrate the area, the people, in ways that us whites can't. I need a batman, Sir! No. Seriously, I have this guy who is brilliant in that area. He will assist very much."

This request was totally overruled by PK van Der Byl. Absolutely no blacks must be allowed into the camp. He was now arrogant and contemptuous toward Brett.

The General explained that there would be another briefing from the SAS C/O., Major Coventry. Then he dismissed Brett, who stood quickly to attention, placed his blue beret on his head, saluted the general, and marched out of the room.

He instructed his driver to drop him at the office of Major Coventry, where he knocked on the door and was invited in.

He saluted, greeted and was offered a seat in front of the Major.

"Good afternoon, lieutenant. How did it go?"

"Well, Sir. However, our brass, the ministers, even General Walls do not understand the true inner marrow of our local people. You are aware of the problem near Vila Salazar! The solution is simple. They are a damn good bunch, down there. I have a guy working for me, whose brother is amongst the terrs. They won't let me take him to solve the problem. That was Minister PK, himself, who rejected the suggestion. I can handle it in other ways, but it would be solved in two weeks if I took Hennery."

"Lieutenant you are officially on R&R as of now. Go home for a few days. Phone me if anything relevant springs to mind. I'll arrange your provisions, kit, weapons etc. Give me a list of lads you want to take. I'll arrange the rest. Anything you need tell me. You realize you are going into a hornets nest, don't you? You need Sergeant Willie Divine and Corporal Vernon Thornsby. Off you go, lieutenant. Your departure is scheduled for Tuesday next week. Have a good rest, boy. It'll be the last you get for a darn long time."

Brett stood to attention. Saluted the Major and marched out. He would be on "Twin Streams" by the evening.

The helicopter circled over the rust-red cliff. An elephant was visible through heat haze, standing under a distant tree, fanning, cooling himself with his ears. Brett looked out from the front right seat then signalled an open grass patch for the pilot to land. It was on the highest plateau above the cliffs.

The grass waved, flattened, as if in humble submission, creating a perfect circle, each reed of grass pointing outward. Slowly the magnificent machine was lowered to land. The pilot spoke into his radio mouthpiece, cutting the motors speed to an idling tremble. The rotor blades slowed, not stopping. Brett indicated approval, removed his headset, debussed from padded comfort onto the ground. Three troopers followed from the rear seat, quickly establishing an all round defence, on guard, protecting the helicopter from possible attack.

Brett scanned the horizon, heat haze preventing meaningful visual achievement. He did notice three buffalo at rest on the outskirts of a thicket of trees. He signalled the pilot a "thumbs up." The rotor blades were brought roaring into action, lifting the 'green machine' gently up, then by virtue of lifting the tail, a forward thrust propelled her down and forward into the gorge of the Lundi river, and out of sight.

The other helicopters arrived within minutes, in flight formation, landing a zone signalled by Brett. A sergeant and a corporal and nine troopers debussed, removing heavy back packs, water containers, trunks of dry rations and steel boxes of ammunition. Two Troopers were armed with MAG machine guns, the others with FNs, phosphorous grenades, and 32Z grenades, in containers and secured to their webbing and belts.

Within minutes the helicopters lifted individually, following the same routine and direction as the lead pilot had taken. Quick decisions were made by each trooper locating places of preference from which to re-orientate. Brett assisted, moving packs and boxes to camouflaged concealment.

The camp, high above surrounding forest, grassland and the river, could be a tourist paradise. The area was surrounded by an abundance of wildlife, the big five, Lion, Elephant, Buffalo, Leopard and Rhino. It afforded panoramic views of terrain virtually uninhabited by man. Brett stood amongst his silent men, inhaling the ambiance, the aura of tranquillity, the sheer magnitude, and variation of scenic beauty, as they scanned their world – in search of hidden evil.

Camp catering remained an individual responsibility. Rations were distributed and responsibilities were delegated and absorbed with enthusiasm. Brett was supported by 12 Troopers, Sergeant Willie Divine, Sergeant Tony Hahn and Corporal Vernon Thornsby. This was a group of 16 carefully selected men who had achieved the toughest selection challenges of any present day fighting unit. These were the finest fighting men available. He had high regard for them all. Their respect of Brett as their leader was supreme.

Brett scheduled the first day to three patrols of four men each. He would lead three men out the following morning, being dropped at a place he pre-marked on the pilot's map.

The helicopter settled slowly on the landing zone, in the first light of dawn. Two Patrols were ready to leave and the pilot took his instructions from Brett, marking points on the map clipped to his flight suit upper thigh. The men em-bussed and the helicopter lifted out, turning westerly, flying low over the tree tops. It returned within 20 minutes and took the other patrol out in a south westerly direction.

On returning Brett climbed with his backpack and rifle into the front right seat, leaving space for three troopers in the back. The green machine lifted off, flying directly over the village of Chief Gono. Brett instructed the pilot to hover high over the village for a few moments. He sat observing the people flowing out from their huts, from under tree canopies, from every possible place of overnight shelter. There were many more inhabitants than when Brett had previously been here. The people were waving and excited to see the helicopter. Brett was moved by an historical emotion as he saw the old chief step out from his hut, turn looking upwards to the helicopter, shielding his eyes to the rising sun. Brett spoke into his mouthpiece and the pilot gently glided his machine down to the eastern side of the village. When they were at treetop level, Brett stepped out onto the gunnel plank normally reserved for the machine gunner. He shouldered his rifle and dangled the rope ladder over the edge. The village people descended with hysteria. They were joyful, curious, whistling, shouting welcome and chanting as Brett lowered himself, dropping the final eight foot to the ground. The helicopter lifted up and turned eastward, disappearing over the trees and away.

Brett waved in acknowledgement of the village enthusiasm, and walked a fast pace towards the village, setting course direct for the door of the hut of chief. He was impressed by security as elders surrounded him in smiling goodwill, preventing his approach to the chief.

Brett spoke in the tongue of the n'Debele king, Lobengula. He explained that he could not remain long. The chief would remember him as the man that killed the leopard! The message moved fast, mesmerizing the village to sudden silence. Curiosity beat the chief. He could not contain his inquisitiveness. He walked out, hunched, leaning heavily on a walking stick.

Brett stopped some five paces in front of the elderly man, greeting him in the dialect in which they had communicated on the previous occasion. The wrinkled face features of the chief exploded into youthful joy. He had fewer teeth, but seemed content. Brett lunged forward offering his hand and received the gentle shake of an aged man. "Kunjaani, Nkos" was splashed out from an almost toothless mouth, smelling strong of fermented beer of millet. The old man pulled Brett by the arm, insisting that he enter the hut for privacy. The masses remained in silence outside. Brett leaned his FN rifle against the wall and sat on a low wood carving designed for this purpose.

The Chief had aged, now older than elderly, and explained his additional wrinkles and loss of teeth, blaming human greed and stupidity. He laughed easily, nervously, and from deep within. Peleele-Pasi had become a member of the village and had fathered two sons and a daughter. He had been loyal to his wife, but had not kept to the agreed bridal payment, 'lobola.' He had recently been behaving in strange routines, sometimes disappearing from the village for days, then unwilling to explain anything. Brett requested to see him immediately. The messenger was instructed accordingly and disappeared at speed to call him.

Peleele-Pasi had heard that the helicopter carried the white spirit, who was now in conference with the chief. He became terrified, his facial colour draining to a sallow grey. He decided to remain next to the simmering three legged pot of water, and wait to see what happened.

The messenger arrived, skidding to halt, excitedly stuttering a message from the chief. He had to escort Peleele-Pasi back to the hut of conferences. Nervous but pleased to be seeing his friend and old-times mentor, he stood then moved through the people. He was again being idolized by the village youth, revered and respected for his closeness with "white spirit."

In celebrated humble submission he entered the dark hut, extending subservient reverence first to the chief, and then to Brett. His nervousness had been unfounded. He was received as a brother, a returned prodigal son and a friend. He squirmed in his guilt at having deserted the ranch, his brothers and his employer, but this was not mentioned, and never would be.

Brett permitted time on trivialities, small talk and family matters. Then, witnessed by the chief, his elders and a messenger he asked "Tell me about Sauros? What are you doing with him? What is your plan? Are you pleased with the things you have done together?"

Guilt and shock replaced his broad open-mouth smile. Momentary aggression replaced his jovial friendliness. To dispel all aggression, Brett turned quick to laughter and family unity. He brought goodwill from Naison, Hennery, Gauto and Braziwa. The moment was right! The message was good and Peleele-Pasi felt surrounded, embarrassed and shame. Being in the presence of the chief made him nervous; a feeling of being on trial in Court. His speech faltered, his voice cracking and a tremble developed in his hands. He had entered this hut as a respected hero. He would probably leave as a despised hyena! Humiliated, his eye contact appealed for Brett to be gentle. Because of old times the interrogation suddenly changed to a family discussion of their youth, of olden times. It was left, distinctly clarified that nothing was finalized. Present respite would be available so to mature any prospect of remorse. This discussion would continue at a later date.

The swirling sounds of the helicopter rotor blades and the screaming jet engine interrupted the meeting. Brett stood quickly. He moved close to the still seated chief and put his hand on the wrinkled upper arm. He imparted warm greetings, assuring that he would return. The old man rose to his feet, not accepting that Brett leave without partaking of refreshment. Brett declined graciously, firmly, that he could not fly the helicopter unless his body was free of contamination. He assured that he would return within days, leaving a friendly spirit. He departed out of the low hut door, followed anxiously, closely by a pleading Peleele-Pasi.

As their eyes attuned to the bright rays of daylight Brett spoke softly to Peleele-Pasi. He had to meet with Sauros as an extreme urgency. The only remorse that Peleele-Pasi could demonstrate would be to arrange such a meeting very urgently. Brett would return to the place on the village outskirts, in the shade of the tree under which the first approach to the village had been arranged, celebrated with fresh fruits of the forest. The place they had met the chief on the first occasion. Peleele-Pasi agreed, and a time was scheduled. The chief was notified of this agreement, through his senior messenger. His support and approval was relayed back to Brett almost immediately.

Peleele-Pasi followed Brett to the hovering sounds of the helicopter, metaphorically clinging to historical forgiveness and family compassion. Brett was walking at a hard pace so as not to delay the green machine, but he afforded an attitude of compassion, maybe more sympathy, to this little fool who had so easily been persuaded into activities of an evil system. He sternly dismissed Peleele-Pasi when the helicopter was in sight. He instructed that the meeting would occur at mid-day on the third day from now. Peleele-Pasi agreed, offered his cup-hand-clap respectful departure and turned, running, sprinting to his hut, wife, children and refuge.

The helicopter had landed in an open clearing and troopers were alert in all round defence, lying flat on their bellies, facing outward. The rotor blades were turning but the machine was silent, motor off. Brett sat alongside the pilot, who had removed his headgear, making notes on his leg-pad. These two men were of equal military rank, but the pilot was several years older than Brett. Distinct friendship was developing as they got to know each other.

"We have just seen a huge bull elephant with tusks that must weigh in at 80lbs, pouring rivers of blood with every step. We left him standing, but obviously agonized. It looks like he has been shot with rifles set on automatic. His entire body is drenched. I followed his blood trail at 60 MPH, and he has obviously been walking several days. I do think we should put him out of his misery."

"Wait here. I'll be back in minutes. I'll arrange for bearers to carry the meat. We must take a couple of guys in the chopper. They can return and direct bearers to the carcass. I must inform Chief Gono. He will appreciate some meat, now." Brett jumped out, grabbing his FN and sprinted back to the hut. He passed through the messengers, and ran on, into the hut. He explained very quickly what had to be done; stressing that the sooner the animal was shot the closer it would be for moving the meat. The chief was grateful, clapping instructions through to his elders and messengers. The village became a hive of activity. Brett called for Peleele-Pasi and one other strong youth to accompany him in the helicopter. They responded quickly and joined Brett at a fast trot back to the helicopter. A group of about a hundred village men armed with axes and sheath knives, machetes and blades of razor sharp steel followed Brett to the helicopter, and then continued running in the direction of helicopter flight.

Unbeknown to Brett, Peleele-Pasi had already sent a messenger to summon Sauros into meeting with himself and Chief Gono.

Two troopers remained unseen at the landing zone of the helicopter as it lifted, moving eastward low over the treetops. Peleele-Pasi was terrified as he observed from his outer seat, the craft lifting away from the ground, turning at the same time. Trooper Steyn grabbed his wrist and cuffed it to a centre ring adjacent the seat-belt buckle. This was a precaution in case of this first time traveller being overtaken in fear. The other man was in the centre seat, secured into a seat belt. He could not do anything drastic in the event of panic, but he was not disturbed by the experience. Rather, he was observing wide eyed with an expanding smile as the air speed increased, and tree tops filed past at unbelievable speed. Peleele-Pasi remained in controllable fear, no longer showing panic.

Just ten minutes into flight when the pilot pointed out the elephant trail, the big brown, splashed markings, the flattened swath of blood drenched grass and then the lonely, pain-filled giant of the wild. They circled low over the animal which continued in direction apparently oblivious and undisturbed by the helicopter. He bashed directly into shrub and thick bush, at times being deflected by tree girth too big for his weight. Brett told the trooper to aim for a head shot direct into the brain and to action his shot only when certain of a precision shot. Brett readied himself for the same position, explaining to the pilot to hover at a safe altitude. Both Brett and Trooper Steyn aligned their sights, Brett out of the right door, the trooper out of the left door. The giant lunging animal was in agony, but had powerful running strength, forward mobility. Blood was oozing from several parts of the animal, creating areas of blended blood bubbles dripping freely, leaving unmistakable trail and occasional pools of dust filled fluid. The animal was moving as if disengaged from reality, determined only to move, and move fast. Moving several thousand pounds, breaking bush at aggressive speed.

Peleele-Pasi regained his composure, looking interestedly, with a wide open mouth, at unfolding events. Both rifles were almost focused; the pilot handling the helicopter in a slow forward motion just 20 feet above the enraged and pained animal. The target was fast moving and difficult because of the bush, scrub, trees and forward movement.

Then it happened. The Elephant broke bush into open grass area. Both rifles seemed to fire simultaneously. Like a volcanic eruption from the roof of his head a dark fountain sprayed high and the giant animal swung his head from left to right, continuing to move forward at speed. Both rifles exploded again and this giant piece of African flesh crashed headlong into the dust. The animal rolled over, ending stretched out, dead. The helicopter hovered above as the final kicks of a legend repeatedly thrust through thin air.

The side of the carcass had no less than 100 holes of rifle shot, some oozing blood, some oozing fermentation of gut blended with green liquids and some oozing yellow pus, surrounded by buzzing flies and dislodged maggots falling, wriggling. The pilot hovered a little longer, moved off about 200 long paces to one side and gently settled his machine to the ground. Peleele-Pasi looked gormless, seeking release from his cuff. Trooper Steyn snapped open the clip-lock and set him free. The pilot indicated attention to the turning rotor blades, reminding Trooper Steyn of the dangers to these first time passengers.

They hurried to the elephant carcass, obedient to instruction of caution from Brett. The animal was definitely dead. Brett approached, with his rifle at ready, Trooper Steyn remaining as back-up from some twenty paces away.

Brett left instructions with Peleele-Pasi that the tusks were to be removed, taken to Chief Gono for custody, from where Brett would collect them in a few days. The meat must be cut into manageable sections, carried back to the village for the Chief to distribute. The skin should be salted, cleaned and pegged out to dry in the sun. The skin would remain the property of the Chief. Brett would arrange delivery of sufficient salt for the task.

The carcass had been shot, almost certainly with machine guns set on automatic. It appeared there was no purpose in the shooting because not a single shot had been placed near kill regions, the heart, the spine or the brain. There were bullet holes in the head, legs, rump and stomach, with majority puncture wounds in the gut. Festering wounds and fly filled maggot sores evoked flesh-rot and putrification. The animal stank, gangrenous, horrific. This did not perturb the men who were about to consume this meat. Peleele-Pasi cleared an area and lit a small fire under a fallen trunk of deadwood. This fire would certainly burn for several days.

Peleele-Pasi and his aid spoke briefly and Peleele-Pasi selected to return in the helicopter to direct the porters quickly to the carcass. As the green machine returned to the village all eyes were searching for the outgoing porters. First they saw a small cloud of dust, then the men running at a canter. It was an impressive sight to see about 100 men running in unison, cheerful, and fresh. The pilot lowered the helicopter for Peleele-Pasi to out, and then climbed to the treetops returning to collect the unseen troopers near the village.

They wasted no time clambering into the helicopter, returning to the camp at the crest of the cliffs. As they gained height over the village, Trooper Len Mathews leant over to Brett and said “Sir, just before you got back, a Charlie Tango – ‘Communist Terrorist’ ran past us carrying this AK47. He ran straight towards the village. He chucked this weapon in the grass. Literally, threw it on the ground as he passed us. Was tall, big bastard, looked bloody strong, wearing baboon skin kit. He's in the village right now, Sir. He is going to feel an idiot when he can't find his rifle. I didn't take him out because he's probably the guy you are looking for, to speak to."

Brett acknowledged this information with gratitude, as he looked back, inspecting the AK47. "Thanks, Len. Well done. It would have cocked things bad if you had shot him. This way is better. I am meeting him in three days. I think he'll talk to us, but if not, I'll get his brother to get it out of him. We may have to slap him a bit. Sounds like he has 'gotten rotten'."

Chief Gono had been reliable, honest and grateful to Brett. But he also inherited traditions: spiritual, cultural, survival, and emotional. Among these was a natural inclination to absorb and believe what he was told. After all, people had no reason to lie or be deceitful. Men may exaggerate for reasons of valour, but nobody would deliberately lie! It would serve no purpose.

Sauros had told him of grand gifts, abundant wild fruits, quantities of fresh meat in daily supply if he would support 'chimurenga,' the 'war' against the 'gurumende' – the government. The elderly mind of this congenial, fragile leader was easily manipulated through impossible promises of simple 'extras' contributed into his routine. Brett had never made a promise. He had fed the village with prime flesh of kudu, elephant and he destroyed the curse of the area, the man-eating leopard. Sauros had promised many extras. The chief believed what he was told, and what he saw. He never suspected that the white spirit was the adversary of his new found friend. This was, after all, the brother of one of his own people, the brother of the black spirit who had accompanied the white spirit years before. His new found friend was simple, wore baboon skin clothes, was fit, strong like a man should be, and he had promised many things. Surely, the white spirit and the black spirit were good. They both provided for the village. They both spoke gently and showed respect for others. Surely they would be friends. Why, then had Peleele-Pasi insisted on secrecy in meeting the chief? Something was not right.

Jelly-like facial wrinkles on the old man looked a picture of corrugated desert ripples, moving, elasticized, travelling the road of confusion.

Chief Gono sat close to the fire in the centre of the room. He was cold, but the day was hot. Men had gone out to porter in the meat of a legend. The village would eat well this day. He needed warmth as he anticipated, awaiting the arrival of Sauros.

The senior messenger spoke in a deep, quiet baritone voice, almost whispering, from outside the hut, telling the chief that Sauros had arrived. The old man was relaxed, comfortable, and confident of his authority, confused by strange events, relationships and clandestine activity between his people. He smiled as he thought that he must be getting old.

He was about to experience and witness a fragment of core evil beyond human comprehension.

The helicopter had been recalled to Chipinga, by Major Cutter. It would remain away for a few days. Brett sent three troopers, each carrying coarse salt for the village. They were instructed to leave it in the personal care of the senior messenger, and return to base camp as quickly as possible.

In a pre-briefing Brett included, "Your attention is alerted to maximum security. Our arrival has surprised a gang of terrorists who have been lying low, probably recruiting or training others. They have been alarmed and we can expect action. Delivering this salt is very important on a psychological front. Carry it in your pack, with your rifle at ready. I don't expect them to attack yet. The terrs will not be expecting you at this time but you may surprise them and suddenly find yourself surrounded. Only one guy must go into the village, and this is like going into a hornet nest. The village is about three hour's fast walk from here. Be back here before dark. Good luck."

All they carried was a map, radio, packs of salt, rifles and ammunition. The men left: focused, strong, fit and fast.

Sauros had been in the hut with the chief, angry and very nervous. Extended discussions had contested the chiefs meeting with Brett. Why had the helicopter been here? "Did you, Chief Gono, call the army against me? Why are they here? How did they hear of my activities?" The helicopter motor sounded close, very close, then the accelerating engines and clacking rotor blades passed very low, directly over the hut, loudly heard, but unseen. They did not move from within the hut.

Protocol, tradition, tribal custom and all subservience was forgotten. Sauros addressed the Chief in despicable tone with contempt and anger. The old man had never experienced insult of this nature. He summoned the messenger, seated outside, to come in and witness the discussion. This compelled Sauros to a heightened anger. He stood tall over the old man, who was seated low, hunched close to the fire. They spoke n'Debele.

"You did call the army. You have destroyed the plan. You are not a Chief of the people." The messenger drew close to intervene, remove Sauros. Age and physical strength ridiculed the effort. Sauros pushed him to one side. Losing balance he fell to the floor. Then Sauros kicked with every strength, as hard as he could muster, landing a booted heel hard on the jaw of the unsuspecting Chief. The old man fell, sprawled on the floor, with his outstretched arm falling hard in the fire, penetrating deep into burning coals. Sauros jumped on his fragile chest then kicked him hard in the stomach and slapped him, full open handed, smoothing the wrinkles on his aged face. The messenger moved as quick as his elderly muscles could manage, but Sauros punched him hard in the solar plexus, expelling all air, winding him as he fell awkwardly over a log-stool, landing too hard for an old man.

With the two elderly men sprawled on the floor in agony, the chief badly burned on his wrist and forearm, Sauros kicked the door open, smashed the hinge, flattened the door to the ground, and ran out. He was enraged, very nervous, attitude verging on uncontrollable insanity. He ran to where he had left his rifle and he couldn't find it. Panic struck. He searched a wider area. Quick actions, jerk actions, looking behind stumps, kicking rocks, looking to where he knew it was not.

Momentarily he regained composure, standing tall with both hands on his hips, thinking. One final quick search revealed nothing. He shouted out loud, a trumpeting sound, directing his call to the sky, sounding human attempt to imitate an Elephant. His call was heard by two of his female recruits who were both attending to domestic chores in the village. They responded quickly in search of this coded urgency.

The village was almost empty. Every youthful man had gone in search of the elephant meat. The village had little movement, apart from an isolated women washing pots or hanging clothes out to dry or casual, stoking coals in preparation to cook meat that would arrive later in the day.

In a mood of killer aggression Sauros ran back toward the village, meeting two youthful girls running towards him. Their anxiety hyped on seeing Sauros moving so strong, fast, determined towards the big hut. “Wa’ita se?” “What's the matter?” they asked. Sauros stopped, pleased to see them. “Run fast; bring me a very sharp blade. Quick. I will be at the big hut.” The girls scampered off. Sauros, sleek and fast arrived amongst several elders surrounding the hut door, some women some men, all well aged. He pushed and pulled the confused onlookers, throwing elderly men and women like discarded rag dolls, to the ground. He grabbed the Chief by the arm, dragging him out from the hut then, throwing him hard to the ground he shouted, “Where is my gun? What have you done with it?” Kicking the Chief in the face and realizing a futile situation, he turned on a very old women, grabbing her by the throat, screaming into her face, “where is my gun, you stole it, where is it?” He tightened his grip on her throat, pressing his thumb deep into her oesophagus. Her legs buckled, under her feeble weight. He lifted her high by the neck, and then threw her hard to the ground. Her body lay crumpled, motionless, bleeding from the mouth, sweat-stained and bent over a small boulder.

Surrounded by confused and agonized elders, he broke loose moving towards the two girls, now running fast towards him. They were aware of an emergency, but had no idea as to what was happening or why. They were simply responding to the distress call of Sauros, their mentor, good instructor and man of strength. They were brandishing knives and a machete, running arms outstretched trying to get the scathing tools into his hands – oblivious as to why he needed them.

He grabbed the machete and instructed the girls to obedience. He grabbed the closest elder woman, who was standing bent at the shoulders, naked from the waist upwards. He grabbed a knife with his free hand and tested the blade. He threw it at the girl, pegging it as a dart into her naked abdomen. Screaming loud he could now be heard at distance, "I said a SHARP knife," and he grabbed the knives offered by the other girl. She was terrified, as was everyone. She had not comprehended the turmoil, but the people had witnessed her running, handing the knives to Sauros. He selected the sharpest, instructing the girl to hold the head of the old woman. He used his weight and full strength to hold her head to his thigh, leaning his elbows, forcing her into total submission. He plunged the knife sideways into her mouth, slicing her cheek, penetrating between her teeth, cutting up to her ear. Removing the blade and cleaning it dry from blood on the clothes of the agonized old woman, he pried open her face flesh, slicing a huge segment of cheek flesh which fell to the floor. She was gargling in her own blood, trying everything to move, overtaken in agony. Her bloodied, hacked face revealed a full side of teeth blended with dust, spit and nasal discharge. Sauros released her, propelling her off his thigh hard to the ground. He picked up the cheek-flesh from the floor, spat on it and threw it onto the coals of a nearby fire.

The elders had watched in terrified disbelief as this enraged lunatic carved their peaceful lives into pages of history. They were absolutely distraught, mesmerized and stilled to unbelief.

The knife-blade had penetrated the girl through thick outer muscle of belly, embedding a full blade length. She had winced in pain, overtaken by automatic reaction to remove the offending blade from her body. A scrawny looking older than middle aged woman approached to help her. Sauros had swung the full force of a flat handed slap, sending this woman crashing to the ground. It was the young girl's grandmother who Sauros now had in his grasp, and this young innocent girl was in panic. The wound appeared small, now bleeding only slowly. Sauros lifted her by the arm and threw her towards the fire – and the grilling flesh. She now landed, sprawling to rest very close to being burned. Sauros grabbed the grilling flesh from the coal and turned it, throwing it burned side up, back onto the coals. He looked at the young girl seeing tears running off her face. He looked into the mass of elderly people surrounding them, and he jumped up onto a rock, peering down at his audience, who were all too terrified to move or speak.

He threw all the knives into the fire, keeping the machete in his stronger right hand. His n'Debele voice boomed down. "This is our land and we will rule. You are all old, have done nothing for your children. They live like animals. Shame on you and especially, shame on your chief! The animals belong to us and the trees and the birds are for our use. If you are obedient to me you can have it all. If you are obedient to that helicopter you will live like hyena for ever. Now, hear well! I instructed this girl to bring me a sharp knife. Disobedience has cost her a small cut this time. Next time she will hang from a tree held by the very flesh of her disobedience – with everything about her female body cut out for the vultures to play with as she watches. To be eaten, just before she dies.

Understand me and live. Disobey my words and every one of you will eat his own flesh."

He skipped down from the rock to the fire, flicking the now grilled cheek flesh toward the young girl lying in agony at the fire side. "Eat it," he barked. She shook her head, refusing, and sobbed out loud. He swung his heel hard down onto her thigh, landing a vicious thud midway between her groin and her knee. She screamed, appealing to Sauros in desperate facial expression. Again he commanded, "Eat it." Her hands shaking, her body trembling, her fingers reached to the flesh lying in the sand. She lifted it into her mouth, and bit it. "Chew it and swallow, get it deep into your spirit. You will never disobey me again." Tears streamed from her face. She sat shaking her head from side to side as she ground away at the flesh. Then she broke. She spat the flesh from her mouth and lay howling, then sobbing on the ground, rolling in agony, now sobbing uncontrollably. Sauros kicked her in the groin and again on the back of her head. Then he lifted the machete and swung it hard, whistling through the air, he directed it slicing into the skull of the frail old body lying bent and broken over a rock at his feet. This was the body of the senior wife of Chief Gono.

Standing tall and proud he observed the people. Not a single eye looked at him. Old bodies all around; wrinkled skin, quivering mouths, bent fingers; trembling hands wiped tears into the dust. In shocking disbelief the village had been raped, savaged to the core. Shaking heads shed silent tears.

Sauros ran from the village, stopping for a last frantic search for his AK47 rifle, continuing at determined athletic pace.

The troopers arrived near the village having maintained a steady trot from the base camp. In consideration of terrorist presence they selected an approach from a different direction.

Two men guarded from behind, one worked a slow unseen hunters approach. The three remained close to each other, cautious, observant and silent. As trooper Steyn closed in on the gathered men and women, expecting celebration and a pleasure at his presence, he was alerted to the tragic scenes and human pain. He returned to discuss things with the others. They called Brett on the radio, receiving no response. Their motto "Who Dares, Wins" prompted a decision to storm the village. They grouped close, approaching like stalking leopards. They arrived amongst the silent, traumatized elders, having not been detected until the last instant.

They witnessed the results of the visit by Sauros. A fragile girl remained sobbing near the fire, holding her hand over pain on her torso. The painful old frame of Chief Gono was hunched over the broken body of his wife. He held her hand between both of his, gently rubbing, clapping and humming a gentle tune. The rugged fighting men of the SAS were horrified.

The return to base camp was faster, as they trotted the well used route used by the village women when collecting water from the Lundi River. Brett had achieved radio contact with Chipinga base camp. Major Cutter had responded in his usual efficient and friendly manner. He had arranged additional troops and a helicopter to arrive early the following morning.

The search for Sauros started early, pre-dawn. Brett landed two units of six troopers each very close to the village. He then located Peleele-Pasi and a messenger; spoke briefly with the chief assuring him that medical attention was en route to the village. The old man was solemn, confused, dignified and very grateful. Peleele-Pasi had been absolutely mortified at the conduct of his brother, and anxious to assist in his capture.

With the messenger and the now highly air worthy Peleele-Pasi safely strapped into the back seat of the Alouette, they lifted barely above tree tops and moved eastward. The messenger was disorientated by this birds-eye expanse below and distances seemed out of proportion. Within minutes and with input from Peleele-Pasi they located the nomadic bunk type grass shelter from where Sauros had been recruiting and training.

Sauros had not slept at his camp, but about a mile away. When he heard the helicopters he abandoned everything, preferring to run. The mile separating him from his camp was far when on the ground, but the many very alert eyes in the helicopters were quickly attracted to a running being on the ground. Within minutes Sauros was detained securely in the helicopter, relieved of his every possession, including his clothing. His ankles were widely separated, cuffed to legs of the aircraft front seats. His wrists were individually cuffed to the backrest of the rear seats. The seat belt was tightly secured around his waist. He could barely move, and was deprived of vision with a black blindfold hood. Despite aggressive protestations this remained well secured. Peleele-Pasi sat next to him, strapped into the outer seat. The messenger was returned to the village in the other helicopter. Brett took the front seat, sat turning back, facing Sauros the duration of the return flight. Peleele-Pasi was incensed at what his brother had done to the village. He repeatedly slapped Sauros, occasionally punching him on the nose or crushing his manhood.

When they arrived at the base camp it had been decided that removing this prisoner from the helicopter would be much like releasing a captured lion from a cage. Peleele-Pasi was escorted, considered as a guilty party, isolated into an interrogation tent. Sauros was escorted, well shackled into another tent, where he remained shackled and was tied down secured on his back, lying flat on two metal trunks. He remained naked

Brett called the office of General Walls and remained on radio alert for several hours. When radio contact with the General was concluded he went to the interrogation tent of Peleele-Pasi. After short consultation with Corporal Vernon Thornsby, he ordered his release. Together they went to see Sauros. Peleele-Pasi was now more infuriated, having been slapped and treated as a prisoner because of what his brother had done.

He stooped low stepping into the tent. His rage was evident the instant he saw his brother. He walked directly to a pair of workshop pliers lying on a trunk in the corner of the tent. He jumped at his brother and secured the pliers to his left testicle. Quietly he asked, "What have you done? What have I done that you turn like a cobra against us all? Why, why, why? Slowly he squeezed the pliers handle, extracting an indescribable agony from the throat-sounds of his brother. His brother's manhood lay limp, flopping from side to side as Peleele-Pasi realigned the pliers and applied more pressure. He was relentless, not wanting to finish the pain too soon. He continued squeezing, applying pressure, then releasing it. Brett was horrified at the circumstances he was witnessing. He left the tent, with a short nudge to the interrogating trooper, who followed Brett out. “This is simple family justice. Leave them alone for a few minutes.”

The agonizing pain caused Sauros to scream and yodel and bellow and pass intermittently out of consciousness. Then, when Peleele-Pasi could control his anger no more, he clenched his jaw and squeezed the pliers with all his might. The testicle burst lengthwise in the scrotum and Sauros bellowed like a wounded Bull Buffalo, prolonged, then lost consciousness.

Peleele-Pasi came out from the tent and said to Brett “I have left the other half for later. He must never forget what he has done this day. Sir, may I return now to my village?”

Sauros was imprisoned in Salisbury maximum security prison for several weeks pending recuperation and legal trial. Chief Gono observed the burial of his wife amongst the trees in which he first met Brett. Medical officers from the Bubi river military camp of Major Buster Johnson were sent to repair the broken bodies remaining in the village. Although Chief Gono recovered from the agony of a fractured femur and collar-bone, he never recovered the psychological devastation of witnessing the death of his wife and lifelong friend.

Sauros served five years in prison after his trial, being released in October 1973. During his confinement he underwent several surgical operations, and used this time studying, becoming a medical doctor. On release from prison he left the country, joining up with his friend in Mozambique, Josiah Tongogara. From there he went to Czechoslovakia where he completed his doctorate and further terrorist training. He knew he could never walk a free man amidst his own people. He changed his name in accordance with the shameful principal of the 'chimurenga' – 'war,' thereby protecting his future identity. In the mind of every good living, Honourable citizen of Rhodesia this new name, Hitler Hunzvi, would become the most dreaded name in history, followed closely by the name Robert Mugabe.

Hitler Hunzvi became better known as Hitler Chenjerai Hunzvi, the militant leader of the war veterans of Zimbabwe. He instigated much violence and cruelty and led the barbaric invasions onto commercial farms throughout the country.

These pivotal events changed the lives of every Rhodesian forever. A hand full of characters inverted the bowl of Godly governance, replacing it eternally, with indiscriminate mass murder, torture, suffering and starvation. This peace-loving people are being drowned in a satanic black spirit. Gallant men and women, mostly black Africans, gave limbs, life, and sweat in pursuit of good living. The world observed and decreed from distant boardrooms of marble and gold; supported what it did not understand, initiating the most successful theft in history. Yes, theft of an entire nation. The world imposed Mugabe on the peoples of Rhodesia in ill-conceived comprehension.

It is this platform that propelled the political deceptions, torture chambers, deathly dungeons, executioner's mortuary and national graveyard now called Zimbabwe.

Courageous, disciplined and well principled, Honourable men and women with an esteemed determination, strength and resilience now flounder homeless, psychologically destroyed and destitute. A majestic well structured vessel called Rhodesia has been holed, not held, sunk and not supported, destroyed not developed, divided not united, doomed to eternal dependence and almost non productive lives.

Merit or demerit, as leaders become led, scales imbalance, vessels invert and “evil” is called “good”. This would not occur if our trusted world leaders used their wisdom and authority wisely, accepting and conforming to Gods guidance – whilst sailing their own ship.

The support of the British government for the terrorist actions led by Robert Mugabe will never be comprehended by those who understood and fought the gallant fight to preserve civilization; those who resisted the front line of terrorism that was so strongly supported by Harold Wilson. But Rhodesians and Zimbabweans simply pray "Father forgive them for they know not what they do. In fact, in foreign policy, they have not even a vague idea." Their leaders are led by the mob!

The efforts of Rhodesians under the leadership of Ian Smith were determined to prevent terrorism, and the expansion of such organizations as al-Qaeda. The efforts of interfering foreign powers did not understand the elementary issue, so Zimbabwe is now a springboard for the highest bidder to launch whatever terrorist activities they may require. As a hunter would say, "get your ducks in a straight line……. before you fire."

TONY MORKEL

Zimbabwe Darkness – The Enemy Within

Sable Publishing House
Email: SablePublications@yahoo.co.uk

The sequel to Rhodesian Dawn - Zimbabwe Darkness, ZIMBABWE DARKNESS – THE ENEMY WITHIN is the inside tale of greed, privilege and events in the corridors of political power, revealing elements of Mugabe's influence and the instruments of psychological manipulation that have brought the nation of Zimbabwe to its' knees.

Dark days in Zimbabwe

By LAURA THORPE
newsdesk@chardandilminsternews.co.uk

BOOKS rarely evoke so much emotion as when they are written from personal experience, and Tony Morkel's 'Rhodesian Dawn, Zimbabwe Darkness' has the capacity to grip the reader with its keen eye to detail and emotive language.

As a third generation Rhodesian, now living in Ilminster, Mr Morkel experienced life at a time when Africa was struggling in a conflict of power, and this is portrayed in his book through characters and situations which reflect Tony's life. The book is a moving tale born from personal experience and historical fact.

The story follows three main characters — Arthur, Southey and Brett — three generations and their differing experiences in a wild country.

Use of imagery is particularly effective where the author describes hunting scenes to draw the reader into the action.

■ **TONY TELLS:** Ilminster writer, Tony Morkel, with his book.
PHOTO: Laura Thorpe

"The front-runners of the herd were in sight now, and it seemed as if the horizon was a giant wave of anger; rumble; rage and thunder all crashing directly towards them. Moonlight washed over the battlefield, giving floodlit view to the spectators — clinging to their grandstand. Hennery called loudly to Brett, demanding his immediate climb up the tree. He shouted that the raging river of buffalo was too vicious a storm to challenge. Brett smiled, sent back a 'thumbs up' and called back, shaking his head, but his shouted refusal was drowned out by the herd.

"He had his .318 rifle at the ready; was bull faced and focused as always; ready, whatever may happen."

The book is interjected with moments of humour as well as sadness, and the author even explores his own creativity with a poem entitled 'Crocodile Pools'.

'Rhodesian Dawn, Zimbabwe Darkness' will appeal to historians and to those who enjoy adventure, and for those who want more — Tony Morkel's sequel 'Zimbabwe Darkness — The Enemy Within' is available from July.

'Rhodesian Dawn, Zimbabwe Darkness' is published by Mr Morkel's own publishing house, Sable Publishing, based in Ilminster. The book is available from Ile Bookshop, Ilminster, WH Smith and other bookshops.

The Evening Telegraph -- Review by Darren Holden

This two-part novel by Rhodesian émigré Tony Morkel is concerned with how Zimbabwe, once one of the most advanced nation-states in Africa has found itself under the heel of the despotic Robert Mugabe and his ZANU-PF Party, and how the country has descended into land disputes, violence, famine, disease and poverty.

The first novel, "Rhodesian Dawn, Zimbabwe Darkness" charts the rise and fall of the colony of Rhodesia as seen through the eyes of three generations of the male line of the De La Harp family taking us from early colonialism to the start of the Civil War period.

Arthur, the pater familias of the De La Harp family is first encountered in 1888 as a brave 14-year old embarking on an epic trek as a pioneer and entrepreneur from South Africa to Rhodesian territory.

His son Southey establishes the family empire, whilst the story of the third in the line Brett De la Harp brings us up to the modern era, with his tale of how the colony became mired in horrific inter-racial and tribal conflict, and how international politics conspired to set the colony on the path to civil war.

Arthur's adventures through South Africa and Rhodesia are dramatic conflicts against nature and disease and work well on their own as 'big trek' stories so beloved of the South African region, his journey and Brett's tale on the pursuit of Sauros (in real-life notorious 'war-veteran' leader Hitler Hunzvi) are absorbing highlights of the book.

Some readers may be put off by the brash, patriotic and proud, heart-on-the sleeve style that Morkel employs.

My caveat would be, if you are looking for an unbiased or particularly comprehensive history of the Rhodesian conflict, this obviously isn't the book, but as a personal account of certain periods of family and political history it works well and the enthusiasm and passion in this book make up for any minor faults of style.

I found it refreshing to read and as his first novel in the series it did it's job perfectly well in that it has whetted my appetite for the second book, where I think the authors background will give us an interesting and much-needed account of the betrayal and sense of loss that Rhodesian ex-patriots feel.

Darren Holden